Sacrificed

CALI

TERRI ANNE BROWNING

The Rocker Universe Timeline

Reading Order

Playlist

- "Psycho Crazy" by Halestorm
- "Explosions" by Three Days Grace
- "Waiting on the Sun" by Citizen Soldier
- "Devil Doesn't Bargain" by Alec Benjamin
- "The Steeple" by Halestorm
- "A Scar is Born" by Three Days Grace
- "Hope It Haunts You" by Citizen Soldier
- "Can Anyone Hear Me Now" by Anthony Mossburg
- "Only Love Can Hurt Like This" by Paloma Faith
- "Hold My Hand" by Lady Gaga
- "Worth the Fight" by No Resolve
- "Good Without" by Mimi Webb
- "Terrible Things" by Halestorm

- "Always Been You" by Jessie Murph
- "Save Your Story" by Citizen Soldier
- "Wrapped Around Your Finger" by Post Malone
- "My Drug" by Anthony Mossburg

Trigger Warning

SOME CONTENTS IN THIS BOOK MAY BE
TRIGGERING TO SOME READERS.

*Please proceed with caution if you are easily
triggered by assault of any nature.
To avoid triggers, you should avoid the Prologue, as
well as Chapters 9-11.*

Wait!

Have you read *Heartless Savage* yet?

If not, either pause and read it now—or risk serious spoilers.

If you have, then **Happy Reading**!

Hugs,

TAB

Prologue

CALI

USING a headband to keep my long, dark hair back from my face, I stared into my mirror. The LED lights surrounding the rectangular glass showed me a sight I was expecting, but I still hated. The bruise along the left side of my jaw would take some extra contouring to disguise, but I'd become a pro at hiding the proof of what a nightmare my home had turned into.

My gaze flickered to my camera that was positioned to record my makeup tutorials, but I would have to wait until I'd covered the bruise before I could hit record. If I didn't hide the evidence of Manuel's latest beating and it got back to my stepfather, the next time my stepbrother got his hands on me would most likely be the last.

Covering up the injury hurt and was especially hard when I had a little swelling. But it wasn't the first time I'd had to hide the hate that was inflicted upon me. The beatings had been coming more frequently, each one more brutal than the last. I'd made the mistake of trying to ask for help from Matias, my beloved stepfather, once and quickly learned my lesson.

My stepfather had slapped Manuel in front of all their men when I confessed that my stepbrother had used me as a human punching bag one night. Matias had left for the States on business directly after, thinking that would be the end of it. He was gone for two weeks.

Just enough time for me to be able to walk upright again when he returned.

The house I'd grown up in since my mother married Matias when I was five had slowly become my prison over the years. It had been a gradual process, starting with just slaps when my mom first got sick and Matias was always away with her at the hospital. Then she died, and Matias started hiding his pain at the loss of his wife in work. The slaps had turned into punches, and those punches had become full-on beatings in the past year.

That was why I'd started the makeup tutorial videos on social media. At first, it was just in hopes of getting a sponsor or two that would pay me to use their products. But I'd gotten lucky by gaining over two million followers within a few short months. I had nearly a dozen sponsors and my own money coming in.

Money I planned on using to get as far away from the Ramirez family as soon as I had enough saved to rent an apartment in the States.

I would miss Matias, but missing him didn't outweigh the survival instinct screaming at me that I needed to get far away from this place—fast.

The eye makeup recording I did after my foundation was in place didn't even need editing, so I posted it before reading through some of the comments on the video I'd posted the day before. I didn't just do videos of getting ready in the morning. I liked to play around, turn my face into that of one of the celebrities I admired. My love of art had come in handy, and the majority of my following had been accumulated because of my ability to transform myself into nearly anyone.

There were over three thousand comments on the video from the day before, which would make my sponsors happy. It would have made me smile if my jaw weren't hurting so badly, despite the anti-inflammatory pain medication I'd taken when I'd first gotten out of bed that morning.

After flipping through the comments, liking a few as I went, my attention was snagged by the picture of one of the commenters. Hot guys left me messages on my posts and in my DMs all the time, but I'd learned to ignore them for the most part. For one, many of them were a good twenty years older than I was. For another, they usually just wanted me to sext them and send them nudes.

Typically, I just scrolled on by the guys in the feed, but for some reason, my finger lingered on his picture before clicking on it so I could have a better look. Blond hair cut short and styled in that slightly unkempt way that most guys favored. His green eyes glared into the camera. I traced my index fingernail over his strong jaw and his naturally pouty bottom lip. I had no way of telling how tall he was, but I found myself imagining him towering over my five-four.

My heart gave a little flutter, and I let myself fantasize that this guy, this Garret Hannigan—if that was his real name—would storm the gates surrounding the Ramirez mansion and sweep me up into his arms. That he would take me away from the nightmare of this dreadful place. He would protect me from Manuel.

I would be safe.

Maybe even loved?

Then my finger accidentally exited out of the

blown-up version of his profile picture, and I saw what he'd posted.

The fantasy I'd been building in my head only moments before turned to smoke, and I felt bile rise into my throat as I read the vile things he was going to do to me. Inhaling slowly, I read the long comment, taking all of it in.

Garret Hannigan had a reason to hate my stepfamily, if he was to be believed. Matias had sent someone to kill his little sister, a girl who was important to the Vitucci crime family. That name was very familiar to me. I'd heard it many times. When a member of the family would come to Bogotá for business, I would have to stay in my room the entire time they were visiting, but Manuel often ranted about them.

Mostly about Ryan Vitucci.

My stepbrother particularly hated Ryan, whom I'd seen pictures of online. It was no wonder Manuel disliked him so much. With just a glance at the young Italian American, it was easy to tell that Ryan was everything Manuel wished he could be. Smart, incredibly handsome, and, above all else, competent.

Manuel was an idiot. He was Matias's heir, but my stepfather was already in despair of leaving his life's work to his son. Everything he'd worked so hard for would be gone before the dirt even settled on his grave if Manuel was left the Ramirez businesses and fortune once Matias died.

Feeling sick, I started to close my social media app when a notification for a DM popped up. Needing something to take my mind off what I'd just read—even if it was a dick pic from some random guy—I clicked on the message icon.

Nova: *After seeing the comment my idiot, disgusting brother left you, I attempted to beat some sense into him for you and the greater good of the female population. If it doesn't work, I'll continue to do so until he pulls his head out of his ass.*

For some reason, despite the pain in my jaw, I found myself smiling.

Me: *Don't worry about it. I get crap like that from guys all the time. I'm not scared of some punk in another country who thinks he can get to my stepdad through me. I have other things to worry about than what some nobody like your brother fantasizes about doing to me. He's just pissed he doesn't stand a chance with me.*

After I hit send, I closed the app and stood, trying to forget the feeling I'd first experienced when I saw Garret's picture. The sickness swirling around in my stomach continued to linger, but not as strongly after Nova's message.

Neither of the Hannigan siblings was what I

should have been worried about. Not when I opened my bedroom door and found a seething Manuel standing there.

I opened my mouth to scream when he stepped menacingly over the threshold into my bedroom. But the scream didn't have time to leave my throat as he pounced on me.

The smell of his breath hit me in the face as he grabbed me by the back of the head. His fingers twisted and pulled, ripping strands free as he jerked me around by the hold he had on my hair and dragged me from my room.

"Manuel, let go!" I cried, gripping his wrist in an effort to at least ease the pain of his hold, if not get him to release me. "Please. What did I do? Why are you so angry?"

"Shut the fuck up, you little whore," he snarled as he shook my head from side to side while he marched me down the hall to his own bedroom. "Vitucci's little asshole thinks he can run his mouth? Well, I'll give him exactly what he wants."

I gulped, my gaze racing around the entire room in fear. I'd never been in there before. It was a mess. Empty bottles of beer and liquor littered the floor and the bedside tables. The bed itself was unmade, the sheets looking as if they hadn't been changed in weeks. He refused to allow Maria or any of the maids inside while he was home, so they had to wait until he left the mansion for more than a day to clean.

On the desk near the window was a small pile of a white substance with several lines already measured out. I shuddered, not daring to look at my stepbrother's eyes to see how blown his pupils were. Not only was he drunk, but he was high. That was never a good combination.

And with Matias not home, I knew this was going to be bad.

Manuel pushed me forward until I was standing at the end of his bed. Then he tightened his fingers in my hair and shoved me forward, tearing my scalp open as I fell facedown on his bed.

I cried out in pain and fear, praying someone would come to help me, but I already knew they wouldn't. No one ever did. There was no one who cared enough, and even if they did, they would only end up worse off than I was.

Breathing hard, Manuel grabbed one of my arms and pulled me up the bed then flipped me over so I was on my back. He cuffed my wrist to the head-board. I whimpered at how tight the shackles were, but while I was distracted by the pain, he moved down the bed and strapped something around my ankle.

By the time he had all four of my limbs tied

down, he was sweating because I'd tried to fight him. Picking up a pair of huge shears, he stood at the foot of the bed and laughed maniacally down at me.

"Now, the real fun begins," he said with an evil grin.

Cali

PICKING up the tray loaded with a pitcher of beer and two baskets of wings, I was about to turn to walk away from the bartender when someone called my name.

"Hey, Lis."

I shifted my head to find the girl who worked the section beside my own standing a few feet away, leaning her forearms on top of the bar. She was popping gum, with her shorts, like my own that were more like a thong, climbing up her crack and show-casing her ass cheeks. The tops we wore were barely any better. Mine at least covered the majority of my boobs, but she was taller and more well-endowed than me, leaving the undersides of her tits on display as well as her cleavage. I wore a bra, but my coworker didn't see the need.

Since she got about twice as much in tips as I did, I could understand why she went without the bra, but I had reasons for keeping my bra on that had nothing to do with the embarrassment of a possible nip slip.

"Yeah?" I asked, a little annoyed that she was stopping me from doing my job. Time was money as a waitress. It affected my tips if I took too long to get back to my customers. I wasn't there to make friends, so I didn't chitchat with anyone who worked there. Not even my roommate, who was currently on the main stage dancing.

Kim and I weren't close. She'd gotten me the job waiting tables at Cherry Bomb Gentlemen's Club, but that was only because it would help me cover half of our bills. When we were at work, she pretended not to know me. We even left separately each night. Normally because Kim went out with some of the other dancers once their shift was over, and I went home to shower and fall into a coma-like sleep until it was time to get up for work again.

The other waitress popped another bubble, taking her time answering. "Just thought I'd warn you that tall, blond, and grumpy is back in your section."

Goose bumps instantly popped up along my entire body, but I mentally shook myself and shrugged like it didn't matter to me before continuing on my way. I kept my gaze on the table where the beer and wings belonged, a flirty smile on my face as I walked in my sky-high heels and swayed my hips with each step, something I'd learned early on got me better tips.

The two men at the high-top table watched me come toward them. The dark-haired one licked his lips, and I winked as I placed his wings in front of him first, knowing it would bring me a few extra bills when I brushed my chest against his arm as I moved around him to place his friend's wings in front of him.

The dancers were strictly hands off unless the customer shelled out the cash for a private dance. For the waitresses, flirty, physical contact was particularly encouraged. I hated to touch or be touched, but giving guys the impression that they had a shot with me earned me enough in tips each night to cover my part of the bills and allowed me to set a little aside for a nice nest egg.

With the pitcher of beer between them, I lowered my tray and touched the redheaded man's arm. Every inch of exposed skin turned bright red at the contact, in true ginger form. If I had a soft spot for the male population, I might have felt sorry for his inability to hide his emotions. "You fellas need anything else?" I asked, giving them each a pouty smile.

"We're good for now, darlin'," the dark-haired one said, his eyes on the low neckline of my top.

I didn't mind showing off the tops of my boobs. It was the undersides that would freak people out. The scars were hard for me to stomach, so I could only imagine how a complete stranger would feel when he saw the ugly pink lines Manuel had left behind.

The entire time I stood there talking to them, I could feel eyes boring into me, so I lingered, letting the two men get a good look at my front and bottom. If I wanted to stay in NYC, I had to pay my bills, and this was better than getting naked on stage like Kim did. When I walked away, I let my fingertips trail over the dark-haired man's back.

I could feel the aggression coming from *his* general direction. I took my time checking on my other customers before finally stopping at the huge round booth where Garret Hannigan always sat.

The first night he came in, he'd been with half a dozen other men in suits. Every single one of them had an air about them that I recognized only too well. The slight bulges under their jackets shouldn't have made it past the bouncers, who would have wanded them and then patted them down before letting them through the door. Yet there was no mistaking the guns they carried.

It didn't surprise me, though. They worked for the Vitucci family, after all. And I was all too aware of the power that name carried, not only in New York, but across the entire country. If they didn't want to hand over their guns, they weren't going to, and no one was going to make them. I wouldn't have even been surprised if the Vituccis or the Donatis or even the Volkovs owned Cherry Bomb.

Surprisingly, they had all been respectful. All of them had been more interested in drinking, eating, and watching whichever dancer was on the main stage than me. All of them except for Garret. He'd spent the night watching me, and I'd thought it was because he knew who I was. I'd been tense that entire night, thinking he was going to call me out for being a Ramirez, even if it was just as the late Matias Ramirez's adopted daughter.

But he hadn't mentioned anything about my being Calista Ramirez.

Even more surprising, each time one of his friends even looked twice at me, he would snap at them, and they would turn their gazes back to their food or the dancers.

When they left that night, I'd gotten over a thousand dollars in tips from them combined. Garret's number had been wrapped up in the wad of twenties he'd personally left for me.

The next night, he'd returned, alone. He sat in the same booth, never once looking at the dancers on the stage, and flirted with me. And that was how it had been every night for the past two weeks.

At first, I thought he was just fucking with me, like he'd done back when I was a teenage social medial influencer. The messages he would send me, not just comments he made, but the DMs he would drop in my lap, on top of everything else I was already going through at home, had been the second worst thing that had happened to me— every damned day—until Nova had helped me escape.

But I saw no recognition in Garret's eyes whenever I looked into them. Just a hunger that shook me. I didn't want to feel anything but hate and disgust for the asshole, yet my body had its own plans. My second archnemesis was the only person to ever cause this reaction, and I was seriously struggling with how to digest that.

Placing my order pad on the tray I was still holding, I cocked my hip and gave him a tight smile. His glower turned darker. "Why do I never get the bright, flirty smiles like every other jerk-off in this place?"

I liked that I could annoy him, but I kept my face neutral as I waited patiently for him to give me his order, although I already knew what he was going to say. Every night, it was the same thing. Macallan whisky, neat. Cheeseburger, no tomatoes. Side of loaded cheese fries. For thirteen straight nights, that was what he'd ordered, without a single deviation.

If his mom knew he was eating like that every single night, she would be after him with a wooden spoon. But he didn't know that I was acquainted with Felicity "Flick" Hannigan. He had no idea I'd spent the previous summer in his hometown, recovering from a broken jaw and the emotional trauma that had been accumulating for years.

Even if he did, I doubted he would care. I might have only met Garret in the flesh very recently, but my past knowledge of him told me he was a narcissistic asshole.

When I didn't speak, he muttered a curse. "You haven't called me."

Instead of answering, I scribbled down his usual order. "Your drink will be over, and I'll have the cook get started on your food."

Turning to go, I tried to put him out of my mind so I could focus on work, but before I could take the first step away from his booth, he wrapped his huge hand around my wrist. I stiffened, but I told myself to relax. This was not Manuel. I was safe here. Garret Hannigan wouldn't physically hurt me.

Would he?

He'd threatened to many, many times. But that was just him being a keyboard warrior—or so Nova had told me. His sister had assured me Garret would never put his hands on a woman with the intention of violence. And if he ever did, she and their mother would make sure it never happened again.

Heart pounding with fear and memories of how Manuel would have already jerked me down beside him in the booth raced through my mind. He would have taken delight in the terror that was undoubtedly shining out of my eyes. And then he would have done things to me that no one would have seen beneath the table.

Panic made my breathing come in sharp gasps, and I began to tremble as I glanced down at where Garret's fingers were wrapped around my flesh. There was no chance he missed the way my pulse was close to two hundred beats a minute.

"Hey." His voice sounded far away, but because it didn't have that thick Colombian accent to it, I was distracted enough to lift my terrified eyes to look at his face.

He'd stood and was in my personal space, standing over me despite the six-inch heels that were part of my waitress uniform. With his right hand still wrapped around mine, although gentler now, he lifted his other to touch my cheek. "Take a deep breath, little Lis. I swear on my life that I will never harm you."

Seeing his green eyes helped remind me that this wasn't Manuel. My stepbrother's eyes were an ugly brown color, not the warm hunter green of Garret's. I swallowed and attempted to regulate my breathing.

"I'm sorry," Garret murmured after a long moment passed, and my heart rate finally slowed to something that wouldn't cause my heart to explode at any moment. Lifting my hand, he kissed where his fingers had been. Every fine hair on my body rose in reaction. When my nipples instantly hardened, I had to swallow a gasp. I hadn't reacted like that to anyone—ever. I thought Manuel had killed that urge in me. "I didn't mean to frighten you."

"I-it's okay," I choked out, watching as he skimmed his thumb over a faint scar on my wrist. I remembered that injury well. Matias had been away, and Garret had made yet another comment on my social media that had baited my stepbrother. Manuel had dragged me down to his room, thrown me on his bed, tied my arms above my head with barbed wire, and—

Shutting down that horrible memory, I tugged my wrist free from his grip. "I-I, um, I'll just get this order in and be right back with your whisky."

Garret

A FEELING I was unused to experiencing settled in the pit of my stomach as I watched Lis walk away. I hadn't meant to scare her, but there was no mistaking how frightened she'd been when I'd suddenly grabbed her.

In the two weeks that I'd been coming to Cherry Bomb to see her, I'd never seen her be anything but sassy. Nothing seemed to faze her.

Guilt churned in my gut, and I gritted my teeth as I retook my seat. But my gaze fell on her ass as she walked toward the bar, and like every other time I was presented with that back view, my body turned to stone. When she walked out of view, I tilted my head, keeping those ass cheeks in sight until she reached the bartender. I couldn't hear what she said, but I could read her lips as she called out for my drink before punching my food order into the computer at the end of the bar.

The entire time I had my eyes on her, I was acutely aware of every other motherfucker in the vicinity looking at her too. Especially the two jerk-offs at the high-top with their hands dirty from their hot wings and their cheap draft beer quickly disappearing.

As I'd sat there waiting on Lis, watching her with her other customers, I'd been ready to pull out my Glock and put a bullet in every fucker's skull. Acid had burned in my throat and stomach as she'd touched them flirtatiously, letting her fingers trail over their arms or backs, pressing her tits into them.

It wasn't something I hadn't seen before. Every night was the same bullshit, and I knew it was so they would leave her better tips. A waitress's tips were her livelihood, something I was all too aware of. My family owned a bar back in Creswell Springs, California. And my aunt Quinn co-owned Aggie's, the best restaurant in all of Trinity County. For the waitresses who worked for her, even though they were well paid, how much they earned in tips was sometimes the difference between making the difficult decision to pay rent that month or buy groceries for their families.

But the girls who worked at Aggie's wore jeans

and tops that covered everything. Lis, however, walked around with her tits about to pop out of the top of her shirt, exposing her flat stomach. Her shorts barely had enough material to cover her pussy in the front and a string up her perfect ass. Some of the other waitresses wore fishnets under their shorts, but Lis wasn't one of them.

I could have called Adrian Volkov and requested he change the waitresses' uniforms. He was a silent partner in the club, and if he made a suggestion about the work attire, it would happen. But I didn't want to draw unwanted attention to my regular visits to Cherry Bomb. Volkov would start questioning why I was there so often, and then when he found out about my interest in Lis, he would gossip like an old lady with Ciro and Cristiano.

It would take less than a day for the news to get back to my folks, and I wasn't ready to examine what I was feeling for the sexy little waitress, let alone field questions from my mother about the tiny goddess who had captured my attention so thoroughly.

The bartender placed the glass of Macallan beside Lis. Picking it up, she placed it on her tray and started back toward me. My gaze drifted up and down her body with each step she took. Without the heels, I figured she was about five-four. Her hair was down, which I loved. The glossy locks ended just above the small of her back in silky waves that I ached to run my fingers through.

As she neared, customers at one of her other tables stopped her. She put on that flirty smile she'd never once graced me with as she listened. Pulling out her order pad, she scribbled something down before winking at the fortysomething man and continuing on toward me.

Placing the tumbler in front of me, she gripped the tray with both hands so hard her knuckles turned white. "Your food should be out shortly."

"Who hurt you, Lis?" I snapped, unable to take that she had become so nervous with me. She flinched at my harsh tone, and I groaned. "I'm sorry, sweetheart. It's just, the thought of someone putting their hands on you pisses me off."

She huffed and took a step back. "I'll make sure you get your ketchup too. But maybe tomorrow night, you should order a chicken entree or perhaps a salad. All that red meat is bad for you."

I felt my lips twitch and fought a grin. "You worried about my heart, blue eyes?"

That earned me another sexy little huff, but I was happy to see that she eased her tight hold on the tray. "Whatever. Eat what you want. I'll be back when your food is ready."

As she walked away, the grin won, until she

stopped at the high-top and started touching the thicker, dark-haired douchebag's arm. Her laughter reached me, and I itched to pull my gun and pop the bastard between the eyes. But I'd promised Ciro and Cristiano I would do better. That I'd stop letting my anger get the best of me.

It had been a struggle, until I walked into Cherry Bomb one night and set eyes on Lis. Between her blue eyes that couldn't quite hide the past that haunted her and those slight curves, I'd felt like I'd had reality slammed into me. I wanted her, but it was more than that.

I wasn't the type of guy who was empathetic; I couldn't sense what people needed the way my little sister could. And even if I could, I didn't have much of an urge to fix the things I knew needed fixing for them. Yet with Lis, all I wanted to do was make whoever had hurt her to the point that she'd nearly had a panic attack when I'd grabbed her pay. That motherfucker needed to die, and I needed to be the one to take his life from him.

And still, that wasn't enough for me. I wanted to toss her over my shoulder and carry her out of that club. Drop her into my bed and keep her there so that I knew where she was and that she was safe. She would stay there until I built us a house, possibly beside the one Ryan wanted to build for my sister behind the mansion within the compound's walls.

Nova was great with everyone. Sweet and gentle —to the point of annoyance at times—but she would get along just fine with Lis. My sister would welcome my girl into the family, make sure she was comfortable, and ensure that the others treated her with the affection and respect that she deserved.

Those thoughts gave me a moment of pause. They were gigantic ideas that I'd never considered before in my entire life. But for some reason, they didn't scare the ever-loving fuck out of me like I would have expected them to. I wasn't sure if it was because I was ready to settle down in general, or if Lis was simply that special.

Her laughter reached my ears again, causing my entire body to react, and I knew the answer in that instant.

It was Lis.

She flirted with the two men at the high-top for a few more moments before checking on her other customers. Once they were taken care of, she went to the kitchen to grab my food. I kept my eyes on her every move, and even when she was out of sight in the kitchen, my gaze didn't leave the swinging doors until she reappeared. A feeling in the pit of my stomach told me if I didn't keep my eyes on her every second, she would disappear and I'd regret it for the rest of my life.

The closer she got to my booth, the slower her steps became, and I had to clench my hands into fists beneath the table to keep from jumping up and snatching her out of this damn club. Anytime she wasn't behind the closed doors of a bedroom—our bedroom—she needed to be covered from neck to ankle. Every inch of that alabaster skin was for my eyes only.

But instinct told me if I tried to do any of that shit, she might shank me, which only put another grin on my face.

Yeah, Lis would fit in just fine with my family. Both the one that I worked for here in New York, and the one back in California.

She placed the plate with the burger in front of me, then the basket of loaded cheese fries beside it, before dropping a bottle of ketchup within reach. "No tomatoes on the burger, yet you smother the thing in ketchup?"

I picked up a fry with cheese, bacon, spring onions, and sour cream all over it. "I like what I like," I told her with a wink.

Heat filled her cheeks before she rolled her eyes at me. "I hope you have a cardiologist lined up for your thirties."

"See? You are concerned about my heart, blue eyes." I lifted another fry, but instead of stuffing it into my mouth, I brought it to her lips. To my delight, she didn't even hesitate before taking a bite—and none too gently, nipping my finger in the process.

I groaned as her teeth sank into the backs of my index and thumb, my cock so hard, the tip started leaking. Her aggression was just as sexy as that sweet innocence I sensed right below the surface. "Ah, baby," I murmured. "You just sealed our fate."

Cali

WORKING from six in the evening until two in the morning, on my feet the entire time in heels, was enough to cause me agony.

The moment I stepped into the dressing room and kicked off my shoes, I released a moan right along with half the other waitresses. Before I even started changing into my street clothes, I sat on the bench in front of my locker and started rubbing the arches of my feet on the tennis balls I kept to help with the pain.

While everyone else rushed to get out of their uniforms, I just sat there with my eyes closed as I tried to release as much of the ache from my feet and toes as possible. Eventually, my stomach started to grumble, and I began to yawn. Tossing the yellow balls into the bottom of the locker, I exchanged my work clothes for a thick sweater, jeans, and the coat I'd found for a steal at a thrift store a few blocks from my apartment.

Once my sneakers were tied up, I slipped my hands into the thin gloves I'd bought at the same shop as the coat and then placed earmuffs over my ears. They were childish, with little pink kitten ears on the top, but I'd gotten them for two dollars.

Ready for the cold late-December weather of NYC, I grabbed my cross-body and slung it over my shoulder before using my foot to close the locker door. I didn't keep my tips in my bag, but in the bottom of my shoes, something Kim had also taught me after I'd gotten my purse snatched the second week I'd lived with her. But that was back when I worked at the diner close to our apartment, so the thief hadn't gotten nearly as much of my hard-earned cash as he would have if he'd taken it after one of my shifts at Cherry Bomb.

My stomach was starting to growl louder, and my mind was on the cup of instant noodles I planned on making as soon as I got home. Licking my lips at the thought of food, I walked out the back door, giving the bouncer a nod when he called a goodnight. I lifted my hand, ready to flag down a taxi. It would have been cheaper to take a bus, and because it was before five in the morning, I could have asked the driver to drop me off at the corner where my apartment was. But I was exhausted and decided that the cab fare was worth it to get home faster so I could fill my empty stomach sooner.

But instead of one of the yellow cabs stopping for me, a huge black SUV braked right in front of me. Instinctively, I took several steps back, my hand going into my bag to reach for the can of bear mace I'd acquired from Jack Hannigan when I lived at Salvation back in Creswell Springs.

The back window powered down, and Jack's cousin sat there, watching me. Just as he'd done all night inside the club. I'd felt his gaze on me every minute I was on the floor, dropping off food and drinks to my other customers. The only time I'd gotten a break from the goose-bump-inducing thrill of his eyes on me was when I had to go to the kitchen or took a single bathroom break to pee sometime around midnight.

Garret hadn't left until about twenty minutes before we closed, much like he'd done every night for the past two weeks. But this was the first time he'd approached me after club hours.

Just because I knew who he was, I didn't release the hold I had on the spray can. Bear mace was essentially illegal in the state of New York, but the man sitting in the decked-out SUV wasn't exactly a law-abiding citizen. The Vitucci family could play it up to the media that they were legit these days, but I, of all people, knew better.

After all, they had taken over my stepfather's cocaine fields after his death and were now the single biggest coke supplier on the East Coast, if not the entire country. I didn't doubt that made the Mexican cartel unhappy, but not even they had the balls to take on the Vituccis. And Garret not only worked for the crime family, but he was also related to them through Ciro Donati.

In a word, that made Garret Hannigan untouchable.

But if I spray him with mace, would I technically be touching him?

That question flashed through my mind, and I actually had to fight a smile. Amused, I released my death grip on the can, but I didn't take my hand from the bag—just in case.

"It's cold. Let me drive you home." It came out as a command, and I grasped the mace once again, until he said the one word I never thought I would hear from his lips. "Please."

Unable to hide my surprise, I pulled my hand free of my bag—minus the mace—and took a small step closer to the SUV. As I did, he opened his door and stepped out onto the sidewalk. Another wave of surprise hit me at how courteous he was being. I knew he wasn't drunk since he'd only had the one glass of Macallan all night, but this was leaps and bounds away from the version of Garret I'd come to know—not just over the past two weeks in person, but in the years he'd tormented me on social media.

Taking my hand, he helped me into the back of the SUV and then slid in beside me. I moved as close to the other door as possible, trying to put more distance between us. There was a partition between the back of the vehicle and the front where the driver was. As Garret closed the door, he hit a button, lowering the divider just enough to speak to the man behind the wheel.

Fear hit me hard and fast when he gave the driver my address.

"How the fuck do you know where I live?" I demanded, already reaching for the door handle.

Garret pressed his lips into a hard line before shrugging. "I may have followed you a time or two."

"Followed me," I repeated in a squeaky voice before my anger returned. "You mean you've been stalking me!"

"Ensuring you got home safely," he amended.

"Following me like a creeper without my permission," I gritted out. "That is basically the definition of stalking."

"The definition of stalking is to pursue or approach something in a stealthy manner," he stated matter-of-factly. "Or did you mean stalker? That is defined as a person who harasses or persecutes someone with unwanted and obsessive attention. I have to admit that I do find myself becoming more and more obsessed where you are concerned, but I don't believe I've harassed or persecuted you."

"Are you a walking dictionary?" I muttered, shocked at how he'd just defined the two words verbatim.

He grinned. "Something like that. I was able to graduate at the age of seventeen, despite skipping more classes than I actually attended because I have an eidetic memory. I read something once, and it gets stuck in my head forever."

"Just words?" I asked cautiously, wondering if he did remember me and had just been bullshitting me by pretending not to recognize me, or if he really did not have a clue who I actually was. "What about people? I know it's a leap in the opposite direction, but I ask because I watched a Korean drama where the main character had prosopagnosia, which is basically face blindness."

"I don't just have to read something to get it in

my brain, but yeah, it's mainly restricted to words. I've never even heard of prosopagnosia, but I do sometimes have trouble placing where I've seen people before. My sister, she can place any celebrity in every movie she's ever seen. But unless they are people I have a vested interest in, they're just blank faces to me."

"Sounds more like a narcissism problem to me," I muttered.

Garret threw back his head and laughed. "Fuck, blue eyes. I think you and my sister would get along really well."

I rolled my eyes to hide what I was feeling. Nova and I did get along. I loved that girl. She'd been my hero, the person who had saved me from what would have surely been a fate worse than death. Nova was my guardian angel and best friend.

When Matias got sick, I had known it was only a matter of time before he died, and then there would be no one left to protect me from Manuel. The beatings...and other abuse...had gotten worse with each passing day. Once his father passed, Manuel would have done anything to get his hands on my portion of the inheritance, which would have meant he would have tried to marry me. And then once he had the business shares and money in his grasp, I would have been useless to him.

It had been only a matter of time until he killed me. But Nova snuck me out of the hotel my step-brother kept me locked in while he was at the hospital every day with Matias, gave me her credit card, and told me where to go to get the help I needed to heal from that last beating that had left me with a broken jaw and even more emotional scars than ever before.

There was no way I could ever repay Nova for what she'd done for me, or the people at Salvation who'd had a hand in helping me heal afterward.

Warm, rough fingers touched my cheek, and I flinched away from the contact on instinct. Garret instantly dropped his hand. "Sorry. I didn't mean to startle you."

I swallowed down the knot of emotion that always filled my throat whenever I thought about the events of the previous summer. "I-it's okay. I was just lost in some old memories."

It was dark in the back of the SUV except for the passing lights of other vehicles and streetlamps. One flashed over his face when I lifted my eyes to look at him, and I saw his green orbs darken with an emotion I didn't understand. "Obviously, they were bad memories," he said in a gentle tone. "Who hurt you, Lis?"

He'd asked me that earlier in the evening as well,

and I hadn't answered him then. But for some reason, I found I couldn't keep the words locked away this time. "My stepbrother," I said with a shrug. "It got so bad that I eventually ran away from home."

"Does that mean you're all alone in the city?"

"I don't have any family left," I answered, instead of telling him the pathetic truth that I had zero people I could rely on in NYC. At least until Nova moved to the East Coast permanently. If she moved here. From the last few times I'd spoken to her since her birthday, I wasn't so sure if she was still going to make the move. She hadn't confided in me, but I'd gotten the impression that her relationship with Ryan was up in the air.

If she stayed in Creswell Springs, then I would continue to be all alone. It was fine. I was used to not having anyone I could trust or depend on. I'd been taking care of myself ever since my mom had gotten sick. Matias had been a decent stepfather, and I'd never doubted that he cared about me, but the loss of my mother had destroyed something in him. Even before he'd died, he hadn't truly been present.

"What about friends?" Garret persisted.

"None that live in New York." I realized that telling him just how alone I was could be dangerous, so I was quick to mention Kim. "I have a roommate, though. We watch out for each other." That was a huge lie. The only thing she watched out for was the money I contributed to the bills.

"You need more than just one person watching out for you," he muttered unhappily. "I don't like you being without security. I'll have to assign one of my men as your bodyguard." He grunted, his face scrunching up in concentration. "I don't trust any of those fuckers not to try something with you, though. I'll speak to Ryan about it, get you one of his most trusted men to—"

"I don't need a damn bodyguard," I snapped at him, crossing my arms angrily over my chest. "I've been doing just fine on my own since moving here at the end of the summer."

No way was I going to tell him about getting my purse snatched. He didn't need to know that. He was already talking crazy, and if I mentioned the mugging, he was likely to lose his shit. I'd had all I could handle with guys going ballistic at the least little thing.

"Don't argue with me on this, blue eyes," he growled. "How am I supposed to sleep at night if you aren't protected when I'm not around?"

"Easily," I huffed. "You are just some guy I wait on at the club. We mean nothing to each other, Garret."

He balled his hands into fists, and I tensed,

waiting for the first blow. But instead of lifting them to strike me, he flexed his fingers before popping each knuckle one at a time. "Don't say shit like that, Lis. I know you feel something for me. What's between us, this chemistry, it's too strong for it to be one-sided."

I turned my head, looking out the side window, hiding away. "I don't know what you're talking about."

"Bullshit," he snapped. "Pretending is for little kids, and we're both grown-ass adults. Tell the truth. Admit it. Out loud. You like me coming into the club every night. You like that my eyes are always on you. You enjoy driving me fucking crazy with jealousy by touching those bastards who think they actually have a chance with you. But we both know they don't. Because the truth is, you want me."

"I—"

"Don't. Lie." He grasped my waist and pulled me onto his lap. I went as still as a statue, scared of what was about to happen, yet oddly turned on to the point that my panties had become uncomfortably wet.

Another first for me. I'd thought Manuel's abuse had killed those kinds of urges and needs in me. But as Garret placed me so that I was straddling his lap, and I felt his hardness flex against my core, I had to bite my tongue to hold back a moan.

Holding me in place with one hand curved over my ass, he lifted the other to tenderly tip my head back. "I'm not going to hurt you, Lis. Fuck, I just want to be near you. We can take things as slowly as you want, but please, just give me—*us*—a chance."

Garret

LIS REMAINED silent as we stepped off the elevator on her floor. I stayed back a few steps, allowing her to lead the way to her apartment. It wasn't the worst part of the city, but the security in the place left a lot to be desired. There hadn't been a doorman, but at least it didn't have those damn intercom things that went to each apartment. Too many lazy people in the world would let anyone they didn't know into the building just to stop someone from constantly buzzing them until they got what they wanted.

And then those freaks could easily get in and hurt Lis.

I was already making notes on the upgrades that needed to be made to the place. Doorman. Better lock on the front door. Cameras—everywhere. It wouldn't take more than a day to get everything taken care of, even though it was New Year's Eve. I just had to call Ryan and get one of the tech guys over there to make it happen.

Lis stopped in front of an unmarked door. I'd been so focused on the security updates that I'd completely missed the fact that none of the apartments was actually marked. That was just as unsafe as the lack of a doorman. What if she had an emergency and needed EMT assistance? They couldn't readily identify where she was, and that was unacceptable.

Whoever owned the building would be getting a visit, that was for fucking sure.

She paused in the act of twisting the key in the dead bolt. Nervously, she looked up at me. "Why are you growling?"

"I don't like that the doors are unmarked," I explained. "That's dangerous."

She finished unlocking the door and twisted the knob. "I know. I told the super about it the first week I was here, but then he started bitching at my roommate and me. The next month, the rent increased by two hundred dollars." Shrugging, she pushed the heavy door open. "Kim nearly kicked me out, but I've been covering the extra costs, so she calmed down. I haven't mentioned the lack of identifying markers for the apartments again."

I gritted my teeth. First, the super, I promised myself. And then the owner of the building. Both were going to get visits, and neither was going to enjoy it.

Putting aside the need to inflict violence on those two scumbags for the moment, I followed Lis into the apartment. The living room was clean, with only a few decorations to give it a somewhat lived-in feel. None of the pictures on the walls had Lis in them, but there were a few things spread around the room that reminded me of her. Like the fuzzy pillows on the couch. They were gray and looked soft to the touch, but firm.

The urge to drop down and rest my head on them was nearly too strong to resist, but then I heard Lis's stomach grumbling. "You should have said you were hungry. We could have stopped for something to eat."

"It's fine. I have some instant noodles—"

My glower cut her off, and I imagined it was the same look my mother would have given me had I said the same stupid thing. Instant noodles? Felicity Hannigan would have taken a wooden spoon to my ass for simply thinking of eating such trash. Shaking my head at Lis, I walked into the kitchen, which was just off the living room, and opened the fridge.

There wasn't a lot to choose from. It was obvious shelves were split, with Lis and her roommate having a side each. One side had eggs, a few veggies, and a single steak. It was a cheap cut, but still, it was protein. There were also bottles of water and diet soda. Then there was the other side, which held a few bottles of water, two cans of a cheaper brand of diet soda, and nothing else.

My gut knotted. "Which side is yours, blue eyes?"

She ignored me as she opened the pantry, and from what I could see, it, too, was split into sides. One side had cans of soup, popcorn, and a few other snacks. The other had packs of ramen, cups of noodles, and a few other cheap microwaveable items. Lis took a cup of noodles off the shelf and started to open the lid, but I snatched it out of her hand before she could pull it up.

"Hey," she whined. "I'm hungry."

"And I'm going to feed you," I assured her, returning to the fridge to pull the eggs and steak free.

"No, wait!" she cried. "Those are Kim's. She'll get mad if we eat her food."

I started searching for a frying pan. "I'll replace everything we use."

"But she'll come home and see—"

"Lis, I'll have every shelf in the damn fridge filled to capacity within an hour. But you're hungry now, and there is no way I'm letting you eat a cup of fucking noodles." I searched for oil and seasonings. Once I found them, I nodded toward the door. "Go shower and get comfortable while I make your dinner."

"But…"

"Please," I murmured softly. "Let me feed you."

She nibbled on her bottom lip, but after a slight hesitation, she huffed and stomped out of the kitchen. While I was heating the pan, I heard the shower turn on from somewhere close by and tried not to imagine her standing under the spray of water naked.

Needing to take my mind off what was happening just a matter of feet away, I cooked the steak before frying half the eggs in the carton. The entire time, I was on my phone, ordering the groceries. I didn't know if a store would deliver this late, so I texted my driver to pick everything up.

By the time Lis walked into the kitchen with her damp hair hanging down her back, dressed in pajama shorts that went all the way to her knees and a matching long-sleeved top that was almost as long, the food was ready and my driver was on his way to pick up the groceries.

"It smells delicious," she said grudgingly as she sat down at the small table where I'd laid out two loaded plates with a half a steak and three eggs on each. I'd found a loaf of whole wheat bread and toasted several slices. I placed the stack of toast on the table between the plates, along with some butter. "Kim is going to kill me."

"Don't worry about your roommate," I commanded, taking the seat across from her. "Eat, blue eyes."

Rolling those eyes at me, she picked up her knife and fork and cut into the steak. I watched her take the first bite, almost holding my breath as I waited to see if she liked it.

The moan that left her lips made my cock hard as steel. As she chewed, her eyes rolled back into her head. "Oh God," she muttered. "I haven't eaten anything this good in…" She broke off, leaving the rest of what she was going to say hanging while she took another bite.

"In?" I urged her to finish what she was going to say, but she kept her gaze on her plate as she busted the yolk of one of the eggs and dipped a slice of toast into it. "How long has it been since you've had some-thing home-cooked, Lis?"

"A while," she said with a shrug.

"Days?" She took another bite of steak. "Weeks?"

That didn't get me an answer either, and my gut only tightened more. "Months?"

Huffing, she shrugged again. "Sometime in August. I don't remember what day specifically, okay? Happy now?"

"No, baby," I whispered, so the rage boiling inside me didn't spill over into my voice and scare her. She'd been eating nothing but cheap junk for months. It wasn't her fault. She was living on a budget, one that was even tighter after the damned super raised the rent. But if I'd known, if I'd had an inkling that she was out there in the world and needed looking after, I would have scooped her up in a heartbeat and taken care of her. "That sure as fuck doesn't make me happy."

Lis stabbed her fork into the steak again, cutting with agitated slashes. "It's cool that you can cook. I don't know many guys who know their way around a kitchen."

Jealousy hit me like an anvil falling on my lap. Jaw clenched, I took a bite of my own food. "My mom made sure I knew the basics before I hit my teens. I'm no chef, but I can pull off a full meal that will satisfy the taste buds while not killing anyone with food poisoning."

Her lips twitched with the ghost of a smile. "That's always a plus." She took another bite and slowly chewed before speaking again. "I only know how to use the microwave, for the most part. And I can boil water without causing too big of a mess. My mom died when I was a little girl, and we had a cook who handled every meal. I tried to learn to cook a few times, but…" Her face darkened, and she lowered her eyes to her plate with a half shrug. "I learned quickly not to get caught anywhere outside of my room if I wanted to stay out of my stepbrother's way."

I dropped my utensils on the plate, balling my hands into fists beside it and causing her startled eyes to jump up to meet mine. "Give me his name, blue eyes," I growled. "I'll make sure you never have to worry about that motherfucker ever again."

Her brows puckered, and she squinted at me for a long moment, studying me curiously before her expression cleared. "He doesn't matter anymore. That's part of my past now. I have a new life without having to fear every step I take within my own home."

"I'm happy for you, baby," I told her honestly. "But I need to eradicate this bastard. If he hurt you even once, then he doesn't deserve to breathe."

She considered me for another moment before licking her lips. "That is weirdly sweet, but I don't want him dead. At least…" She sighed. "At least not right away. I want him to suffer before his death. I want to take everything he's ever wanted away from him before he meets his end."

"I can make that happen," I promised. "Just give me his name, Lis."

"No." She picked up a second slice of toast and soaked up the rest of her yolk with some of the steak's juices. Stuffing a huge bite into her mouth, she dropped the rest on the plate and folded her hands over her stomach with a contented groan. "That was delicious," she said around the food in her mouth, making me fight a grin even as my rage at her stepbrother continued to boil inside me.

"What time does your roommate normally get home?" I asked, needing the distraction. I either wanted to go out and kill her stepbrother or pin her to the nearest wall and fuck us both blind.

Lis glanced at the illuminated clock on the microwave. "It varies. I heard her talking to some of the other dancers while I was changing. They were making plans to go out for drinks. I bet one of the whales offered to keep the party going somewhere else. 'Drinks' is normally the code they use when that happens, so they don't get in trouble for meeting up with a customer after hours."

"And you're not worried about getting in trouble

for letting a customer take you home?" I asked curiously.

She rolled those gorgeous blue eyes at me. Maybe she thought it would annoy me, but all it did was make my cock leak. I loved her sassiness. "Puh-lease. It's no secret you are more or less related to someone high up within Cherry Bomb. No one even bothers to pat you down before they let you in. If you're special enough for that, then no one is going to give me shit for letting you drive me home on a cold winter's night."

"I like that you think I'm special."

An adorable snort-like laugh escaped her. "Of course that's all you heard. We both know you're a gangster, Garret."

"Do people even use that word these days?" I mused. "I've been called a thug plenty of times, but no one has called me a gangster before. I like it. Sounds kind of badass."

"I take it back," she said with another cute snort. "You're no gangster. You are one hundred percent a pain in the ass."

Garret

AFTER MAKING sure the side of the fridge that belonged to Lis was filled—and her roommate's eggs and steak had been replaced—I knew I had to head home. The sun would be up soon, and I needed a few hours of sleep before handling the super and apartment building owner.

But every time I decided it was time to tell her goodnight, I couldn't bring myself to open my mouth, let alone stand up from where we'd been sitting on the couch with the television on. She didn't have cable, but there were a few streaming services available. When she said they were all her roommate's accounts and she could only watch them when Kim was out, I ordered a flat-screen for her room that would be delivered before she had to go to work later that night.

I planned on setting it up and signing in to all of my own streaming accounts for her to watch what she wanted, whenever she felt like it. Until then, I had other things that needed to be taken care of.

When she yawned, I finally forced myself to move. Getting to my feet, I took her hand and led her to the door. "Make sure this is locked up tight when I leave."

Her eyes flickered with something that resembled disappointment, and I stored that away for later. But then she rolled those gemlike blue eyes. "Sure thing, Dad."

I tapped her under the chin with my index finger. "I'm going to wait on the other side until I hear all the locks engage."

"I stand behind the pain-in-the-ass observation I made earlier," she grumbled.

"You wouldn't be the first to say that to me," I told her with a grin. "Get some sleep. I'll see you tonight."

"I thought all gangsters worked at night. If you're spending every night at Cherry Bomb, your boss must be getting pissed at you for slacking on the job."

"I'm not a gangster, baby," I teased as I bent my head to brush a kiss over the top of her head. She was so much shorter than me in her heels at the club, but barefoot, she was even more so. I basically had to fold myself in half just to get to the top of her head.

As my lips grazed her, her hands flew out, pressing against my chest. I could feel how tense she was, but she didn't push me away. Instead, she clenched her fingers in the material of my shirt, as if she was undecided on what to do. Kissing her one more time, I took her hands and untangled her fingers as I stepped into the hall outside her apartment. "If you need anything, you have my number."

She lowered her lashes and gave me a stiff nod.

"Dress warm for work tonight."

"I'm not a child, Garret," she said with an annoyed huff. "I know how to take care of myself. I've been doing it for most of my life."

"I'll send a car to drive you to the club." When she opened her mouth to argue, I turned in the direction of the elevators, calling over my shoulder, "Sleep tight, blue eyes."

"Pain in the ass," I heard her grumble seconds before the door slammed shut. I paused, listening for the locks to engage. Once they did, I continued on my way. Before I could press the call button, the elevator doors slid open, and a girl I vaguely recognized from the club stumbled off.

Her hair was a tangled mess, her clothes in disarray, and her makeup smeared under her eyes and around her mouth. I stepped back when she nearly bumped into me, causing her to grab for the wall instead. I gave her an annoyed glance before walking onto the elevator.

"Rude," she muttered, and I saw her sway as she continued down the corridor toward Lis's apartment.

My driver was waiting downstairs, and I got in the back, my phone already out as I started making arrangements for later in the day. I was so focused on what I was doing, it took a few minutes for me to realize I was home and the sun was breaking through the clouds.

After I gave the driver instructions for later, he nodded before I stepped out. I yawned as I walked into the building, mumbling hellos to the men on duty beside the elevators. I got grunts in return, all of them having just come on shift but still only half alert because of the early hour.

The ride up to the apartment I shared with Ryan was over in a blink, and to my surprise, my sister came running toward the elevator as I was stepping off. "When did you get here?" I asked, part of me happy to see her.

I hadn't seen or spoken to her since her birthday the month before. Maybe I should have called her and apologized, explained that I'd lied about what I'd said. That she'd believed me when I'd said Ryan was hooking up with anyone was funny as hell, but she had, and I regretted hurting her.

"I'm not here," she said, her voice emotionless as she stepped into the elevator. "You didn't see me."

Noticing what she was wearing, I stopped the doors from closing. "You can't go out in that," I snapped. Stubborn little girls were going to be the death of me. Grumbling under my breath, I shoved my knit hat, gloves, scarf, and coat into her hands. "It's freezing out there. Do you want to catch pneumonia?"

Her green eyes flickered with surprise, and I mentally cursed myself that she would be shocked that I actually cared about her well-being. It hadn't always been like that with us. I'd always loved my baby sister, but after we both realized that New York was where we were meant to be, things had started to change. I hated living in Creswell Springs when I knew that my soul belonged in NYC. Yet, for Nova, she seemed to make the best out of any situation, and she grew content during the times we weren't on the East Coast.

It annoyed me that while I was miserable as hell, she was able to laugh and have the time of her life. We didn't belong in that small-ass town. We needed the big-city life and our mother's Italian side of the family to thrive. I wanted to hate Nova for her ability to carry on with her life as if things didn't feel like they were put on pause whenever we weren't in New York. Over the years, it more or less became my mission to make her as miserable as I felt when we were stuck in Northern California.

Grimacing with regret for how I'd treated her over the past few years, I walked toward my bedroom, in need of a shower and a little sleep. Before I reached my door, Ryan's opened, and he walked out, Nova's coat in his hand and his phone lifting toward his ear.

"I gave her my coat and things," I informed him. "She won't freeze."

His dark eyes narrowed on me. "You're home late."

"I'll be late getting home tonight as well." I glanced at Nova's coat. "I'm going to assume you have plans with my sister."

He grunted but gave me a nod. "Did you know she was in town?"

"Didn't have a clue until I saw her just now. Does that mean you didn't know either?" His clenched jaw confirmed he didn't. "You two haven't been talking?"

"We're good now," he hedged.

"But you weren't before?" Guilt tightened my gut. Shit, had I done more damage to my sister's heart than I realized?

"She was mad at me. Someone told her I was fucking my old secretary."

That someone was me, but obviously, Nova hadn't told him. Otherwise, I knew I already would have been in a wooden box back in the family cemetery in Creswell Springs. Either there or fish food for all the aquatic life in the Hudson River. My baby sis was loyal to a fault. She'd been protecting me all her life, and even though I'd lied and said things that had hurt her, she still loved me enough to protect me.

I didn't deserve her, but I planned on trying to change that.

"I need a few guys later today," I told my future brother-in-law. "The bigger, the better."

"You in trouble?" he asked, deadpan.

"No, man," I assured him. "My girl has a shitty landlord and super. I need to make sure that they know they can't play games with her or her safety. I also need your best tech. The whole place needs a security upgrade. My brain is on fire, thinking she's not safe in her own home."

"Everyone will be waiting downstairs for you by noon," he promised. "And if you need anything else, just let me know. Pop can make a few calls if you need him to."

"This should take care of the problem, but I'll keep that in mind in case it doesn't." I shot a glance at the closed elevator. "Are you going to be with Nova?"

"Pietro is with her right now. I'll join her later. I have a few things to handle first. Plans to make for tonight."

Brows lifted, I glanced back at him. "Does that mean you're going to ask her to marry you tonight?"

"I asked last night," he admitted sullenly.

"She turned you down?" I asked in disbelief.

"No. She just wants to wait longer than I'm prepared to. Damn stubborn little angel."

I couldn't help snickering. "She's a Hannigan. Of course she's stubborn."

Cali

AN ANNOYING TAP-TAP-TAP WOKE ME. It sounded like construction work rather than someone knocking, but since it also seemed to be coming from my front door, I had no choice but to get up and see what was going on. Especially when Kim started kicking at the wall that separated our rooms and yelling for me to see who it was.

Grabbing my favorite old cardigan—another steal I'd found at a thrift store—I wrapped it around myself as I walked half blind through the apartment and opened the front door. It took me a few seconds to realize what I was looking at as the guy in jeans and a long-sleeved shirt stood in front of me, frowning. He had a drill in one hand and what looked like a number in the other.

"Miss Brewer?"

It took a moment for me to remember that was my new last name. I wasn't Calista Ramirez any longer, but Lis Brewer. I even had a different birthday and social security number, thanks to Gracie Hannigan.

"Miss Brewer, are you well?" the man asked again, sounding concerned.

I blinked a few times, dispelling the memory of when Gracie had handed me the envelope with all my new credentials in it before I'd gotten on the bus that would take me back to New York. I missed the pseudo-family I'd made back in Creswell Springs. Not just Gracie, her husband Hawk, and their son Jack. But all the other women who had lived at Sanctuary and many members of the Hannigan clan.

It was lonely in the city on my own. Which, I told myself, was why I'd allowed Garret to stay so long when he'd brought me home after work. Fuck, it was the excuse I was going with, and I wasn't going to allow myself to think about it any deeper than that.

"I'm okay," I told the man before me. "But, um, what are you doing?" I glanced down the hall in either direction. The guy with the drill wasn't the only one present, however. There was a guy at the stairwell installing a security camera. When I glanced at the other door for the second set of stairs, I saw a camera was already in place. It was one of those high-tech cameras, too, that did a full 360 of the entire area.

"Did the building get a new super?" I mused, more to myself than the man standing in front of me.

He smirked down at me. "Let's just say the current guy in charge saw the error of his ways for not properly protecting his tenants."

I felt a sudden pounding behind my eyes that came on so quickly, I nearly groaned at the pain. "Fucking gangsters," I growled. "You work for Garret Hannigan?"

"Sometimes," he said with a shrug. "More often than not these days, I take my orders from Ryan Vitucci, though."

"Of course you do," I grumbled, crossing my arms over my chest angrily. "How much is my rent going to go up now? Huh? You know, I like having a little extra spending money in case of emergencies, and this is going to eat away at that nest egg I've been trying to build. You go back to Garret goddamn Hannigan and tell him—"

"Whoa," the man before me said with a strained laugh. "You should say whatever you need to directly to him. I'm just doing my job, lady. No need to bitch at me for earning my pay."

"I'm sure you earn every one of your blood-covered pennies with ease," I snapped. Stepping back, I slammed the door in his face and stomped through the apartment to my bedroom. Snatching my phone off the charger, I swiped my thumb over Garret's recently added information and waited.

"Blue eyes!"

I barely had time to catch my breath at how happy he sounded to be hearing from me before I remembered the reason for my call. "What the fuck are you doing?" I snarled. "Do you realize how much my rent is going to go up with all these added 'security measures'? I have no doubt that you either roughed up my super or threatened to in order to get them put in place."

"Lis, baby, calm down." He tried to soothe.

But I was suddenly finding it hard to catch my breath. "You ruined everything," I got out between gasps. "My roommate…is going to be so…so mad. I'll…have to…to find somewhere else…to live."

"No, no, sweetheart. Just listen," he urged. "Your rent isn't going to go up. I'm taking care of all the upgrades personally."

"Don't…lie." I dropped down onto the end of my bed when my vision grew dark around the edges, fighting the panic that was attempting to consume me. It had been so long since I'd had an attack, but this was too much. He was too much. I never should have let him bring me home the night before. I never should have let him stay. All he'd ever done was hurt me. Maybe it had only been behind a screen, with a keyboard, but psychological pain was still pain, damn it.

Then I remembered who exactly I was dealing with and what he was capable of when he wasn't trying to scare little girls on the internet. "Is the super in the hospital? Is he even still breathing?"

"He might have a permanent limp," he said after a pause, his tone reluctant and maybe a little petulant. "But he completely deserved it. I also got your rent lowered back to its original price. The owner saw the error of his ways and was generous enough to reduce it."

"Oh fuck." I sucked in a deep breath. "I won't have to wait for Kim to throw a tantrum over this. They're going to evict me. I'm…going to…to be homeless."

"Goddamn it, Lis!" he exploded, and I couldn't control the flinch at the harshness of his tone. "I will be there in fifteen minutes. Until then, you stay right where you are and put your head between your knees. If I get there and you've passed out because of this fucking panic attack, I'm going to—"

The phone went silent before he could finish the threat. I gaped down at the phone in my hand. Oddly, my panic attack had started to ease, but I was

TERRI ANNE BROWNING

still shaken from the fear of what was most likely to happen after he'd gone all gangster, threatening my super and the owner of the building.

Manuel had done shit like that all the time when I lived in Colombia. He'd throw his weight around, thinking he was just as powerful as Matias, and piss off the wrong people. Then things would go straight to hell, and afterward, once Matias was done chewing his ass out and embarrassing him in front of all their men, I'd pay for it with another beating.

Shivering, I wrapped my arms around my middle, trying and failing not to remember the beatings...and other things my stepbrother used to do to my body. I had scars, all of them hidden in places Matias never would have seen, but every time I saw my naked reflection in a mirror, I was transported back to the moment I'd gotten each one.

Closing my eyes, I reminded myself that Manuel wasn't a part of my life any longer. I didn't have to see him—not until I was ready to shell out the vengeance I deserved. He couldn't hurt me.

I was safe from his tyranny, the terror of his abuse.

Taking slow, deep breaths, just like I was taught in therapy at Sanctuary, I felt my heart rate calm down. The sweat that had started to bead on my skin began to cool, and the weak, sick feeling I'd been fighting only moments before eased.

When I opened my eyes, I jerked, my shoulders straightening as I found Garret dropping to his knees in front of me.

"How did you get in here?" I demanded, shifting my head back when he tried to cup my face in his hands.

"I'd tell you, but you won't like the answer, so I'm going to keep that to myself for the moment." He pushed my hair back from my face, and I couldn't help flinching, even though his touch was gentle.

His green eyes darkened, and he dropped his hands to his thighs. "I need you to listen to me. Visiting the super and the apartment building owner, that was only to protect you. I won't ever do anything that could potentially harm you."

As tall as he was, even on his knees, he was basically at eye level with me. I frowned at him and, after a few moments, realized that he believed what he was saying. Then again, he worked for the most powerful crime family in the country. Anything he said or did, his family and future brother-in-law would back him up, so there was nothing for him to fear.

It was why he'd never been worried about the possible backlash for all the horrible things he'd said to me over social media when we were teenagers. But he had no idea that with each threat he'd made to harm me, my stepbrother had carried it out. Every single one.

Logic told me to hate this man, but in my heart, I knew who the true villain was. Words were just that, but actions were a different story. Garret had only been taking his anger and frustration out on me after what Manuel had done to Nova in Matias's name. What Manuel did to me, he didn't really need a reason for.

I could have breathed wrong on any given day, and it would have set my stepbrother off. My brain told me I shouldn't blame Garret for what my personal monster did to me.

And damn it, I was tired of being all alone.

Swallowing with difficulty, I forced my muscles to unclench and surprised us both when I threw my arms around Garret's neck. I pressed my face into his shoulder, hiding the emotions swirling around inside me. "Thank you," I whispered. "For trying to help me. I...I don't know if you did, or if you made it worse, but either way, thank you."

He slowly folded his arms around my back, and I felt him turn his head. The graze of his lips on my temple caused my arms to squeeze around him subconsciously. "You're going to learn that I'm here to make everything better, blue eyes. I won't allow anything or anyone to hurt you ever again."

I wanted to laugh at how stupid it was to believe him, but instead, I buried my face deeper into the material of his suit jacket and held on for dear life.

This would most likely end in disaster, but right then, all I cared about was that, for the first time in forever, I wasn't alone. I had someone to hold me, who wanted to protect me.

Not hurt me.

Not make me cry.

And I ached for that so damn bad.

Garret

ONCE THE TV was mounted to Lis's bedroom wall and I had all the streaming apps set up, I tucked her back into bed. She insisted she was going to work later, even though I'd asked her to quit. If she wanted a job so damn badly, I would find her one. But she was stubborn as hell—just like every other female in my life.

When she told me I could either accept her job and stick around, or keep harping on it and get the fuck out of her life, I shut my mouth. There was no fucking way I was letting her go, and I could wait until I was able to talk her into quitting that fucking job. Until then, I'd just have to spend every night she was at work watching out for her.

Instead of letting my possessiveness get the better of me and ruining what we could have before we even got started, I kissed her brow and let myself out of her apartment. As I walked down the hall to the elevator, I noted the lettering and numbers over each door, as well as the two cameras over each stairwell door.

Ryan's tech guy had taken care of everything; he'd even sent me a link to the feed for the entire building so I could keep an eye on my girl. And then I'd told him to send the bill to the building's owner. Something he was all too happy to pay after the visit I'd paid him and that fucking super earlier in the day.

The broken hand I'd given the dickhead who ran the apartment building had changed his attitude really quickly, but that was nothing compared to the busted knees I'd left the property owner with before he'd gotten on board with making sure all of his tenants were safe. He'd been seconds away from calling the cops on me when I'd casually let it slip that I worked for the Vitucci family. I didn't like to name-drop who my family was, but there were times when it was necessary and just made things easier— less bloody.

Giving Lis a few hours to sleep, I took care of a couple things before I went back to the apartment to get ready for the night. I could hear Ryan and Nova in his room. While some of our family back in

Creswell Springs had always had issues with their relationship, I'd never questioned it. I'd seen it from day one, and even when they were nothing more than best friends, I had still known they would end up together. My sister was strong as fuck, but deep down, I knew even as hard-ass as Ryan was, he was nothing but a lifeless body without Nova.

After a shower, I pulled on a suit, styled my hair back from my face, tossed a scarf around my neck, and slid my arms through the sleeves of my coat as I walked out into the living room. I'd already had a dress, shoes, and a new coat sent to the club for Lis after her shift. She might have insisted on working, but that didn't mean we couldn't have our own New Year's celebration afterward.

"Holy shit," my sister exclaimed as she came out of Ryan's room, and I turned to face her. "When did you learn to dress like a *GQ* model?"

Pausing to tie my scarf, I took in what she was wearing. The long-sleeved black dress had a diamond-like shimmer to it, making her look like one of the sparkly angel ornaments on the Christmas tree we would put up as kids. Her blond hair was curled and pulled over one shoulder, while her makeup was more than I was used to seeing on her. With the heels she wore, she had at least six inches of extra height, but that still put me a good ten inches above her.

She was so tiny, even shorter than our mother, because of how premature she'd been at birth. When she was born, that was the first time I could ever remember being scared. As I'd watched Mom's belly grow, my excitement had built and built. I would have a brother or sister like Lexa and Max did. I would have someone who was mine and only mine.

But then Mom had gone into preterm labor, and I'd heard the adults whispering that we might lose my tiny baby sister. She was in the hospital for so long, it felt like forever before she got to come home. There were rumors of possible side effects from Nova's being born so early, but thankfully, other than a weak immune system the first few years of her life —and how small she was—she'd had no other issues.

"You look beautiful," I told her without hesitation as I pulled my gloves from my coat pocket and slipped them on. "Ryan, man, you're going to have your hands full trying to keep those bastards off my sister tonight. Call me if you need help."

"Where are you going?" Nova asked when I started for the elevator, a teasing note in her voice. "Do you have a hot date or something?"

"Or something," I said, fighting a smile. "It was good to see you, Nova. I figure we won't see each other again before you head home, so give Mom a kiss for me." When I reached her, I paused and

71

tapped her gently on the nose before lowering my voice. This apology was long overdue. "I'm sorry I've been a dick, sis. By now, you probably know I was just blowing smoke with what I said on your birthday. I have no excuse other than I was being an asshole, and I hope you can forgive me."

Nova blinked her green eyes, looking so much like a smaller version of our aunt Raven that it was a little terrifying. She touched my forehead as concern filled her gaze. "Are you sick?" she gasped, her voice dropping dramatically, causing a pang to hit my chest. Fuck, I missed her. "Are you dying, Garret?"

Regret filled me. "I guess I understand why you would think it would take something life-changing like a death sentence to make me be nice to you." I wrapped her in a hug and squeezed her tight. "I'm sorry, sweetheart."

I held her for a long moment before kissing her forehead and stepping back, continuing on to the elevator.

Walking into Cherry Bomb, I took note of how crowded the place was. There wasn't a free seat at the bar or near the stages, and only one table was free but it wasn't in Lis's section. It took a few moments before I found my girl in the crowd, but when I did, I started walking toward her before I even realized my feet were moving.

Six guys were seated in my usual booth. Even as I moved through the crowd, I could see that they were all obviously drunk. The one sitting on the outside of the circular booth closest to where Lis stood, trying to set baskets of appetizers down on the table, was looking at her ass like he wanted to eat his dinner off it. His lips were moving, and even over the noise of the hundreds of people in the club, I could hear his friends laugh at whatever he said.

Lis gave him a tight smile but took a half step back from the table, looking... Not scared, but definitely uncomfortable. I increased my pace, physically pushing people out of my way as I hurried toward her. Several feet away, I saw the motherfucker lift his hand, and I knew exactly where he planned on putting it.

Before he could make contact with her ass, I grabbed his wrist and twisted and then pulled it back. It didn't break, but his scream was enough to stop the conversations of those around us. Still holding on to him, I jerked him to his feet and folded his arm behind his back before bending him over the tabletop.

"Garret," Lis scolded, but I didn't miss the hint of relief in her shaky voice.

"In this club, it's hands off unless the girls decide

they want to touch you," I gritted out, squeezing his wrist a little harder. "Did the lady touch you?"

"She was shaking that ass in my face, man," he said, too drunk to understand that his life was in serious danger. "Girl was begging for my handprint on those round little cheeks."

"Hey, man, we're just here to have a good time," the guy sitting in the middle of the round booth snapped at me. "You're killing our vibe."

I lifted my gaze to his, and whatever he saw in my eyes had his Adam's apple bobbing as he swallowed. Behind me, I sensed movement and then felt Lis step closer to me, her fingers twisting in the material of my coat. I grabbed a fistful of hair of the guy who had been about to slap my girl's ass and jerked him into an upright position before shoving him toward the three bouncers who had finally made their way over to the table.

"Escort them all out," I instructed. "Put them on the banned list."

"But—" one of the bouncers started, but I shot him a glare.

"Do I need to call Volkov?" I gritted out, and the huge man gulped.

"No, Mr. Hannigan. We'll take care of them, sir."

I stood there with Lis at my side until every man at the table was out the door. Once they were gone, I untangled Lis's fingers from my coat and lifted her hand to my lips. "Are you okay, blue eyes?"

She inhaled slowly, seeming to gather herself, but moments later, she released an annoyed huff. "I could have handled that on my own, you know."

I never once let her see my amusement as I nodded. "I know, baby."

She rolled her eyes and started picking up the full baskets of wings, onion rings, and other appetizers that she'd placed on the table only minutes before. "I'll get your order put in."

I slid into the round booth. "I'll have the grilled chicken wedge salad," I told her as she lifted the last basket and placed it on her tray. "And whatever diet cola is available."

Her eyes widened at my request. "No Macallan?"

"In a few hours, it will be a new year. I figured I'd start early on the new me." I winked when she shook her head at me, causing her long dark ponytail to swing over her shoulder. Seeing her smile, I nodded to the food on her tray. "Add their shit to my bill."

"No need," she said with a smirk. "The one you got up close and personal with gave his card to start a tab."

"Did you get the clothes I had sent over?" I asked, changing the subject when the memory of that fucker's hand hovering over my girl's ass replayed through my head.

"They're beautiful. But I don't get off until two."

I shrugged. "Doesn't matter. We'll make our own party. I just want to see you in that dress, babe."

She studied me for a long moment before taking a step back from the table with a smile. "Grilled chicken wedge salad and diet cola. What dressing?"

"Whichever one my woman thinks is the healthiest for me."

Cali

AS SOON AS my shift was over, I took my time changing in the locker room. The garment bag hung from the hook inside, and I just stood there for several minutes, staring at it. I should have been wondering how Garret Hannigan knew my size, but instead, all I could think about was where he intended to take me.

It was well after two in the morning, and the club had a tiny disco ball that had dropped at midnight. All the dancers had come out onto the floor and kissed a few of the customers as "Auld Lang Syne" had played through the speakers. I'd been standing at another one of my tables, putting their drinks in front of them, when I'd felt someone come up behind me.

I'd known it was Garret before I even felt his

hand on my arm. Slowly, I turned to face him as confetti had fallen around us. When he lowered his head, I'd turned to stone. Kissing was not something I'd been interested in experiencing. Not after what Manuel had done to me. For half a second, I'd wondered if it would feel good, but then the fear had started to choke me as unwanted memories assaulted me.

Garret must have seen the panic on my face, because he cupped my cheeks in his giant hands and then lowered his head, pressing his lips to my forehead. "Happy New Year, blue eyes," he'd murmured just loud enough for me to hear over the music and buzz of the crowd's combined voices.

"H-happy New Year," I'd stuttered, my heart doing something funny in my chest. He gave me a reassuring smile and returned to his booth, where he picked up his second glass of diet soda of the night.

As he sat there, his green gaze had captured mine, and I'd slowly relaxed. After several long moments, I'd finally returned to reality and gotten back to work.

With fingers that trembled, I finally unzipped the bag and nearly gasped at how beautiful the dress was. It was shimmery and long-sleeved, with a high neckline, but the hem was short and would hit right above midthigh. Taking it off the hanger, I saw that the back was low-cut, going all the way to the top of my panty line. Frowning, I looked through the rest of the items and saw a nude backless, strapless bra. There were also shoes that matched the dress and a long Burberry coat.

Having grown up in luxury, I knew exactly how much the entire contents of my locker were worth. That one outfit cost more than everything in my closet back at my apartment combined, with a few thousand dollars left over. I could have paid my rent for months—fucking months—with the money spent on the shoes and coat alone.

The year before, I wouldn't have even blinked at the expense of all the designer clothes. But I no longer had that luxury.

I hadn't been the one to spend the money, however, and it wasn't like I was about to explain to Garret why I was squeamish about the cost. He still hadn't shown a single sign that he recognized me, and at this point, I could only assume he was completely clueless as to who I'd been before I became Lis Brewer. I hadn't fully believed him when he'd said the night before that he could remember every word he read but sometimes had issues with faces.

But apparently, that wasn't a lie. He didn't remember me. And that made it easier for me to step into the dress and slip the thousand-dollar shoes onto my already aching feet. The feel of the Burberry coat on my back was enough to make me moan, and I wasn't surprised to find gloves in the pockets.

If he didn't remember me, then I wasn't going to hold his past treatment of me over his head. It was time to let that shit go anyway. I had to stop pretending I didn't like Garret. We were kids back then. Kids did stupid things.

Ugh. I was standing there making excuses for a guy. Which was ridiculous. I hated women who did that. Overlooked the verbal abuse a man—or anyone else—put them through, for whatever reason. Yet there I was, doing just that.

Because I was attracted to the asshole.

Grabbing my purse, I pulled out my phone and debated calling Nova. She would guide me through this without judgment. Plus, I needed to hear her voice. She'd texted me not long after Garret had left my apartment the previous morning to ask about her brother visiting the club, but I hadn't heard from her since. She was my voice of reason, the only person to selflessly risk their own life to save me. The girl was so damn sweet and the most precious person in my life. She was also smart as fuck and wouldn't have hesitated to let me know if I was making a mistake or not.

"Yo, Lis!"

I jerked at the sound of my name being called from the door. Turning, I saw the locker room was empty, but there was a shadow of one of the bouncers near the entrance. "Yeah?"

"Mr. Hannigan is worried about you. Everything all right with you in there?"

"I'm fine," I called back, returning my phone to my purse and slinging the strap over my shoulder. My hair was still in a ponytail, and my makeup probably needed to be refreshed, but Garret was just going to have to take me as I was or drop me off at my apartment.

Walking over to the mirror, I examined myself in the expensive outfit. Even with a few flyaway hairs from my ponytail, I looked good. But then again, it was hard not to with the clothes I had been given. Sighing, I redid my ponytail, even though I'd told myself I wasn't going to worry about it only moments before.

My makeup had held up, so I gave one last shrug at my reflection and turned for the door. Only to stop in my tracks when I caught sight of Garret walking into the locker room. He paused mid-step, almost stumbling when he saw me. The way he licked his lips was a compliment all its own, especially when the pupils of his eyes enlarged and he inhaled sharply.

"You look amazing," he said in a raspy voice. "I was going to take you out, but right now, I don't know if I can share all this beauty. I want it all for myself."

Heat filled my cheeks, and I quickly lowered my gaze, busying myself by putting on the gloves. I heard his footsteps, but I didn't look up until his fingers touched my chin and gently urged me to lift my head.

"Tell me what you want, blue eyes," he murmured. "If you want to go out, I'll take you anywhere so the world can see how beautiful you are. If you want to go home, we can go there. Grab some dinner on the way and hang out in your room watching movies or shitty sitcoms until the sun comes up. Or we can go back to my place. My sister is in town. Maybe it's too soon to introduce you to any of my family, but Nova is special."

I quickly swallowed to get moisture back in my mouth. "You paid for all these clothes just to take me home and hang out in my pajamas?"

"It's just money, baby. I bought them so *I* could see you in them. It doesn't matter to me who else sees you—or doesn't." He skimmed his thumb over my chin and up my jaw. "But maybe on your next day off, you'll wear this dress when I take you to dinner?"

Say no. Say no. Say no.

"Okay," I whispered, ignoring the voice screaming in my head to end whatever was going on between us, then and there. Instead, I let him take my hand. "I want Chinese for dinner."

Garret

THERE WAS a Chinese restaurant open all night just a block from Lis's apartment. She ordered our food on the ride back to her place, and with traffic so crazy from partiers celebrating the ball dropping still crowding the streets, the delivery guy was waiting for us when we stepped off the elevator.

I pulled out my wallet and extracted several bills, exchanging them for the food while Lis unlocked her door. She walked into the apartment, and I followed moments later with the three heavy bags of food.

"Kim is out, but I don't know when she will be home." She made a face. "Want to eat in my room, so she doesn't bother us?"

"I want to do whatever you want," I assured her and followed her into her room. There was a rainbow rug at the foot of her bed, and I set the food on that before shrugging off my coat. "Get changed, babe. I'll unload these boxes and grab us some drinks."

Pink tinged her cheeks, but she grabbed a few clothes from her closet and quickly made her way to the bathroom while I did as promised. By the time I returned to her room with bottles of water and cans of diet soda, she was already sitting cross-legged on the rug. Chopsticks in hand, she was licking her lips hungrily as she considered the options and what she wanted to taste first.

Having already kicked off my shoes, I dropped down beside her on the floor and offered her a drink before leaning my back against the bed frame and stretching out my long legs. I watched her as she finally picked up the container of chicken lo mein and twirled her chopsticks into the noodles before stuffing a bite into her mouth.

The way she licked sauce off her lips had me forcing back a tortured groan, and I quickly made my own selection from the containers to distract myself from the dirty thoughts I was having of her luscious mouth wrapped around my cock. But the memory of the stark fear I'd seen in her eyes when I'd leaned down to kiss her at midnight made me keep my hands to myself.

I'd seen that look before. In the eyes of some of the women who sought protection from their abusers at the safe haven of Sanctuary that my aunt ran back in Creswell Springs. My mom had made both Nova and me work there from time to time when Aunt Gracie needed extra hands.

Some of those women, they started trembling as soon as a man walked into the room, their eyes like a feral cat looking for any and every possible exit they could use at the first sign of violence. My gut would twist every time I saw them react like that to me, and to have Lis look up at me with the same fear in her eyes had torn at something in my chest.

It had told me that she'd been hurt in more than one way by her abuser, and I knew without a doubt that I needed to take things even slower than I'd originally thought I would have to. I never wanted to see that look in her pretty blue eyes ever again when she saw me.

Grabbing an egg roll, she stuffed half of it into her mouth and chewed like she was starving before wiping her fingers on her pajama pants and picking up her new TV's remote. Selecting Netflix, she clicked on her avatar that we'd made for her earlier that afternoon and then skipped over several suggested shows and movies before picking *Pokémon*.

I stiffened at her choice, the tips of my ears already burning. "Are you trying to make fun of me, Lis?" I grumbled, hating that I felt embarrassed.

She shifted her head to look at me with a frown. "How could I possibly make fun of you, gangster?"

I gritted my teeth, not wanting to admit it, but the confusion on her face seemed genuine. "I was obsessed with this show when I was a kid."

"Me too!" she exclaimed with a laugh. "Actually, I go Pokémon hunting all the time." Grabbing her phone off the foot of the bed where she'd tossed it earlier, she opened it to show me the game app.

I picked up my own phone and showed her the app on my home screen.

"No way!" she cried in envious disgust, snatching my phone out of my hand. "How do you have three Uxies as well as a Mesprit and an Azelf? That's not even fair. I've only seen one Uxie in all the years I've played this game, and it ran away before I could capture it."

Fuck.

It was right then, in that moment, with her eyes glowing with excitement and jealousy, that it hit me. Without a shadow of a doubt, I knew Lis Brewer was made for me. Not only was this girl beautiful, but she was a little bit of a geek just like I used to be—and, if I had to admit it, still was. There was no other woman in the world more perfect than she was.

No matter what happened, how long it took for me to get her to trust me, I would make her fall in love with me too. Because now that I'd found her, I couldn't imagine my life without her in it.

"What?" she muttered when she realized I was just sitting there staring at her. Pink filled her cheeks, and she dropped my phone back into my hand. "There's nothing wrong with liking anime. I read manga too," she said, lifting her chin at that stubborn angle I'd come to adore. "Make fun of me all you want, but I'm not embarrassed that I like what I like."

I set my phone and carton of orange chicken on the floor and slowly lifted my hands to cup her face. "I'm going to kiss you now, Lis," I told her, giving her plenty of time to pull back if she wasn't ready.

The wheels started moving in her head, and I could practically see in her eyes that she was arguing with herself over whether she wanted to allow me to kiss her. But by the time my hands touched her soft cheeks, she hadn't shifted away. My breath caught, and I lowered my head, still going slow enough to give her time to get away from me if she wanted to.

My lips grazed tenderly over hers, tasting a little bit of the chicken lo mein she was eating, along with something else. Something...addictive. In my teens, I'd been bored and stupid. Drugs were easily available if you knew where to look, and I'd had plenty of cash to buy whatever I was in the mood for. I never allowed myself to get too attached to any of them, though. I just needed something to do to pass the time until I could get out of Creswell Springs.

But the flavor of Lis was too much. One taste and I fell in over my head, already drowning, craving that next hit. I thrust my fingers into her hair, tilting her head back just enough so that I could deepen the kiss. Nipping at her bottom lip, I was rewarded with her opening her mouth so that I could dip my tongue inside.

The full force of the drug that was this girl took root in my mind, making me an addict for her. There was no cure for the sickness that afflicted me. No antidote to wean me off. Not even the best rehabs could have helped me get over the need that wrapped its hooks around my every nerve ending and tightened more and more the longer I kissed her.

Lis made a sound, and I instantly jerked my head up, unable to determine whether the noise had been in pleasure or fear. Breathing heavily, I looked down at her through my lashes. She gasped, her chest rising and falling rapidly.

Fuck, she was even more beautiful with her lips swollen from my kiss. Pink darkened her cheeks, and her eyes glazed with the same need that throbbed through my veins. But there was more than just want in her blue gaze. The fear made me want to punch something, preferably whoever had caused her that fear in the first place.

"Garret..." she panted, touching trembling fingers to her lips.

"Tell me who hurt you, Lis," I pleaded, a desperate man who only wanted to protect what was his. She deserved to have every last person who had ever caused her harm or fear annihilated, their entire bloodline put into extinction for daring to make her so much as flinch. "I swear to God, I'll kill him. You won't ever have a reason to be scared again."

She clenched her eyes closed. "Whether he's alive or dead, he will always live on in my head. He haunts me," she whispered, but I still heard it. Shame. There was no reason for her to experience that particular emotion. The only one who should be ashamed was the one who had hurt her.

"Do you...wanna talk about it?" I asked hesitantly.

I heard her gulp, and after a moment, she slowly lifted her lashes, and that small show of strength made me so damn proud of her. "The beatings started before my mom died. I wasn't even a teenager yet."

"Was it only your stepbrother? What about your dad?" I guessed, clenching my hands at my sides, but she shook her head.

"No, he died when I was a toddler. Mom remarried, and my stepfather was good to me. But his son…" She shuddered and seemed to curl into herself right before my eyes. "I'm sorry."

"There is nothing to be sorry for, blue eyes." I lifted one hand and stroked my index finger down her cheek. "He beat you?"

Lis caught my hand and clutched at it as she gave me a tiny nod. "At first, it was just beatings. But as I got older…"

"He raped you?" I rasped, trying to contain my growing rage.

I felt her tremble, but she gave me a dry laugh. "He couldn't get his dick hard enough to rape me with it. I don't think he was into girls. Hell, I'm not sure what he was into, but he got off on making me hurt. He would use whatever was on hand to…to…" Her voice shook, and I wrapped my arms around her, tucking her head to my chest as a sob escaped her throat.

The rage burned even hotter through me. It was like nothing I'd ever felt before, an inferno of anger and the need to make her stepbrother bleed the way he'd no doubt caused her to bleed. To hear his cries—his fucking screams—in pain and terror before I ended his pathetic existence and spared the world another day of him walking the earth.

Inhaling slowly, I tried to gather my control so I didn't scare her. I wanted her stepbrother dead. If anyone deserved to meet the angel of death, it was that fucking bastard. But Lis had already had enough fear in her life, and I didn't want to be the reason she felt it again.

When I felt like I could speak without growling, I tipped her chin back so I could look down into her face. "Baby, you have nothing to be scared of when you're with me. I will never let anything or anyone hurt you again."

"I-I think I know that," she said after a few long moments.

"Good. If you haven't already figured it out, I care about you, blue eyes." I stroked my thumb over her bottom lip, wanting to kiss her again, but refusing to rush her. "I want to make you mine—" Fear filled her eyes before I could even finish. "But I swear to you, I can wait until you are ready."

"Garret," she muttered, pulling back and shaking her head.

"However long it takes, I don't care. I'll wait for when you are ready, Lis. I'm not going to rush you. This? Us? We will move at your pace. If all we do for the next week, month, year—fuck, the next decade— is sit here on your rug every night after you get off work and eat takeout while we watch anime, I'm there for that. But I can't walk away from you. I won't. Not when I care this much."

She licked her lips nervously. "But what if… What happens if I'm never ready for…that?"

"However long you need," I vowed, my voice full of earnestness. "I'm not going anywhere, Lis."

Cali

I BENT and tossed my hair over my head, fluffing the thick tresses. I'd just finished taking the curling iron to it, having spent the last two hours getting ready for dinner with Garret. He hadn't given me a chance to back out of my promise to go out with him on my next day off, but that had taken longer than expected.

Many of the waitresses at the club had gotten sick the last three weeks, and I'd picked up every shift my manager offered. That meant I hadn't had a single day off since before New Year's Eve. Garret wasn't happy that I was working so much, but my little nest egg was growing more and more with each shift, so I wasn't going to let him pull rank and go above my manager's head to Adrian Volkov to demand I have a day off.

With the other waitresses now back to work, I'd been ordered to take the next four days off. Part of me had wanted to argue that I only needed two, but my feet begged to differ. I really did need the extra time off to recover from all the nights in those damn heels.

Even if I was going to be spending the night in shoes just as high as the ones I worked in. But I was oddly looking forward to it. For the past three weeks, Garret and I had been having dinner after each of my shifts. Seated either on my rug or in my bed, eating whatever takeout I'd asked for that night, watching every episode of *Pokémon*.

There was nothing romantic about it. He never once tried to touch me in any way that would even suggest he wanted to take things further than just two friends spending a little time together. When he'd made the promise to take things as slow as I was comfortable with, I hadn't completely trusted him, but he proved himself more and more with each passing day.

Over the last week, I'd found myself sitting closer to him. Each night, the physical distance between us would decrease a little more. The night before, I'd even fallen asleep with my head on his shoulder. I didn't remember closing my eyes, but when I'd opened them close to sundown, I'd awoken feeling more well rested than I had in forever.

Garret was gone, but there had been a rose on my pillow with a note scrawled in his oddly neat hand-writing, reminding me of our plans for dinner.

As I'd lifted the flower to my nose and reread the note, butterflies had started fluttering in my stomach. The petals of the flower had brushed over my lips, and I was instantly transported back to the night he'd kissed me. The memory of his lips on mine as he'd taken his time, being tender at first and then steadily more demanding.

He wouldn't have known that it was my first kiss. I'd never allowed anyone as close as I'd let Garret. There was no way he could have possibly under-stood how torn I'd been as sensations I'd never felt before had swarmed me. I hadn't had a single sexual urge from the first time Manuel had violated me. And for a few moments, frozen in time, I'd been so turned on from Garret's kiss that I'd felt my sex become wet.

That was when I'd gotten scared, when the shame had hit—along with the fear. The places where he was making ache were the same places my step-brother would shove painful things into. While I'd felt my panties dampening from Garret's kiss, it all came back to haunt me…

SACRIFICED

"Now, the real fun begins," Manuel said as he stood over me.

I struggled against the cuffs on my wrists, kicking my legs as much as possible in an attempt to release myself from the restraints around my ankles. But the more I moved, the tighter they became.

"That's it, whore. Keep struggling. Soon, you'll cut off the blood flow to your hands and feet." He laughed with glee at the thought as he used the shears to cut off my clothes.

In no time, I was completely naked on his gross bed. The smell of stale alcohol was so strong it nearly made me gag, but that was nothing to the fear making my stomach roil. With my clothes lying in tatters beneath me, Manuel picked up a wedge-shaped cushion and shoved it under my bottom so that the lower half of my body was lifted.

Throwing the shears aside, he grabbed a broom that was lying on the floor and broke the handle across his knee. My gaze clocked his every movement as he walked over to the desk where the lines of coke were already measured out. He snorted two of them before coming back to the bed.

His blown pupils went straight to my exposed bottom, and the grin he gave me nearly made me vomit.

"Please, don't," I whispered, so scared I began to shake.

My plea fell on deaf ears, though. He pressed the smooth end of the broken broomstick against my rectum. I *screamed as he forced it in. "Please stop! Please, Manuel. I'm sorry. Whatever I did wrong, I'm so sorry!"*

"A whore like you can take bigger than this up the ass. Just like your mother."

Sweat coated my body while tears poured down my face as I tried to breathe through the pain. Closing my eyes, I tried to block everything out. The way he seemed to be getting off on hurting me, the sound of his laughter, the pain that thankfully started to become nothing more than a burning ache.

Suddenly, he pulled the broomstick from my bottom. My eyes snapped open, hoping that the torture was over. But as he tossed the broken wooden handle aside, he picked up one of the empty beer bottles.

One of his knees pressed into the mattress, and he put the tip of the bottle to the entrance of my sex. My scream echoed through the entire mansion as he shoved it inside...

Nausea had swirled around in my stomach, and I couldn't hide my fear as I'd cried out against Garret's mouth.

My mouth had felt swollen and I could still taste Garret on my tongue, but all I could think of was the blinding pain. I was thrown back into the moment when I was helpless as my stepbrother had raped me with a beer bottle.

Garret had tasted like the orange chicken he'd been eating, but there had been something beneath the Chinese food, something richer, with a hint of spice. But I couldn't enjoy it because I was still reliving the way I'd begged Manuel to stop, to please, please, not hurt me anymore.

And he'd only gotten more excited.

The beer bottle had stayed inside me while he'd slapped my face and then punched me in the stomach. Over and over and over again until I'd passed out.

I'd woken up lying in the shower in my bedroom hours later. My entire body was one huge throb. The ache between my legs was nothing compared to the agony of my abdominal pain. Slowly, I'd curled into a ball and just lay on the cold tiles, weeping. No one had come to check on me, and I'd eventually gathered the strength to shower off the blood before limping into my room to dress myself.

The pain was so bad that I'd still been crying silently as I'd snuck out of the house and made my way to a doctor's office several miles from Matias's mansion. I was scared I had internal bleeding, but the doctor had X-rayed me and assured me nothing vital was damaged.

He never once asked how I'd gotten the bruises. Everyone in the area knew who I was, who my stepfamily was. They were aware of how often Matias was home, that it was just Manuel and me up at the house. And every single person in a one-hundred-mile radius was just as terrified of him as I was.

So the doctor kept his mouth shut, stitched a few places that needed stitching, and sent me on my way.

It wasn't the last time I had to see that doctor. And if he'd thought keeping his mouth shut would keep him alive, he'd been wrong. Because the last time I'd needed medical assistance, one of my step-brother's men had followed me and called Manuel. He'd shown up just as the doctor was finishing the stitches on the undersides of my breasts where Manuel had taken his blades to me, cackling while I'd sobbed and bled all over his white sheets.

After that first time, he always changed his sheets to the white ones when he hurt me. The sight of the bright red on the pristine white cotton excited him.

Manuel took one look at the needle and medical thread in the doctor's hands and put a bullet in the man's head. Then he'd taken me back to the mansion and locked me in my room for three days with no food. The only water I was allowed was from my bathroom sink, so at least I didn't die of dehydration.

Even as I tried to shake those memories away, Garret had been making promises. He'd kill whoever had put the look of fear in my eyes if I just gave him a name. But I didn't want him anywhere near

Manuel. My stepbrother was a psychopath. He might be stupid as fuck, but he was also dangerous.

And I already cared about Garret too much to risk losing him to the monster whose greatest pleasure was to make me cry.

Those awful memories had slowly faded a little each night over the last three weeks, though. As my trust in Garret grew, the hold Manuel still held over my psyche faded a little more, too.

Stepping into the sexy shoes, I licked my lips in anticipation of this date. Garret might not have labeled it as that, but I could tell he wanted to.

I secretly did too.

But more than anything, I was hoping for another kiss.

Once I had my new coat on, I grabbed the nicest bag I had—a cute little black clutch that was yet another thrift store find—and walked out of my bedroom. As I did, Kim came out of her own room, dressed for work in a pair of matching sweats, her hair up in a knot, and her duffel bag full of all her work outfits tossed over her shoulder.

She took one look at me and stopped in her tracks. I didn't miss the envy in her eyes as she raked her gaze over me from head to toe, her nose flaring when she noted the Louis Vuitton shoes that I was wearing. She pressed her lips into a hard line as she lifted her eyes back to mine. "Finally giving that pussy up to Volkov's lackey?"

I smirked, her jealousy amusing me more than anything else. "My man is no one's lackey." I stepped around her. "He has his own men he's in charge of. Didn't you know? His future brother-in-law is Ryan Vitucci."

She made a choking sound, and I bit back a laugh as I walked toward the door. Making sure my keys and phone were tucked into my clutch, I opened the door and instantly heard a deep growl.

Head snapping up, I met Garret's green gaze, and my need for another taste of him doubled. He was always in a suit, but when he hung out with me in my room, he usually tossed his jacket aside and rolled up the sleeves of his shirt and undid the top few buttons. I liked seeing the ink on his arms and what little peeked through on his chest.

None of his tattoos was showing at the moment. He was wearing a long black coat over a black-on-black suit. I couldn't help wondering how soft the material of his black button-down was, and before I even realized what I was doing, my fingers were skimming over his chest.

His breath hissed out in pleasure as I let my hand travel lower. But then I felt the hardness of his gun tucked into the holster beneath his suit jacket and jerked my hand back.

"You can't go without that thing for even one night?" I sassed him as I stepped over the threshold and closed the door behind me. I heard Kim mutter something snide behind me because I'd closed the door in her face, and I bit the inside of my bottom lip to keep from laughing.

"I don't go anywhere unarmed, blue eyes," he said, putting his hand to the small of my back as we walked toward the elevator. "You should at least know that much about me by now."

"Fucking gangster," I grumbled, but from the tilt of my lips, he could easily tell I was teasing him.

"You look gorgeous," he said, lowering his head to kiss my temple. "It's going to be hard for me to share all this beauty with the rest of the world tonight."

"We don't have to go out," I told him, leaning back against the wall of the elevator. "I would have been all too happy to stay in and eat takeout again."

"I may not like other dickheads looking at my girl, but I'm not going to keep you locked up in your room every night. That's Ryan's way of thinking, not mine. If he had his way, my sister would stay locked behind the compound's walls for the rest of her life. Not that Nova would let that happen." He captured my hand and entwined our fingers. "You deserve a night out, baby. Let the bastards look all they want. I know that, at the end of the night, I'm the one you're letting take you home."

I gazed down at his hand holding mine. In comparison, his was twice the size of my own. Long, thick fingers wrapped around slender ones. His hold was firm, yet gentle—the same way he always held me. His touch had a possessiveness to it, but there was also the tender way he touched me. The combination was enough to make me want to curl up in his arms and allow him to erase the trauma of my past— the memories that tried to haunt me day and night.

Pulling my hand free from his made him growl in displeasure, until I grasped hold of his tie and tugged his head down so our faces were so close I could feel his warm breath on my cheek. His eyes lit up with need in a nanosecond, his nose flaring with a want my body was starting to match despite the damage Manuel had inflicted on my psyche.

"Lis…?" Garret breathed, but that was as far as he got before I closed the distance between our lips and pressed my mouth to his.

Garret

I'D HAD SO many plans for the night. First, I would take Lis to dinner, then we would go to any club she wanted. We would have danced until she pleaded for me to take her home, and then we would have grabbed some food to gorge on while we watched TV in her room until she fell asleep.

But the moment her lips latched on to mine, all those plans went up in a cloud of smoke. Grabbing her ass in both hands, I backed her against the wall and deepened the kiss. I hadn't had a hit of her addictive taste for three weeks, and somehow I'd survived the withdrawals from the dangerous drug. Having it explode on my tongue, this time without food masking how delicious she tasted, I was gone before she even opened her mouth enough to encourage my tongue to play with hers.

Her body molded to mine perfectly, my hard cock notched at just the right spot to make her moan when I gripped her ass a little harder and tilted her up ever so slightly. She'd already released my tie to thrust her fingers into my hair, her nails raking over my scalp in a way that forced a groan from me. It felt good—she felt so damn good.

The memory of fear in her pretty blue eyes the last time I kissed her, however, came back to haunt me. Reluctantly, I lifted my head, dreading to see that same expression on her lovely face. Yet when our gazes locked, fear was the last thing I saw.

She licked her swollen lips as she sucked in deep breaths. "That was even better than I hoped," she whispered, touching her mouth, the hint of a smile teasing me.

"You've been wanting another kiss, baby?" I growled and stole another taste before she could answer.

Vaguely I felt the elevator stop, but kissing her was too good, and neither of us noticed when the doors opened and then closed again.

"Really?" I heard someone snap behind us, and I finally lifted my head. Using my body to hide Lis, I glanced over my shoulder to see her roommate standing in the hall. "What a whore," she muttered, glaring at us.

"Takes one to know one," Lis singsonged. Grabbing hold of my tie again, she led me out of the elevator like an obedient puppy. "Have fun at work," she called as she walked back toward her apartment. "I'm sure you won't be home until late. As usual. Smelling like cheap booze and bad decisions. Again, as usual."

"Bitch," I heard Kim hiss, followed by Lis laughing.

The elevator doors closed just as Lis unlocked her door and dragged me inside, still holding on to my tie. I would have never allowed anyone else but this woman to do what she was doing. I wasn't some lapdog to be led around, but fuck if my cock wasn't hard as steel at the way she was pulling me where she wanted.

Lis walked through the small apartment and straight into her bedroom. Once I was inside with her, she closed the door, and for the first time since I'd started hanging out with her in her room, she flipped the lock. With my tie still wrapped around her fingers, she pushed my coat off one shoulder and then the other with her free hand. The coat hit the floor, and she started on my suit jacket before she finally started loosening the knot of my tie.

I didn't so much as lift a hand to help her. My woman had limits from her past trauma, and I was going to let her test them without freaking her out. Because if I didn't hold myself in check, I would definitely scare the hell out of her. Every night, I saw her at the club in that stupid uniform, her ass cheeks teasing me as she flirted with all those goddamn men to get good tips. Only to go back to her place and hang out with her in her pajamas...

Not even a saint could have withstood all that temptation, yet I had. Hell would freeze over before I broke my promise to Lis. However long she needed, I would wait. Because she was worth it.

From the way she was undressing me, I got the impression that maybe she was ready to take things further. Even if it was just to play around, I was okay with that. Fuck, I was so ready. If her kiss was enough to make me an addict, the taste of her pussy was going to end me.

I was already shaking for that stronger hit. All that sweetness on my tongue, dripping down my throat. I'd bet this was how a heroin addict felt when they hadn't shot up in a few days. There I'd been, weeks without the taste of her delectable lips; the possibility of getting my mouth on her pussy would surely kill me.

Even though I was about to die for just a drop of that sweetness on my tongue, I didn't rush her. My hands stayed at my sides even as she pushed my holster off my shoulders and then reached for my belt. It was only then, when she saw the outline of my cock along the inside right seam of my slacks that her fingers paused and began to tremble.

Keeping my eyes locked on her face, I watched her swallow hard, but she continued to undress me. Her pulse at the base of her throat began to beat double time, her cheeks blazing even under her light layer of makeup. It was obvious to me she was nervous, but I didn't know how to make her more at ease. Not without taking over, and I was more afraid of scaring her than if she were to full-on stop because she lost her confidence.

"You're bigger than a beer bottle," she choked out, keeping her gaze lowered to where my cock was growing harder and harder by the minute. Her gaze on just the outline of it was tantalizingly sensual; I was sure the instant she touched my shaft, I would erupt in her soft hand.

But her comparison of my size caught me off guard. Why would she make that kind of analysis between my cock and a beer bottle...?

Then I noticed the sweat beading on her forehead, the way she gulped every few breaths, and I put it all together. I didn't need her to explain, not when she'd already told me some of what that evil bastard of a stepbrother had done to her.

For the first time since we'd entered her bedroom, I raised my hands and touched her face. She didn't flinch away, but it took a moment before she lifted her blue gaze to lock with mine. "I will never hurt you, Lis," I promised her. It wasn't the first time I'd made the vow, but as long as she needed to hear it, I would continue to repeat it.

"I believe that more and more every day," she whispered.

"Good, because it's the truth." I skimmed my thumb over her lips, still swollen from our ravenous kiss in the elevator. "If you aren't ready for this, we can stop now."

Her eyes glazed over. "I want it."

"But you're afraid?" I asked quietly, already knowing the answer but needing her to verbalize it.

"Yes," she said, closing her eyes.

"What do you need from me to not be scared?"

Tears spilled through her lowered lashes. "I don't even know. I've never done anything like this before." Swallowing roughly, she bravely lifted her gaze back to mine. "But I know I want you. I want...us."

"You have me. I'm not going anywhere. We can still go slow. I don't want you to regret anything, baby."

"The only thing I will regret is if I don't—" She broke off, the heat in her face deepening. "I want you more than you understand. These feelings—this need? I've never felt it before, and it's so intense, Garret. It hurts."

I nearly swallowed my tongue at her confession. Reminding myself to stay in control, I pulled my belt free of my slacks and gave it to her. Her brow furrowed, but she hesitantly took it from me.

"What—"

"Put it around my wrists," I offered, placing my hands together. "Tie me up and take what you need from me, Lis."

"No!" she cried, dropping the belt like it was a snake about to strike her. "I-I can't do that. Just the thought…"

"Then tell me what I can do to help make this easier for you because, baby, I will do anything to make you happy."

"I need you to make love to me," she breathed. "I need it slow and easy. E-especially with how big you are."

"I can do that," I rasped. My mouth felt like it was full of cotton, it was so dry. Yet another sign of how addicted I was to her, how desperate I was for my next fix.

"I need you not to laugh at me," she continued,

"or...or be disgusted at some of the scars on my body."

I carefully grasped her by the hips and pulled her toward me. "There is nothing about you that could ever disgust me. And I will kill anyone who laughs at you, blue eyes. Including myself."

She leaned into me for a long moment before lifting her head. "I'm not on anything. We have to use protection."

"Baby, I will always protect you." Taking her hand, I tugged her toward the bed. "I swear I'll take care of you. In every way, until my last breath."

Cali

JUNE

I FELT Garret get out of bed, but I kept my eyes closed, too tired to watch him as he walked into the bathroom. He didn't completely close the door, and I heard the shower turn on. Sighing, I grabbed his pillow and pulled it close, snuggling it like he'd been doing to me only moments before.

From the night we'd first made love, Garret had spent every night in my bed, unless he had to fly back to Creswell Springs for something. But that had only been twice. The first time for Mother's Day, and the second only the week before to celebrate his sister's graduation with her and their family.

For whatever reason, he had come home earlier than expected, and ever since, I'd barely seen him. He came back to my apartment each night to sleep, but he was so exhausted from whatever the hell he did all day that he just took a quick shower and fell into bed with me. I barely got a kiss before he was sound asleep with me tucked against him.

With Garret not at the club every night, and him not trying to put his dick in me every chance he could get—which was basically anytime he wanted, because after how sweet and amazing he'd made our first time, I might have grown addicted to riding his cock—I knew something was seriously wrong. Whatever had happened at work, it was bad.

I tried not to think about what the problem could be that was causing him to inadvertently neglect me when I was typically the center of his entire world. Something churning in my gut suggested I already knew what the issue was—Manuel. But I seriously didn't want to consider that. My eyes and ears had been wide open for any sign of my psychotic stepbrother, and I hadn't seen or heard anything that would suggest he was back in the States or, even worse, trying to find me.

But I wasn't an idiot. I knew even if I didn't see or hear anything, it was still very possible Manuel was just keeping to the shadows, waiting for his chance to strike. When Matias died, I had inherited everything. The properties. The businesses. The money. Manuel had gotten nothing, and by this point, I was sure he'd already blown through his own stash of cash.

He would be getting desperate soon, and I was the only means to his getting the money he thought should have been his by right of birth.

That was going to be my revenge. I just had to wait him out. Once he was dead—which, with how much he liked drugs, could be any day if he overdosed—then I would officially have my vengeance. I would own everything he'd always wanted, without fear that he would try to hurt me to get it back. All that money and power would be mine to do whatever I wanted with. And he would be watching from his pit in hell, hating me more and more, while I got to live happily ever after with everything he couldn't touch.

Of course, the nausea I felt could very well have been for another reason entirely. One I suspected was the real culprit for how sick I'd been recently. But just as I wanted to pretend like Manuel wasn't an issue, I wanted to hide my head in the sand about *that* issue too. My period being two weeks late was nothing. I was fine. There was no way I could be pregnant. Garret wore protection every time we had sex and—

Groaning, I buried my face deeper into his pillow and closed my eyes. And because I was so exhausted, I fell back to sleep right away. When Garret stopped to brush a kiss over my forehead on his way out, I barely felt him, but I found myself smiling in my half-awake state.

Damn it, but I loved him.

I should have probably told him already, but I'd chickened out every time I'd started to. It felt wrong to say those words when he still didn't know who I really was. I needed to grow a pair and just come clean, tell him everything. Who I was. That I loved him. And definitely that he might be a daddy in a matter of months.

Despite all that noise swirling around in my brain, I was too tired not to fall fully back to sleep again.

My stomach growling loudly was what finally pulled me from a somewhat restful slumber. Grabbing my phone, I checked the time—and to see if Garret had maybe texted me. Seeing it was lunchtime, and disappointed that my man hadn't sent a single text, I rubbed the sleep from my eyes with my free hand while finding another contact in my phone and sending her a text.

Me: *So bored. I heard you are back in town. Let's have lunch!!!*

I wasn't surprised when she replied immediately.

NoNo: *When and where?*

Me: *Um, now. I'm hungry. There's a diner near my apartment. Meet me there.*

I shot her the address and then tossed back the covers. Sitting on the toilet, I hoped to see at least some sign that my period had started, but like every day for the past two weeks, it was MIA. Sighing, I took care of business and then washed my hands. Too hungry to delay with a shower, I brushed my teeth then went back into my room to get dressed.

Over the past several months, my wardrobe had been steadily replaced by clothes that Garret had gifted me. He thought he was being sly, but I was onto his game. He was trying to tempt me into quitting my job, but if I really was pregnant, I needed the money I made every night more than ever.

If our two was going to turn into three, then he was more than welcome to take care of his kid all he wanted. But there was no way in hell I was going to let myself become reliant on a man ever again. Growing up, I'd had to rely on Matias to pay for everything I had. When he got sick, Manuel took control over the accounts, and I was lucky if I was able to buy feminine hygiene products each month. My stepdad was dead now, and technically I was the only heir since Matias had supposedly cut Manuel out of the will, but I couldn't get my hands on that money without risking my stepbrother finding me.

Before Nova had helped me run away, I'd had to start rationing my supply of tampons and pads because I wasn't sure if I would get more the next month. Having to wear either of those items longer than I was supposed to was a gross feeling, but I'd had no other choice. Not even our housekeeper and cook, Maria, had been allowed to purchase anything for me once Matias started losing touch with reality. The one time she'd tried to sneak me some from her own supply of tampons, Manuel had slapped her so hard she'd fallen to the floor.

After that, I'd tried to avoid the housekeeper, not wanting my stepbrother to have a reason to raise his hand to her when all she'd tried to do was help me. Until Nova, Maria had been the only one to even attempt to assist me in any way where Manuel was concerned.

Grabbing my purse, I tucked my phone into my back pocket and left the apartment. Kim had been getting on my nerves more and more lately, so I made sure to slam the door nice and loud on my way out. The bitch was a light sleeper and I'd hear all about the noise later, but it put a sly grin on my lips as I walked to the diner.

I'd worked there when I first moved to NYC. The tips had been decent, and I'd gotten a free meal every shift I worked. But in comparison, the money I made at Cherry Bomb was triple each night what I would have made working there.

Entering the diner, I glanced around briefly before walking to a table in the back where I usually liked to sit. The waitress, a new girl I didn't recognize, brought me over a menu, but I waved her off. "I'm waiting on someone, and I don't need a menu. I know what I want, but I'm going to hold off on ordering until she gets here."

"M'kay," she said before walking off to check on her other customers.

The place went through waitresses like they did toilet paper, but the cook had always been the same old man. When I'd worked there, he'd never said much, just flipped the burgers and minded his own business. But damn, they were the best I'd ever tasted in my life.

While I waited for Nova, I played on my phone, hoping I'd get a message from Garret, but nothing popped up from him. It was so unlike him, but other than sleeping in my bed each night, he'd been basically radio silent since returning from California.

Several of the tables around me cleared out before Nova and her muscle showed up. Catching sight of the girl who had become my best friend over the years, I felt happiness fill me and I waved. She spoke quietly to the huge guy in a suit beside her, and he eventually gave a nod before picking up a menu and dropping down at one of the tables far enough away to give us a little bit of privacy, but still close enough that he could eliminate any danger that cropped up.

As Nova neared, I jumped to my feet and wrapped my arms around her as tight as I could. "It's so good to see you," I whispered, trying to mask how emotional I was at getting to hug her again after so long. To hide my tears from her, I eyeballed her body-guard. "Did you have to bring the muscle, though?"

"It's either bring the muscle or not leave the house," she said with a grimace before pushing me back into my side of the booth and sitting across from me. "You look great, by the way. Definitely better than the last time I laid eyes on you in the flesh."

That had been the year before, when Manuel had broken my jaw. I hadn't known that at the time. It wasn't until I got to Creswell Springs and Gracie had taken me to the hospital for X-rays that we'd known just how much damage my stepbrother had caused.

I touched my cheek, remembering the pain of having my jaw wired shut the summer before. "You would be surprised by the changes that happen when you're no longer living with an abusive, sadistic monster."

Compassion filled a set of eyes so like Garret's, it made my heart flutter. "I can only imagine," she said as the waitress came back over. Nova let me order for the both of us once I told her how good the burgers were.

"I worked here until my roommate got me the job at the club," I explained as I picked up my glass of cherry cola. Maybe I shouldn't have been drinking caffeine, but I didn't even know for sure if I was pregnant yet, so it didn't count—at least, that was what I told myself as I sipped it through the straw while the waitress walked away after promising our food would be out shortly.

"I'm going to assume you make bank at that place," Nova commented, and I tensed. "Or you wouldn't be fighting my brother so hard on continuing to work there."

I rolled my eyes, already knowing where this conversation was going to lead. "I make plenty to cover my bills and have enough left over for a little nest egg in case of emergencies. Your brother just wants me to be his kept woman. He says he only wants to spoil me and take care of me. I don't consider it taking care of so much as wanting to control me. I've lived that life, Nova. Never having a penny of my own. Having to rely on some man to provide everything. Beholden to him for every meal, every piece of clothing. I'm never going back to it. If he can't handle me working, he knows where the door is. No one is forcing him to stick around."

"What if you had a different job?" my friend suggested hesitantly.

"I don't need a different job. I'm fine right where I am." I crossed my arms over my chest, clenching my jaw as anger filled me. Not at Nova, but at her brother. He was definitely using his sweet little sister to con me into doing exactly what he wanted.

"What if the job offered better pay and benefits like health care?" she enticed.

"I'd say your brother is using you to try to control me." But the mention of health care had me sitting up straighter, fighting my pride to turn down the offer. I might have had a nice savings, but how long would that money last if I had to pay for all my doctor's visits out of pocket if I did happen to be pregnant? "But I might be interested in hearing you out since you mentioned health care."

"Yeah?" Her smile could have lit up the entire diner.

"Yes," I muttered, shifting my gaze to her bodyguard. He was drinking a cup of coffee and appeared to be reading a newspaper. But there was no mistaking the way his eyes shifted around the diner, keeping everyone in sight at all times, making sure the little angel he was in charge of stayed safe. I swallowed hard and inadvertently leaned forward. "Nova…"

Her green gaze shifted to mine, having been watching her guard just like I had. When our eyes locked, I couldn't blink back the sting of tears any more than I had the power to fight the fear that was trying to choke the air from me.

Nova grasped my hands, her touch offering me a small measure of comfort. "What's wrong?" she whispered.

The lump in my throat was hard to swallow, and I had to put more effort into keeping the tears from falling. I couldn't break. Not now. Not when there might be a life growing inside me who needed me to stay strong. "I think I'm going to need the health insurance," I confessed. "I'm two weeks late."

She lifted one of her hands from mine to slap across her own mouth, holding in a scream. I watched her for a moment, unsure why she was the one screaming. I was the one in emotional overdrive because of what was going on inside my body. But this was Nova. She was an emphatic little thing who loved hard.

After a minute, she seemed to gather herself and returned to holding my hands, her fingers squeezing mine reassuringly. "Okay. There's no need to get upset. We'll figure everything out."

"I'm not worried about me," I hissed, pulling one hand free to wipe away the dampness on my lashes I hadn't realized was there until right then. "Or even the baby—if there is one. I mean, this could be anything, right?"

Nova shrugged, but I knew she was thinking the same thing I was. I was twenty-one years old. The chances of this being something other than a baby might not be zero, but it wasn't exactly likely. I had to face facts. Somewhere along the way, our protection had failed, and now I was knocked up.

Muttering a curse, I picked up my drink and gulped it down, wishing it were something considerably harder than cherry cola. Slamming the glass back on the tabletop caused the salt, pepper, and ketchup bottle to rattle in the basket where they were stored. "Well, I'm not worried about me or the baby," I repeated, trying to convince myself more than Nova. "I can take care of both of us just fine on my own if I have to."

That much, I did know. I was confident that I could raise my child on my own if it came down to it. But I was hoping Garret wouldn't let me down, that he would step up and want to be part of our baby's life. So far, he'd worked hard at showing me I could trust him. But this was different. A child was a lifetime commitment. Not just eighteen years, but for the rest of both of our lives.

"Then what are you afraid of?" my friend asked softly, making me face my real fear.

"Garret freaking out," I said. "He's just now really getting his shit together. I know he's been working hard, trying to show me he's ready for a commitment, but that doesn't mean he won't freak out more if I tell him he's going to be a daddy." I folded one arm over my lower abdomen, instinctively protecting the little life that was growing there. The other, I left on the table, still holding on to Nova's. I turned my hand over, linking our fingers together.

"Don't worry about Garret," she assured me. "I think he might surprise you. But no matter what happens, you and that baby will be taken care of. Ryan and I will make sure of it."

Cali

AFTER MY LUNCH WITH NOVA, and she'd convinced me I had nothing to worry about when it came to confessing all to Garret, I called the club and told them I was sick. I needed the night off so I could work up the rest of the courage I needed to talk to my man when he got home that night.

I was relaxing in my room when I heard Kim leave for the night. Too nervous to eat—or maybe that was the baby—I just lay in bed watching old episodes of *Pokémon*. Hours passed until, finally, I heard Garret come in. He had his own key. Hell, half his stuff was in my closet and dresser drawers. We were practically living together, but I'd been holding out on him, refusing to label it as that. If I did, he would insist I move in with him at the apartment he shared with Ryan Vitucci, and I really wasn't sure I was ready for that.

My bedroom door opened, and he was surprised when he saw I was sitting up in bed. His green eyes brightened, and he practically jogged over to the bed to kiss me. "Hey there, blue eyes." I wrapped my arms around his neck, kissing him back, but it didn't last long before he was lifting his head. "Fuck, baby. You have no idea how much I've missed you."

"I've missed you too," I told him. Licking my lips, I gathered my courage once again. "Um, we need to talk."

He pulled back, his brow furrowing. "I don't like the sound of that, Lis. Nothing good ever comes from anyone saying those words."

I pushed up to my knees and then got off the bed. Taking his hand, I urged him to follow me into the living room. This confession was huge, and I didn't want the sanctuary of our bed to be cursed by whatever reaction he might have to everything I needed to tell him.

"Lis, babe." He laughed a little forcefully, sounding strained. "If this is about how much I've been gone for work lately, I'm sorry. I'll make it up to you as soon as this shit is taken care of. I just—"

"My name is Calista Ramirez. My friends and

family would call me Cali," I said in a rush, and I waited for his reaction.

Garret sat down on the couch, his face going completely blank. My stomach bottomed out, but I swallowed down the nausea that tried to distract me and confessed it all.

"Before I was Lis Brewer, I was Calista Ramirez. My stepfather was Matias Ramirez, and yes, my step-brother—the one who used to beat and abuse me—is Manuel Ramirez. Matias adopted me before my mom died so that I would still have a family. He promised her he would keep me safe, but when she died, he shut down, and I became Manuel's favorite toy to play with and torture."

When Garret didn't even blink at me as I told him, I began to bite on my thumbnail.

What was he thinking? His face was pale, but those green orbs were lifeless.

Tears stung my eyes, but I continued. "Last year, right before Matias died, Manuel brought me with him to New York while his dad was getting treat-ment. One night, he beat me so badly he broke my jaw. The next day, while he was at the hospital with Matias, Nova helped me escape. She sent me to live with your aunt at Sanctuary. They patched me up and gave me a new identity…"

I kept talking even though he didn't so much as

blink once the entire time. Tears poured down my face, and snot was choking me from how hard I was crying, but I didn't give up.

There was only one last thing to tell him.

"Garret, I-I think I'm pregnant," I whispered, silently praying that the news that we might be parents soon would snap him out of whatever trance he'd fallen into. "I-I know we never talked about kids, but—"

I broke off abruptly when he jerked to his feet. Without so much as looking at me, he walked calmly to the door, opened it, and closed it behind him.

My heart dropped, but I stood there, waiting, hoping. Long minutes passed as I just stared at the door, mentally pleading for it to open. But as the clock ticked, ten minutes passed, then thirty. At the one-hour mark, my legs gave out from standing there with my knees locked for so long.

A broken sob left me, and I curled into a ball on the living room floor. Touching my belly, I closed my eyes, but that didn't stop the tears from falling. "It's... It will be f-fine," I promised the little nugget I knew without proof was growing in there. "W-we'll be o-o-kay. I-I won't let anything or any...anyone hurt you, sweet baby."

I wasn't sure how long I lay on the floor sobbing, promising the life growing inside me that I would protect it with my own life until my last breath, but eventually, I began to feel cold, and I knew it was bad for the baby. It took all my strength, but I slowly got to my feet and stumbled back into my room, kicking the door closed and locking it before carefully sitting on the edge of the bed.

Grabbing the pillow that had become Garret's, I lifted it to my nose and inhaled his scent, but it only made me cry harder.

How many times had he told me he would protect me? How many times had he promised to never hurt me?

When I'd needed him the most, he'd just walked away. After everything I'd been through, ridiculously, I'd thought a man who had already hurt me in the past was someone I could put my faith in, that he would take care of his child—and, stupidly, me too. I'd put every horrible thing he'd ever written to and about me on social media all those years ago behind me, because I loved him and had actually believed that he'd grown up. That he'd finally turned into a man worthy of my trust, love, and loyalty.

But he'd let me down.

Nova had convinced me her brother cared about me, and I'd been so sure that she was right.

Instead, he'd walked out that door. Taking what was left of my heart.

Every man in my life who was supposed to love and protect me had done nothing but let me down again and again. Garret was supposed to be different. He was going to be the one who broke the cycle, the one who healed my soul and made me believe in happily ever afters. Instead, he'd been like everyone else. Only this time, it was a hundred times worse. I'd given him my heart willingly, and he'd just thrown it away like it—like his baby and I—didn't mean a damn to him.

My heart felt shattered, but I couldn't allow that pain to hurt the baby, so I locked it down.

Angrily, I tossed the pillow in my hands across the room before curling up in the middle of the bed. I didn't think it was possible to sleep, not with how much I'd been through emotionally, yet I closed my eyes and didn't open them again until the sun was filtering in through my curtains.

My eyes felt swollen as I lifted my lashes, and the nausea was definitely something I couldn't ignore. Groaning, I rushed from my room to the bathroom. I was in there for at least an hour, so sick I couldn't lift my head for the longest time. When I could finally stand, my entire body trembled from the effort, but I did it because there was no other choice. My baby needed me to be strong, and I would be.

Once I was cleaned up, I grabbed a few sports

drinks from the fridge and went back to bed, deciding I would just rest and stay hydrated until I felt better. Then I would go to the pharmacy and get a pregnancy test.

After that…

I didn't know what I was going to do after that, but I'd figure it out.

If nothing else, I still had Nova. As long as I had her, I knew everything would be okay.

Garret

THE BARTENDER PLACED the glass of Macallan in front of me, but when he started to take the bottle with him, I shot him a glare that had him placing the bottle on the bar top beside my glass. Giving him a nod, I picked up the tumbler and tossed back half the contents in one swallow.

I barely tasted the well-aged whisky as it slid down my throat. Around me, the bar was crowded and loud, but all I could see or hear was Lis as she'd urged me onto her couch and then dropped her bomb into my lap.

"My name is Calista Ramirez. My friends and family would call me Cali."

Her words hadn't made sense at first. I thought maybe she was playing a joke, considering all the shit I'd had to do to find Manuel Ramirez over the last week, only to come up with nothing. But then I'd looked at her, really looked at her, and I suddenly realized she wasn't kidding.

Picture after picture flooded my mind from my teen years. Of beautiful Calista Ramirez as she did her makeup tutorial videos. When Ramirez had sent men to kill Nova, I'd been pissed and gone looking for someone to take out my frustration on. Mess with my sister? I'll fuck with whomever your nearest and dearest was.

That was how I'd found Calista—Cali—on social media.

I'd been stoned out of my mind at the time, but not even my impaired brain could deny that she was the most beautiful woman I'd ever seen. She could turn herself into any celebrity with just a little bit of makeup, but when her face was bare, that was when she was at her most enthralling.

It had been years since I'd thought about the girl I'd been borderline obsessed with. I'd lived for watching her videos. Every Instagram picture she shared, I saved to my phone so I could jack off to it later.

But that wasn't the only thing I'd done.

And those memories were what hit me the instant I put it all together. Lis was Cali. The girl I'd tormented because her stepdad had tried to kill my baby sister. Like Nova, who hadn't deserved to have a fucking drug lord target her because of how important she was to his biggest enemy, Cali hadn't deserved the way I'd treated her. Both were innocent in the war between the Ramirez and Vitucci families.

That hadn't stopped me from targeting Cali, though. Every chance I got, I would comment on her videos or slip into her DMs. I'd tell her terrible, sickening things—things that made my stomach churn even as I'd been typing them. How I hoped someone beat her like her stepdad had tried to beat Nova. How she didn't deserve to live.

That I hoped she was raped and left for dead.

I gulped down the rest of the whisky in my glass before picking up the bottle to fill it to the brim. Expensive liquor sloshed over the side as I raised it to my mouth and gulped it down.

Lis had talked and talked, but I hadn't heard a single word she'd said after her confession of who she was. I didn't know how she'd gone from being the spoiled, pampered stepdaughter of Ryan's family's enemy—making him my enemy too—to waiting tables in a strip club and living in that tiny-ass apartment.

The few things she'd told me her stepbrother had done to her rushed into my head as the worst words I'd ever said to her echoed in the back of my mind.

When had Manuel done those terrible things to her? Had he done them because I'd given him the idea when I'd posted that comment on a video?

My glass was empty again, so I picked up the bottle and started chugging, trying to drown out the thoughts. But they refused to be shut down.

Because I fucking knew in my gut that I was responsible for what had happened. I'd put those words out into the universe, and they had become reality. I was the cause of the nightmares that haunted the woman I loved.

And she'd known that. She must have.

Lis had been so unreachable at first, and now I understood why. Yet she'd eventually let me in, given me a chance.

How?

I didn't understand it.

How could that beautiful woman give me a chance, knowing I was responsible for so many of her nightmares?

The bottle, which had been three-quarters of the way full when the bartender had placed it beside me, was suddenly empty. The world began to sway, and I tossed down several large bills, not caring if I gave the man everything in my pocket. Turning, I stumbled through the crowd, bumping into people left and right, getting cursed at and shoved back a few times before I made it to the door.

My driver was waiting where I'd left him, and I climbed into the back, mumbling for him to take me home. As he drove, the whisky did what it always did to me when I had too much. I went from hating myself for what I'd caused to happen to Lis—fucking Calista Ramirez, my drunken brain reminded me—to being pissed that she hadn't told me sooner.

How the fuck could I have been with her for over six months and not realize who the hell she really was? She hadn't changed that much since we were teens. I'd memorized her face back then, but faces didn't always click in my brain, especially when I hadn't seen or thought about them in a long time.

The longer the whisky flowed through my veins, the angrier I got, until all I was seeing was red. My driver stopped outside my apartment building and got out, but I waved him off, snapping, "I can open my own motherfucking door."

"Yes, Mr. Hannigan," he muttered.

Walking into the building, I glared at the men on guard duty. One of them pushed the call button for the elevator, and it opened instantly. Unsteady on my feet, I walked in and had to lean down and blink at the numbers on the panel a few times before I saw it clearly enough. It took three tries before my finger actually connected with my floor number.

My stomach did gross things as the elevator lifted higher and higher, but I burped and swallowed the taste of bile just as the doors slid open. The apartment was in darkness, and as I wavered on my feet, trying to find my room without bothering with turning on a light, I bumped into a table.

The sharp corner jabbed into my thigh so hard the damn thing scraped across the floor loudly. Cursing, I angrily shoved it back even farther before starting toward the direction I figured my bedroom was.

Only to hit the back of the couch.

"Motherfuck!" I snarled and flipped the damn thing just as light filled the room and burned my eyes.

Jerking around, I saw Ryan standing there—with my little sister right behind him.

"What the fuck is wrong with you?" Nova's voice was so loud, my ears rang, but I was too pissed to care that she was obviously mad at me.

What right did she have to be upset? I was the one who had been played. And she probably knew all about it. She and Cali had been friends on Instagram, and I'd catch hell from my sister every time I commented...

I hope you get raped and left for dead.

Rage at her, at Lis—but mostly at myself—filled me, and I tried to focus on Nova. "You…" I stumbled toward her. "You knew, didn't you?"

"Knew what?" she demanded, sounding condescending in my drunken state.

"About Lis…Cali. Whatever the fuck her name is." I took another step toward her, only to stumble into yet another table. Cursing, I picked up the lamp that was sitting there and threw it. The sound of it shattering against the wall did nothing to alleviate any of my anger. "You knew who she really was, didn't you?"

"Garret…" Nova's beautiful face morphed right before my eyes from sneering to sweetly soothing. "Are you really going to tell me you didn't know who she is? How many hours did you spend looking at all those pictures? Don't lie to me and say you had no clue that Lis was Calista."

"I didn't!" I shouted the denial. "She lied to me. For months. I bet you and she had a real good laugh, playing me along."

My heart lurched at the thought, and I couldn't stop the sound that left me as a new realization hit me. The agony was too much, and I slammed my fist down on the table that was still in my damn way. "No wonder that bastard Ramirez is in the city. He's here to take her away from me."

I couldn't let that happen. He'd already hurt her enough. If Manuel got his hands on her again, he was liable to kill her.

"No one was laughing at you, dumbass," Nova snarled at me. "And if you had no clue who she really was, then that is completely on you. Do you even remember how you were back then, Garret? The way you would bully her?" The disgust on her face made my stomach roil. "You were a monster at times."

"No," I tried to deny.

I hope you get raped and left for dead.

Tears filled my eyes. "I wasn't like that—"

"You were."

I started to argue, but the next thing I knew, Nova's hand was smacking across my face so hard, my head snapped back. "You told her she deserved to be raped!"

I hope you get raped and left for dead.

My legs folded under me, and I dropped to my knees, the tears falling faster. The sting of my sister's slap must have knocked some sense into me, because suddenly, I remembered that Lis had other things to tell me, but I hadn't heard any of it.

Oh God, I'd fucked up.

"I said that," I whispered as the full force of my idiocy flooded through me. "I really said that to her."

Stricken, I looked up at my sister. Of the two of us, she was the good one. The one who loved everyone, who always took care of us all—my sorry ass included. "I told her that and so much more, but I never meant it, Nova. I was a bastard to her. How—" Bile lifted into my throat along with the taste of whisky. Quickly, I swallowed it down. "How could she possibly love me when I treated her like that back then?"

"I don't know, but she does." Her touch soothed something inside me just a little, and I felt her wipe away my tears. Hearing her confirm that Lis loved me calmed the rage that was still simmering beneath the surface. "Please tell me you didn't spew more stupid shit when she told you the truth."

"No," I panted, shaking my head, only to cause the world to spin around me. "I didn't say anything. I just let her talk, and then I left."

"Idiot."

Shame had my head dropping until my chin touched my chest. "I know. I'm an idiot who doesn't deserve her." I snapped my head back up, my eyes pleading for Nova to believe me, to help me make this better. If she couldn't fix it, then no one could. "But I love her."

"I'm not the one you should be saying that to, stupid," she scoffed at me.

I jerked unsteadily to my feet. "You're right. I have to talk to her." Tell her how sorry I was. That I'd make it all up to her. That she was the only good thing in the entire world that truly mattered to me. "I have to tell her how sorry I am," I said. "And that I love her. I have to—"

"You have to go to bed and sleep off whatever you took a bath in." Grabbing one of my arms, she turned me toward my bedroom. I leaned on her, letting her help me. That's what Nova did. She was good at it. The best. How could she be so good, while I was such a fuckup?

"You're in no condition to tell her anything right now," she grumbled as she helped me to the bed. "And even if you tried, she probably wouldn't believe you when you smell like tequila."

"I can't believe our dad owns a bar and you can't tell the difference between the smell of tequila and Macallan," I mumbled as I lay down.

"Unlike you, I didn't start sampling the product at the bar when I was thirteen," she reminded me. "Ugh, you drank an entire bottle of Macallan, didn't you?"

"Maybe. Can't remember." I let her tuck me in, not even caring when she gave me a withering look.

"You're stupider than I gave you credit for," she said with a sad shake of her head, reaching to turn off the lamp beside my bed. "Get some sleep, dumbass. Hopefully you can apologize to Cali tomorrow and fix what you broke tonight."

I hope you get raped and left for dead.

More tears spilled from my eyes. "Fuck, I hope so."

Cali

BY FRIDAY, I felt a little better, but not much. For days, the only time I had left my room was to use the bathroom and replenish my supply of sports drinks and bottles of water so I didn't get dehydrated.

My phone had been going off constantly during the days I'd been camped out in my bed, feeling like death warmed over. At least I hadn't thrown up anymore, but every time Garret's name popped up on my screen, bile tried to choke me. Luckily, the anger would help me fight through the nausea, and I finally blocked his number so I didn't have to deal with it any longer.

Nova, on the other hand, was a different story. She called to check up on me at least once a day. Hearing her voice soothed my frayed nerves and even helped me sleep a little during the day. I really hoped she hadn't been kidding about the new job offer—or that it was still on the table now that her brother and I were no longer together. I'd called off from work all week, and the last time I'd spoken to my boss, he'd said if I didn't come back with a doctor's excuse, not to come back at all.

That morning, I'd finally left the apartment and walked to the pharmacy on the corner to grab a few things. Top of my list was the pregnancy test and a case of ginger ale. When I got back to the apartment, I popped a can and poured it over a glass of ice. After chugging half the contents, I took the little bag with the test into the bathroom and peed on the stick.

It was just a formality. I knew without a doubt that I was pregnant, but I wanted the proof to show Garret when I finally faced him again. Not that I expected him to care. He hadn't said a single word the night I'd told him everything, and even though he'd tried to call me and he'd texted, I couldn't get past him just walking away when I'd needed him most.

Didn't he understand I was scared out of my head? I'd played a good game with Nova, telling her I wasn't worried about the baby or myself, but that was all bullshit. I was terrified. My mother had died before she could teach me how to be a good parent, and every other parental figure in my life had let me down to the point that using them as an example had only shown me what *not* to do.

As the second line appeared on the cheap test, I touched my hands to my belly, silently promising my little nugget that no matter how scared I was, that didn't mean I would let him or her down. "I'll figure it out," I vowed. "You have nothing to worry about. Mommy is going to make sure you are taken care of."

I spent the rest of the day resting. A search online about the early stages of pregnancy had said that feeling tired was natural. I wasn't sure if it was the baby or all the emotional bullshit Garret had put me through that was making me want to stay in bed all day, every day, but I knew I would eventually have to push through it and start making money again.

During one of my chats with Nova, she'd invited me out for a girls' night with her and her cousins. I didn't feel much like partying, but I wanted to see Nova. After showering, I put on a little makeup and then pulled on a pair of black shorts to go with my red top. It had been hot and humid when I'd gone to the pharmacy that morning, and I could only assume the heat had gotten worse as the day progressed.

At the designated time, I walked out of my building to find a limo already waiting for me. The muscle that had been with my friend earlier in the week when we'd had lunch together got out and opened the back door for me. He was cordial when he greeted me, and I muttered one in return as I stepped into the back to find my friend and her cousin Ciana sitting together.

"Hey," I mumbled, sitting across from them.

"Hi," Nova's sweet voice greeted, her smile lighting the interior of the limo. Ciana, however, didn't say anything, and when I glanced at her again, it was to find she was asleep with her head against the window. "Are you hungry?" Nova asked, and I switched my gaze back to her. "I thought we could eat before going to the club."

"Yeah, sure," I said with a shrug. "I could eat."

I hadn't eaten much since the last time I'd seen her in person, but my stomach was empty and growly, so I figured I needed to fill the tank. Although I wasn't all too confident that whatever I put in my mouth would stay down, I needed to at least try.

The limo started to move, but the overhead light was still on, and Nova gave me a cautious once-over. "Did you—"

"Yeah," I whispered, not allowing her to get the full question out. "And it was positive."

Ciana sat up straight, looking more alert and a

little startled. "Positive," she mumbled with a yawn. "What were we talking about?"

"*We* weren't talking about anything, C." Nova heaved a sigh at her cousin. "You fell asleep."

"Oh, sorry," the redhead said around a yawn. "But what was positive?"

I pulled the pregnancy test from my purse and showed it to them.

"Wait…" Ciana seemed relieved to see my test. "You're pregnant?"

"That's what the test says," I answered, returning the tiny little test to my purse. "Maybe I should have splurged on the digital test. It could have been a false reading." I didn't doubt the results for a single moment, but what if Garret did? "I guess I'll call and get an appointment at the free clinic, find out if it's true or not."

"If it says it's positive, then it is," Ciana assured me. "It's false negatives you have to worry about. I work for one of the best OB-GYNs in the city. Come in tomorrow, and I'll get you taken care of."

"But tomorrow is Saturday," I reminded her.

"We're open until noon on Saturdays. Come in, I'll get your labs, have the nurse practitioner do your pap, and if my friend in ultrasound is working, we can get some pictures of the baby."

Her mentioning that I might get to see my little nugget lifted my spirits, but then I remembered I didn't have insurance. All of those labs and other tests—not to mention the ultrasound itself—would eat up a huge part of my savings. "I don't have insurance."

"I don't care about insurance," Ciana dismissed. "I can work around it."

"You have insurance," Nova spoke up, and relief flooded me as she continued. "I took care of all of your information with HR and got you sorted."

My mouth gaped open in amazement at my friend. "When? And more importantly, how?"

"Aunt Gracie had all of your new identity information. I told her I was helping you get a job and needed your social security number to get your paperwork completed. She said to tell you congrats on the new job, by the way," she said as she pulled out a little ID badge. "Make sure you stop by HR to sign everything, but your insurance started yesterday, as soon as you were entered into the system as an employee. You'll get your card in the mail in about a week, but it will cover any care you have before it arrives."

"Whoa," I whispered, tears of relief and gratitude filling my eyes. "Nova…"

"I got your back, babe."

———

After stuffing my face with tacos and spending the rest of the evening dancing with Nova and Ciana, I felt lighter by the time we climbed into the back of the limo. Ciana had practically passed out on the dance floor, though, and that was worrisome, but she didn't seem all that concerned for her own health as she argued with Nova about going to the doctor.

I stayed quiet as the two cousins argued about it, but I couldn't help wondering what was going on with the normally vivacious Ciana Donati. I'd only met her one other time. Garret and I had gone to dinner with her, kind of a trial run for meeting his family. But when he'd asked me to go to California for Nova's graduation, I'd chickened out.

Visiting Creswell Springs with him would have opened a can of worms I hadn't been ready for. Neither had he, if his reaction to finding out my true identity was anything to go by.

Ciana fell back to sleep not long after we were on the road, and the driver headed for my apartment to drop me off first. As we rode in silence, my phone buzzed with a text. I pulled it out, only to frown when I read the message.

Unknown: *You can't hide from me now, bitch.*

"Who the fuck is this...?" I muttered as the blood in my veins turned to ice, because I knew down to my toes who it was. But I wanted to deny it.

Nova glanced at me, and I showed her my phone screen.

Her eyes had barely scanned the message when we were suddenly jarred, the limo having been rammed from the left by another vehicle. I screamed, startled by the incident, while Nova rushed to hold on to Ciana so she didn't fall onto the floor and get hurt.

The impact of another car hitting us came again, this time making the limo lurch and then fishtail. The tacos I'd so happily eaten earlier tried to make a comeback, and I fought my gag reflex, trying to keep the contents of my stomach down.

But not throwing up was the least of my problems.

I barely remembered the rest of the roller-coaster ride in the limo. It was scary, the long car hitting and being hit by other cars left and right. The three of us were tossed all over the place, while the noises outside only grew more terrifying. Horns honking, metal crushing, and then there was the gunfire. It came from every direction, but luckily, the limo was bulletproof.

The last thing I remembered, before the world went dark, was Ciana screaming and rambling. Then Nova was wrapping her little body around mine, cushioning it to protect the baby and me from the impact as the limo collided with a tank.

Cali

CONSCIOUSNESS SLOWLY CAME BACK to me a little at a time. I could tell I was on a plane because of the rumble of the engines and that weird feeling in the pit of my stomach I got every time I was in the air. I hated that feeling. Heights weren't my thing, and flying always made me nervous.

But that fear was short-lived when I heard his angry bellow.

"O'Brion tried to pull a fast one on me, but that fucking bitch won't get what she wanted. I took Vitucci's little doll. She might have gotten the redhead, but everyone knows it's the blonde who matters."

I jerked, knowing the sound of Manuel's enraged roar anywhere. As I did, my arm muscles protested, and I fought back a whimper as I lifted my lashes and slowly tipped my head back to see that my hands had been restrained above my head.

I was chained to a bar so high over my head that my feet didn't even touch the floor. My entire body felt oddly numb, telling me I must have been in that hanging position for a while and the blood through my veins had slowed down. From the looks of it, my hands were a weird purplish color, and when I wiggled my fingers, they didn't even tingle—there was simply no feeling in them at all.

The short distraction of figuring out what was going on with my limbs ended abruptly when I felt a punch directly to my left side from behind. I screamed in a mixture of fear and pain. Apparently not every inch of my body was as numb as I had first assumed.

"Do you know how long I've been looking for you, whore?" Manuel snarled, walking around to stand in front of me. I knew better than to answer, but that didn't stop him from punching me again. This time, the blow landed in the middle of my gut, and I cried out again, now more in fear for my little nugget, although the punch knocked the air straight from my lungs. "How much money I spent in an attempt to find you? And all this time, you were hiding with fucking Vitucci and his little bitch."

While he ranted and raved like the lunatic he was,

I tried not to think about the possibility that my stepbrother could kill the baby in my belly. Not wanting to give away my secret—because the bastard would get off on making me miscarry if he knew—I tried to block him completely from my mind. Instead of looking at him, I glanced around.

Only to find Nova across from me. Her arms were tied above her head just as mine were, her head hanging forward, with her blond hair shielding her face from me. I couldn't tell if she was breathing, and from how still she appeared, my heart broke. She was dead. She had to be. There was no way she could have survived the accident and then whatever Manuel had done to her.

Tears filled my eyes, one spilling free, just as Manuel cracked something across my head and everything went dark again.

The next time I was able to open my eyes, I nearly screamed. I knew exactly where I was—back in Colombia. But worse than that, I was in Manuel's torture dungeon. I'd never been inside it, but from the stench of blood, decay, and all-out death, I knew that was exactly where he'd taken me. Not only the smells gave away my location, though. I could see what my stepbrother referred to as his toys hanging on the walls. Saws, pliers, surgical-style instruments that he'd used to make his victims scream so loud the entire mansion could hear them.

As my swollen, blurry eyes shifted around the room, I saw that Nova was across from me again. Her toes barely touched the floor, but her head was still hanging forward, and I couldn't hear if she was breathing or see her chest moving. Tears leaked from my eyes. My friend was dead, and I didn't doubt that Manuel had brought her here to torture me with the sight of her lifeless body.

I took stock of my own body. My face throbbed, and I felt something warm and thick oozing from my nose. I was still tied up with my arms above my head, but at least my feet were on the floor, which gave me a little feeling in the lower half of my body. That was how I felt the cramping, and then the wetness between my legs.

Whimpering, I didn't try to hold back the tears.

This was it. Manuel had finally gotten me where he wanted me. And not only had he killed my best friend—the angel who had saved me from his sadistic ass—but he'd succeeded in hurting my little nugget as well. I could feel the blood trickling out of me, my baby's life slipping away with each passing minute.

The pain of losing everyone I loved was too much, and I cried out again, not even caring if

Manuel heard me. Let him come in and finish what he started. Once I was dead, he'd have what he'd always wanted, and maybe I could find peace with my baby and Nova on the other side.

I wasn't sure how long I remained like that, moaning and whimpering. My nose eventually stopped bleeding, but the cramps got a little worse as time passed. At one point, I lost control of my full bladder and pissed all over myself. That eased a little of the cramping in my lower abdomen, but not by much. And still, time ticked away, hour after hour passed, turning into days with no signs of life. No footsteps overhead. No roar of gunfire as someone tried to rescue us.

It was time to face facts. No one was coming. I'd die in that dungeon like so many other poor fucks had before me.

Then I suddenly heard the sound of chains rattling, and I snapped my head up to find Nova testing the security of her restraints.

The feeling of loss was too much, and I couldn't be completely sure I wasn't hallucinating. But at least I had someone to talk to, even if it was very possible she was dead and I was imagining everything. "I thought you were dead."

"Where are we?" Nova—or ghost Nova, I wasn't sure which—asked.

I licked my lips, only to grimace at the taste of blood on them. "Home," I answered with a shudder. I'd never wanted to return, yet there I was, once again a prisoner in what should have been a safe haven. "Colombia."

"What?" Nova exclaimed. "How did we get here?"

"I don't know," I answered honestly. After Manuel had started beating me, I'd lost consciousness. Which was probably a blessing, considering how bad my body felt. "When I woke up, we were on some cargo plane. Manuel started running his mouth, then to relieve some aggression, he started his favorite pastime —using me as his personal punching bag. Next thing I knew, we were in this stupid room. It's his favorite place in the house. The torture dungeon, as he likes to call it. I've never been a guest, but I've heard plenty of people screaming from this room over the years." I couldn't control the shudder that racked my body again. The pain was agony. "We're going to die, Nova."

At least, I was. She was probably already dead.

"We're not going to die," my friend promised. "Ryan and Garret are probably already on their way to get us right now."

The mention of the man I loved forced a humor-less laugh past my lips. "Sweet, innocent Nova."

Even in death, she was so precious. How could she not see the danger we were in? Or even think that the men she placed so much trust in would ever risk themselves to save us? "You think they will come and rescue us? What world do you live in? We are nothing to them. Out of sight, out of mind. They probably already have replacements for us."

That was how every man was. They didn't think a woman was worth the effort, so they put them out of their minds and found someone else to warm their bed and wet their dicks.

"No." Nova practically growled at me in her vehemence. "Ryan will come for me. Both of us. Just wait and see."

"From what I can determine, it's already been two days. Over forty-eight hours with no sign of your precious Ryan. If they were going to save us, they would have been here by now." I lost strength in my neck, and it bowed until my chin touched my chest. "Just accept it, Nova. We're going to die here. Stop fooling yourself and thinking that any man is a knight in shining armor. That is fairy-tale bullshit our moms tell us when we're little girls to give us hope of a better life."

"You'll see," she muttered stubbornly, reminding me so much of her brother, a lump filled my throat.

"Any minute now, Ryan will come through that door and get us the hell out of here."

"Keep dreaming, princess," I muttered.

Silence descended again, and I was thankful for it. I just wanted to curl into a ball with my pain, but that was impossible, so I channeled my thoughts inward, promising my nugget that after our deaths, I'd get to hold him or her in my arms. We would be safe on the other side. There would be no evil where we were going…

"Hey, asshole!"

Nova's shout startled me so much that it convinced me she was really alive and not a ghostly apparition that was playing tricks on my mind. It also scared the fuck out of me. I knew I wasn't leaving that dungeon alive, but I wasn't sure I was ready to face death just yet.

"What are you doing?" I hissed at the crazy girl across from me. "Are you insane?"

"I have to pee," she said so calmly, I knew she must have sustained brain damage somewhere between the limo accident and waking up earlier.

She had to pee, so she was going to bring my monstrous stepbrother in there to kill us both? It would surely put us out of our misery, but I wanted a little more time to make promises to my nugget before I met the baby on the other side.

Rustling outside the door made my heart stop, but no one came in. With a heavy sigh, Nova shifted, and I watched her fingers clench around the chains above her cuffs. She grimaced in pain but raised her voice louder. "Yo, cocksucker. I'm talking to you, you dickless pussy."

"Nova, you have a death wish," I whispered to her, my swollen eyes begging for her to stop. "Please don't get him in here. He will only beat me again. I can't take much more. The baby…"

"You will both be fine," she said confidently. She adjusted her hold on the chains, shifting the weight on her arms so more was being taken by one than the other just as the door was kicked open.

A seething Manuel stomped into the room, his face twisted with hate—like always. Even through my blurred vision, I could see how huge his pupils were and knew he had been sticking his nose in the coke again. Perhaps he'd even gotten into something stronger since the Ramirez cocaine supply was gone, the Vituccis supposedly having taken over the fields after Matias's death.

"What'd you say to me, bitch?" my stepbrother slurred in accented English. "You dare call me a cocksucker?"

"Your breath sure does smell like you just spat

out your boyfriend's dick," Nova taunted. "You got a little man juice right there?"

My eyes bulged when I watched her touch her tongue to the corner of her mouth, indicating where it was before she actually—fucking actually— smirked at him. "Go ahead and lick it all up, Manny. I'm sure you want to get every last drop."

Oh lord, he was going to kill her first. I knew it. But I couldn't stand it. Helplessly, I watched as he stomped toward her and punched her in the head with his huge fist. Her head fell forward, and I cried out.

"No!" I screamed, needing to protect her. She'd saved me from him once; now it was my turn. "Leave her alone, Manuel. She has nothing to do with this."

Slowly, he turned to face me. "*She* helped you run from me, Calista. *She* is the reason you got away and I couldn't marry you when the old bastard died. All that money, and he left it to his whore's bitch of a daughter."

"I will never marry you!" I screeched so loud that everyone in the mansion must have heard me. "I will slit my own throat before I become your wife."

"You think I *want* to marry you for anything other than to get the money that should have been mine to begin with? I hate you, you stupid bitch!"

He took a step toward me, and I tensed,

preparing for the blow that would finally end my life. But it never came. Right before my eyes, Nova moved as fast as lightning. She lifted the top half of her body and wrapped her legs around Manuel's neck from behind. She cried out, pain twisting her beautiful face, but she didn't release him.

Manuel struggled, an expression on his face I'd never seen there before—fear—as she attempted to squeeze the life from him. Nova tightened her legs, but he somehow turned his head, biting into the flesh of her inner thigh. She screamed so loud, my ears began to ring, but she refused to release him.

Blood began to drip down her leg onto the floor, and her screams came again and again until Manuel went limp in her hold.

Breathing heavily, she released him, and he landed on the floor with his head at an awkward angle. I blinked a few times, thinking my swollen eyes were playing tricks on me, but when I looked again, I met the lifeless gaze of my stepbrother.

He really was dead.

And sweet, precious, little Nova—the girl who was my angel—had killed him.

Cali

IT TOOK me a few minutes to comprehend what had actually happened. By that time, Nova had freed herself from the cuffs and had already started working on my own.

"I need you to do something for me," she murmured, calm as could be as she lowered my hands.

"Anything," I promised, limping forward. My legs hurt from the beating Manuel must have continued after I'd been knocked unconscious on the plane. I could feel the blood oozing from the wounds on my lower legs, but blood was also coming from between my thighs. I didn't have time to think about either of those things, though.

Manuel had men who were loyal to him who

would be after us sooner rather than later, and we needed to hurry before they started shooting.

Nova held out her hand to me. "Pull with all your might." I was confused until I saw the awkward way she was holding her arm. "My shoulder is dislocated, Cali. It has to be put back in before I can get us the rest of the way out of this hellhole."

Dreading what I would have to do, the pain I would have to inflict on her, I still took her hand as she grabbed hold of one of the chains that had restrained her earlier, and I began to pull. "Harder," Nova instructed. "Harder!" she yelled, and I jerked as hard as I could.

Her scream caused my heart pain, knowing I had hurt her when all she had ever done was risk her own life repeatedly to save mine. But then she sighed in relief as the joint popped back into place. It took a few minutes for her to catch her breath before she walked over to Manuel's lifeless body. Blood was gushing from the wound on her inner thigh where he'd bitten her. She paused for a moment, inspecting the area before tearing off a piece of his shirt and tying it around her leg.

There was a gun tucked into the back of his pants, and she picked it up. It was like watching a character in a movie as she popped the magazine out of the chamber, inspecting the gun from all angles, and then popped the magazine full of bullets back in. The entire thing took less than five seconds before she flipped the safety off and took my hand. "Well," she murmured softly. "You know this house better than me. Which way is the bathroom? I really have to pee."

It was crazy, but I had to fight a laugh as I showed her to the bathroom near the stairs that led up to the first floor—I may not have been in the dungeon before, but every floor had at least one bathroom. I wasn't even sure if I was amused or hysterical. The monster who haunted my dreams was actually dead. I'd watched the life leave his eyes as Nova had broken his neck. It was tragic, yet freeing.

We stayed together, and I waited as Nova relieved herself. I took the time to pee as well, gulping when I saw how much blood was darkening my panties.

Hold on, Nugget. Your auntie Nova got us this far. Maybe she can save us from everyone else.

"Wait." Nova stopped me from opening the bathroom door. "Where is Ciana?"

I shook my head. "I don't know anything other than what I heard Manuel and his men saying on the cargo plane. They didn't have her, but there was mention of some woman named Brion taking her."

My friend turned to stone before my eyes, and for

the first time since she'd woken up, I saw real fear in her green depths. "O'Brion?"

I considered the name for a moment, then nodded. "Yeah, that might have been it."

She grimaced but pushed me behind her as we finally started up the stairs. "Do you have anyone you can trust here?"

"He had maybe five loyal men. The rest would have only followed him because they needed the job. All the staff can be trusted. I loved them all." I knew if they had been truly aware of what Manuel was doing to me when I lived there in the past, they would have tried to help me. But like the doctor who would patch me up, they would have all eaten a bullet for it. "They are terrified of Manuel and would probably throw a party now that he's dead…" Despite the danger we still faced, curiosity gave me pause. "How did you do that, by the way? It was scary and beautiful all at the same time."

"Ask me again when this is over," she muttered, a look of determination filling her green eyes. "Do you know which guards?"

I hesitated, trying to remember before nodding. "Okay," she said, her hand tightening on the gun in her hand. "Let's go. The sooner we get this over with, the sooner we can get out of here."

I stayed behind her, my fingers tangling in the

romper she'd worn on our girls' night out. It wasn't so white anymore, especially with her own blood splattered on the bottom half. My legs shook with fear as we climbed the stairs.

"Just say yes or no if we see anyone. But be quick about it. Even a split-second hesitation is too long. It could mean the loss of an innocent life—or our own." She reached behind her and squeezed my wrist, offering comfort, reassurance, but also giving me confidence. "I'm counting on you, Cali."

"No pressure then, huh?" I muttered, and she laughed softly.

"None whatsoever, babe."

At the top of the stairs, two men were standing guard. I remembered them both well. One had been the one to narc on me about going to the doctor. The other had laughed when Manuel had shown him the blood-covered beer bottle he'd raped me with.

"Yes, yes," I breathed. "Yes, yes." I said it a little louder this time, in case she didn't hear me, but it was a waste of breath because Nova raised the gun she held in both hands, pointed and shot first one, then the other point-blank between the eyes before they could even think about reaching for their own guns.

The loudness of the gunfire brought others running from every direction. I had to glance at their faces quickly because they all had their guns pointed at us before they even understood what was going on. I spotted Guzman, who had only started working for my stepfamily a few years before. He'd always treated me kindly, sometimes acting as my personal guard when I left the mansion until Matias got sick.

"No!" I shouted, when Nova pointed her gun at him. She didn't question me and shifted her aim to the next man with a gun. "No," I said again.

An angry shout from our left had my head snapping in that direction, and I saw three more men who were loyal to Manuel charging toward us. "Yes, yes, yes!" I cried, my entire body clenching as I prepared myself for the pain of their bullets as they started flying toward us.

Pop.

Pop.

Pop.

In less than a few seconds, three separate shots, the men were on the floor, their blood and brain matter splattered everywhere—even on a few of the other men who had been close to them.

Seeing their dead bodies, I began to relax. Those were the five I knew Manuel favored. He'd even allowed them to watch a few times when he'd tortured me in his bedroom. And now they were burning in hell right along with their sadistic leader.

Relief made me feel weak. The other men with guns were already lowering their own weapons, staring in gaped-mouth amazement at the carnage that sweet little Nova had caused so quickly and effortlessly.

An angry shout from the second floor was the only warning we got before bullets started to rain down on us. Nova jerked back, blocking my body with her own as best she could while lifting her gun. Two shots, one hitting the man in the gut, the other in the forehead, just as she'd done with the other five men. That was all it took, and then he was falling over the balcony, already dead before he hit the floor with a sickening thud.

Breathing hard, Nova kept her hands on the gun and swung it around, pointing it at the other men, even though their weapons were at their sides. "Anyone else?" she snarled, a momma lion protecting her cubs—me and my baby.

Guzman stepped forward and bowed his head to us. "Welcome home, Miss Cali," he said in Spanish. "We have missed you."

Garret

I SAT SILENTLY on the Vitucci jet as it slowly made its descent into the private airfield in Colombia. Beside me, my dad was crying quietly. He'd rarely stopped since he and Mom were told about Nova. It wasn't me who broke it to them. It should have been, but I was still in Canada when they got to New York after their vacation in Mexico. I wasn't so sure I could have said the words if I had been there, though.

Telling our parents that I'd let Sheena O'Brion take my baby sister, chop her into unrecognizable pieces, wasn't something I felt confident being able to vocalize. Even though I'd seen the proof for myself, speaking the words would make it even more real, and I was already struggling.

There had been nothing of Nova's face left to

identify the broken, massacred body. But she'd been wearing the necklace Ryan had given her for Christmas. The same necklace she never took off. She wore it everywhere, even to bed. And it had just been lying there, in the blood...and other gore. No longer hanging from her neck because her head had been severed from the rest of her little body.

After working for the Vitucci family for years, I'd seen and done some fucked-up shit, but nothing could have prepared me for that sight. I'd lost the contents of my stomach.

What was left of my baby sister had been lying there, more a puzzle that needed to be put back together than an actual body.

As her big brother, I was supposed to protect her, but instead, I'd been out looking for Manuel Ramirez. Then I'd gotten the call from Ryan, and my entire world had stopped. Not only had Ramirez and O'Brion been working together to keep us distracted, they had taken the three women who meant the world to us.

Ciana and Nova had been taken to Canada, where they had killed my sister and tortured Ciana. And Ramirez had taken Lis back to Colombia. Knowing what he was capable of—what he'd already put her through—when I'd been given the choice of going to South America to take out Ramirez once and for all, or head back to Canada for Ciana since she'd been taken yet again, I'd chosen the first option. Even though I wanted to shed some O'Brion blood for what they had done to my family, the chance that Lis might still be alive had me boarding the jet and flying to California to pick up the rest of my father's MC.

Every single brother within the Angel's Halo MC was on the plane, their cuts on and their guns already loaded. We weren't leaving without Ramirez, and once we had him, we were taking him back to Creswell Springs and putting his head on a fucking pike.

Vehicles were waiting for us at the airfield. Since Vitucci had control of what used to be the Ramirez coke fields, we had plenty of men in Colombia, but this was personal. Manuel was responsible for what had happened to Nova, and that meant the MC had first dibs on his worthless hide.

But first, I had to know if Lis was still alive.

We all loaded up, and the drivers stomped on the gas. The plan was to go in hot, break down the gates —just like that fucker Bain O'Farrell did when he took Ciana for the second time—and kill every motherfucker who got in our way.

That plan was pulled out from under us when we were met with an army of men standing in front of the gates, Manuel Ramirez's dead body already lying on the ground in front of them.

Dad, Uncle Bash, Uncle Spider, and Uncle Hawk jumped out of the first vehicle. I followed them with Max, Jack, Elias, and Kingston. Everyone else filled in behind us, their guns already drawn and pointed at the men who stood with their own guns in hand, but they didn't try to raise them in our direction.

"You came for the body, yes?" the one in charge said as he stepped toward the dead body. With the lights from the high wall surrounding the property shining down, along with the lights of our vehicles, we could all see that Manuel had a broken neck.

"Who killed him?" Uncle Bash demanded.

"One of our own," the man said with a shrug. "Take him and go."

I pushed through the others. "Lis…" I swallowed and corrected myself. "Calista. Is she here?"

If I hadn't been watching him, I would have missed the way his features tightened, but in the next moment, his face smoothed out, becoming completely devoid of expression once more. "She was," he said after a brief pause.

My gut clenched. "Where is she now?" I demanded.

Another pause came from the man before he crossed his arms over his chest. "Miss Cali is dead."

I stumbled back, the pain shooting through my body stealing the air from my lungs. Max and Jack caught me, their hold the only thing keeping me upright. "No," I groaned. "I thought—"

"You thought wrong," the man said in heavily accented English. "Now take what you came for, and leave. The way you came up on us, ready for war, we have every right to kill every one of you. But we know what Ramirez did to you and your people. For that reason alone, we will let you go unharmed."

"Did he hurt her?" I choked out. "Was he the one who killed Cali?"

"Yes."

I clenched my eyes closed and sucked in a deep breath. My heart lay cold and empty in my chest, just as dead as the body on the ground. She was gone. The woman I loved had left this world not knowing that I worshiped the ground she walked on, that she was my goddamn reason for breathing.

Right then, it didn't feel like I could draw another breath, but I forced myself to inhale and lifted my lashes. "Elias, Chance, Kingston," I gritted out. "Get the body."

"Are you sure, son?" Dad rasped. "Should we check—"

"She's dead!" I shouted, and he flinched. "Now they're both gone, Dad. I let that fucking bastard take them both from me. All of this, it's my fault. No one has to tell me that. If it weren't for me, my sister and the woman I love would still be back in New York, alive and happy. But they fucking aren't!"

"Garret—" Max tried to break in, but I lifted my hand, cutting him off before he could give me hell. I knew I deserved it, but it could come later. I was holding on by a thread, and if any of them said another word, I was going to take the gun I had in my holster and put a bullet in my own head.

"It's time to go home and bury Nova," I reminded them, surprised I was able to speak through the lump clogging my throat. "She should be at peace, and she can't until we lay her to rest."

"Okay, son," Dad said, putting his hand on my shoulder. "Let's go."

Uncle Bash nodded to the others, and my cousins did as I'd commanded, picking up Manuel's body and carrying it to one of the trucks. They weren't careful as they dumped him in the back, the thud sounding like a bag of wet sand hitting the truck bed.

———

We buried Nova in New York. The Vitucci family had a family cemetery where every member would eventually be interred. There was enough room for generations to come, and because my sister would have been Ryan's wife, she was placed in the plot right beside where he would one day be laid to rest.

Mom was already in NYC since we'd left her there with her cousin's family before going to Colombia for Ramirez's body. Upon my return with Dad, we brought many of his family as well. Aunt Raven and Uncle Bash with their kids and grandkids. My biological uncles, along with their wives, children, and grandchildren. Fuck, nearly every resident of Trinity County showed up to pay their respects as we placed my sister in her final resting spot.

Everyone had always loved her. How could they not? Even when I told myself I hated her because she was content with life in Creswell Springs when our place had always been in New York, I'd loved her. All she'd ever done was try to protect me, from everyone and everything that could potentially hurt me.

Including myself.

There was no way we could have an open casket. Just the thought of my parents seeing their little girl as I'd seen her right after Sheena O'Brion had hacked her into pieces made me shudder. If nothing else, at least we could spare them that much.

At the gravesite, everyone stood surrounding Ryan. Of all the people gathered, including my parents, he was the one I was the most concerned for. He'd shut down when we'd found Nova on that table in Canada. When I looked into his eyes, there was nothing there. No emotion, no soul. It was as if, with the death of the person he considered his heart, he'd lost a part of himself too.

The parts which made him human.

I'd been unable to hold back my tears for days. Not only had I lost my baby sister, but the woman I loved was dead too. I didn't get to have a funeral or even a memorial for her. There would be no saying goodbye to her, except in my heart. The tears and the pain in my soul were never-ending. Yet Ryan, who had loved Nova more than anyone in the world, remained dry-eyed. I didn't see pain on his face or in his dark gaze.

Just an empty ghost walking around in Ryan's body.

Mom stood beside Ryan. She'd been trying to remain strong—for Ryan's sake, she'd said that morning as we'd left for the service. For days, she'd been the strong one, trying to hide her tears from Dad and me. Not even when Aunt Raven arrived did she break down. But as the casket began to lower into the ground, I knew the hold she had on her emotions was starting to slip.

"I can't do this anymore," she whispered. "I-I can't breathe."

Dad, who stood behind her, wrapped his arms around her waist. "Shh, Felicity. It's okay," he attempted to soothe, but the tears that were running down his face made his voice thick.

She jerked out of his arms and stumbled a few steps. Ryan was so out of it, he didn't reach out to steady her like he would have normally done. His gaze remained unblinking on the casket. "I need to go," Mom gasped out, as if she was fighting to get oxygen into her lungs. "I need...air."

The agony in her voice, along with the way she was struggling to breathe, set me in motion. "Okay, Mom," I murmured softly as I put my hand on the small of her back, turning her toward the limos. "I'll take you wherever you want."

She relaxed slightly against me before giving a nod and allowing me to guide her away. I glanced over my shoulder to find Dad right behind us. The tears in his green eyes never failed to punch me in the gut. He'd always been so strong. Fuck, I couldn't even remember seeing him cry at any point in my life up until then.

While I put Mom in the back of the limo, the others started to disperse as well, leaving everyone but Ryan and his parents behind. It was going to take

Anya to get him to leave that grave, but I knew she would eventually accomplish it.

Mom didn't want to go back to the compound, so I told the driver to take us to the airport. There was only one place I could think of that would give my parents any peace. I didn't bother anyone about a private jet, just got three nonstop tickets back to California.

Dad silently cried the entire flight, while Mom held on to my hand like she couldn't bear to let go. The flight attendant kept asking if everything was all right, and I told her to just keep the alcohol coming. There had been four seats left in first class, and I'd bought them all so that Dad could sit alone with his grief.

The flight attendant kept Dad's glass full of Jameson at all times, and I made sure Mom's glass of brandy never got low. I stuck to just water, knowing someone would need to be sober to get us back to Creswell Springs once the plane landed. Even with the aid of alcohol, however, Mom didn't shed a tear, which was exactly what she needed more than anything.

To scream and cry and let it all out.

Hours later, I parked in the driveway of my child-hood home and walked around to the passenger side to open Mom's door. She hiccupped, and I had to half carry her into the house because she was so drunk, but Dad followed behind us as if he hadn't drunk an entire bottle of whiskey on the flight.

The house was silent as we entered, the place feeling lifeless for the first time in my memory. I knew instantly why that was. Nova wasn't there. Nova, who was the life-force for everyone who knew her, was gone. It was like being hit with the realization of her death all over again.

And with it, the realization that Lis was gone too.

Two strong, beautiful women, who had both been the center of my world—even if I had pretended like Nova wasn't at times—were dead.

The pain was hard to swallow, but somehow I got Mom upstairs to my sister's room. She froze outside the closed door, but I opened it and then lifted her into my arms before carrying her to Nova's bed. The comforter was perfectly in place. Her many pillows and a few stuffed animals in the same spot they had always been in.

Laying Mom in the middle of the bed, I stepped back just as the first sob tore through her. Grabbing the little rabbit Nova used to take everywhere with her when she was a toddler, Mom pulled it to her chest and finally released the scream that had been choking her for days.

Cali

THE CRAMP WAS SO small it almost went unnoticed, but after weeks of feeling them every few minutes, I still paid attention to each one of them. It was hard not to when, with each one, I was terrified it was the one that would send me into labor.

Breathing slowly and deeply, I closed my eyes and touched the tiny baby bump beneath my shirt.

Just a few more weeks. Stay strong, Nugget. Don't give up on me, because I will never give up on you. Not until you're in my arms. We can do this. I promise.

As I stroked my hands over the bump, a tiny little kick pressed against my palm, almost as if the baby was responding to my silent message. A small smile touched my lips. My nugget was strong and tenacious, reminding me of Nova so much. I was glad

Hannigan blood flowed through my child's veins, even if I disliked his or her father.

Garret might be a spineless asshole who had abandoned me when I needed him most, but his sister was my superhero. Without her, the baby and I would have died in that torture dungeon. Manuel's evil would still have been infecting the world, and I would have been buried somewhere in the backyard. Instead, my best friend and my child's aunt had not only saved us both, but had taken over the running of the Ramirez businesses.

Once Nugget was born, they would have a future because of Nova.

And because of Nova, I knew my baby would be well taken care of, which was what they would need more than anything. Especially once I was gone.

I didn't need the doctor to tell me that I wasn't going to survive giving birth. With all the cramping and bleeding, I knew that my life was on the line just as much as the baby's was. But that was fine. My life didn't matter. All I cared about was getting through each week until it was safe for Nugget to be born. Once the baby was out, and in Nova's arms, I'd happily leave the world.

I just needed to hold on, let the baby grow and get healthier.

Maria walked into my room with a beaming smile

on her face. "How exciting!" she gushed in Spanish as she brought me a glass of water. It was my third in the last hour, but apparently I needed a full bladder for the doctor's visit. I was officially sixteen weeks, and when Dr. Ortega did his weekly ultrasound this time, he said he was likely to see what the sex of the baby was.

Maria's excitement was enough to produce a small smile from me. "Yes, I can't wait," I told her honestly.

There had already been too many surprises in my life. I didn't need any more. Plus, I needed to know the sex of the baby so I could find the right name for him or her. It was the last thing I could give my child before I died, and I wanted to give it to them as soon as possible. So that Nova would know what her niece or nephew should be called. And I also wanted to talk to my child using their given name until their birth, rather than just calling them "Nugget."

Halfway through the third glass of water, I was hurting from the need to pee. Any difference in pressure in the general area of my uterus was enough to cause cramping, and when the cramps intensified, so did the bleeding. Thankfully, Guzman knocked on my bedroom door and showed Dr. Ortega in.

The ultrasound machine was already in my room. Nova had purchased one to make things easier on the doctor, and us, since I had to have an ultrasound at least once a week. I refused to leave the mansion, and it would have taken several men to get the machine up and down the stairs if they had to haul it to and from the doctor's clinic.

After greeting me, the doctor got straight to work. He never lingered, and I wasn't sure if that was because he was scared to be at the mansion, or if he was simply a very busy man. He was the only doctor around, and I knew he had a lot of patients who needed his attention, but Guzman could be a bit intimidating. And then there was Nova.

Every man who worked for me—and her too now since I'd made her take half of the business as compensation for helping me so much—was more than a little nervous when it came to my best friend. Not that I could blame them. After witnessing just how badass she was, I would have been nervous of her too. Except I wasn't nervous or intimidated.

I was thankful.

If Nova was there to raise my baby after I was gone, then I knew they would not only be safe, but loved and cared for all their life. Everything I wished I'd had growing up.

After the doctor gave me the usual exam, the lights were dimmed, and Dr. Ortega started the ultrasound as Nova entered the room. Seeing her, my heart lifted, and

I held out my hand. She and Maria were always present for the ultrasounds, but this was one of the most important, and I didn't want her to miss anything.

The instant her hand slid into mine, all the noise in my head went silent and I was able to truly enjoy the moment.

"Everything is measuring beautifully," the doctor announced as he continued to type into the machine, taking measurements and making sure my amniotic fluid levels were still good, all while taking a random picture every now and then. "Are you sure you want to know the sex?"

"I don't like surprises," I told him with a huff. "Yes, I want to know who has been kicking around in there."

His eyes crinkled as he smiled down at me. "It appears that you are having a daughter."

"Really?" I squealed, covering my mouth with my hand as tears spilled over my lashes. Happiness I didn't completely understand was zinging through me.

I'd have been lying if I said I didn't really care what the sex was. Part of me had been dreading it was a boy, though, and not because I dreamed of dressing a little girl in beautiful outfits and showing the world my perfect little princess.

After everything that had happened with Manuel when I was younger, and then having my heart broken by Garret, I had little faith in the male population. I trusted Guzman more than most men, but that wasn't really saying much. I would have loved my baby if it was a son, but I wasn't sure if I would—or even could—have loved him as much as I already loved my daughter.

Not that it really mattered. It wasn't like I was going to be around to care one way or the other if it was a girl or boy, but at least now that I knew the baby was a girl, I could bond with her more before her birth.

"Really." The doctor motioned to the monitor. "She seems to want her momma to know who she is as much as you do."

"And you're sure she's okay?" I voiced my greatest worry. "I'm still spotting, and I've been cramping off and on." More on than off, but I didn't want to bring that up. I hadn't shared with anyone, not even Nova, exactly how often the cramps happened.

But the doctor didn't answer, and that bothered me, so I turned to the only person I trusted with my child's life. "Nova, he's not lying, is he? She's okay, right?"

"Doctor?" Nova gritted out, wanting answers just as much as me when he continued to remain silent.

Without looking at either of us, he stood and began putting his things away. "The continued bleeding has not endangered the baby from what I can tell. However..." His shoulders slumped, but I knew what was coming, so I was prepared for it. "I fear you will need a full hysterectomy after you deliver. If we can get you to thirty-four weeks, I recommend you have a C-section and hysterectomy at the same time."

His mentioning of a hysterectomy gave me pause, but I still needed answers. "Wh-why?"

"Between the accident you told me about and then the beating over several days that followed, your womb is barely strong enough to grow the baby as it is." Again, nothing I didn't know. Between the cramps and the bleeding, I knew even one wrong move could put me into labor, and at only sixteen weeks gestation, my little girl wouldn't survive. But I hadn't thought about a hysterectomy as an option.

Not that it gave me any hope of my own survival. Something like a hysterectomy couldn't be done anywhere except in a hospital setting, and there was no way in hell I was leaving the walls that protected the mansion. Not alive or even dead. They could bury me on the property. It was where my mother and Matias were both buried. That way, Nova could bring my baby girl to visit our graves often.

"It is my opinion that carrying this baby to term will put your life in danger," Ortega continued. "That is why I think delivering at thirty-four weeks will be better for both mother and child."

"But why the hysterectomy?" Nova demanded, getting to her feet.

"I truly think there will be no other choice when it comes time. To be frank, with all the trauma that has struggled to heal, I fear she will need the hysterectomy or risk bleeding to death." I wanted to laugh at his observations. He was only now voicing them, when I'd known that practically from the beginning. I could tell I wasn't healing. That the bigger the baby got, more damage was only being added to what Manuel had already caused.

The doctor folded his arms in front of him, looking wary. "The closer she gets to the third trimester, the more danger she will be in as the baby grows and her uterus stretches more and more. It is still bruised even after all these weeks. Quite honestly, it is a miracle she hasn't miscarried. By six months' gestation, she will need to be admitted into the hospital for round-the-clock care."

"No way." I shook my head adamantly before he even finished speaking. "I'm not leaving my home again. I've told you, all of you, repeatedly. I won't go."

Nova bent to hug me, trying to calm me. The thought of leaving the property—hell, the mansion itself—was enough to make my heart start to race. "Cali, I know you're afraid of what's outside of the property gates, but your life is at risk from this."

"I don't care!" I shouted, finally giving voice to what I hadn't told her or anyone else.

I didn't care what happened to me. Maybe part of me even welcomed death. All I was concerned about was getting this baby far enough along that she would survive outside of my body. I clutched at Nova, my entire body shaking from the force I needed to put into my next words. "You can take care of the baby. I trust you to raise her right. But I'm not leaving this house, no matter what he says."

Garret

THE MOMENT it hit me just how bad things were without Nova was when I realized that, between Ryan and me, I was the voice of reason.

It was an unnerving sensation. Ryan was always so in control, so in charge of things. He walked into a room, and everyone turned to look at him before taking a step back because the guy exuded so much power they felt a physical force that pushed them backward.

That was before he lost Nova, however.

Now, he was just a lifeless shell whose only goal was to try to feel. But the only thing that even came close to giving him some kind of sensation was pain. That blankness in his eyes changed the moment he stepped into the circle where the underground fights were held. His opponent would take his place, and a switch would flip within Ryan.

I saw it, and it made me feel physically sick.

Watching him take the hits, the smile that would ghost over his lips as blood covered his teeth. The bruises he had already accumulated and continued to add to. It was hard to stomach. Even more so when he finally decided he'd had enough of letting the other guy pound on him, and another switch flipped in his brain.

The pain was turned off, and all that was left was the pent-up rage he'd been storing from the night we'd found Nova and Ciana in Canada. One second, the other guy would be bouncing around, gloating and showboating that he was kicking Ryan's ass. The next, he would be on the ground, close to unconsciousness—if not death—as my friend pounded his fist into something the poor fuck's mother wouldn't even recognize.

When the referee hesitated to pull Ryan off the other guy, I had to step in. Wrapping him in a headlock, I dragged him back. Thankfully, Bennie and Vito cleared a path to the locker room, because it was a struggle to keep hold of Ryan as it was. If I loosened my grip for even a second, he would have been back on his opponent, and we'd have had to pay off everyone who witnessed the fight—and probably dig a few holes to hide the bodies of those who were too upstanding to look the other way.

The fight tonight had lasted all of three minutes, maybe a little longer. This time, Ryan had only given the other guy the chance at a single punch before he'd lost control and released the rage beast that lived just below the surface these days.

It took just one look from the ref to tell me I needed to intervene, and I was pulling Ryan away— as usual. I wanted to put a bullet in Vito and Bennie for bringing us to the damn underground fights to begin with, but they were still recovering from the last time they were shot. Vito was nearly completely healed, but Bennie was taking longer to recover with his leg.

If Anya found out what we'd been doing every weekend, she would have the twins' heads, along with my own, mounted to her wall.

I almost wished she would. At least then, I wouldn't have to feel the pain that pressed on my chest, making it hard to breathe twenty-four hours a day.

Ryan was in pain. I understood that. But he was missing the fact that everyone else was hurting just as much. Fuck. I'd lost my sister *and* the woman I loved. Two people who were huge parts of my life, gone as if they never even existed. Only the pain in my heart, the constant noise in my head, told me that they had.

Then there was the whole Ciana bullshit. How did I forgive her for what she'd done? If it weren't for her, Sheena and Ramirez wouldn't have gotten close to the girls that night. All three of them would still be with us, not dead or in the hands of the enemy, playing happy family as she paraded around with her ever-growing pregnant belly. She was living the dream, with the father of her children, while Ryan and I were in agony as we tried to find a way to live without the women who had been our entire world.

Pushing those thoughts away, I tossed Ryan a towel so he could wipe the blood off his face. Ninety-five percent of it belonged to the guy he'd just beaten unconscious. While he cleaned himself up, my phone rang, and I quickly answered it, needing the distraction.

It was just one of my men checking in, and I was only half listening to what he was saying. Which was a good thing because I heard Vito and Ryan talking.

"You ready?" my cousin asked.

"Maybe I want another round," Ryan answered, taking the sports drink Bennie offered.

I quickly pocketed my phone. "No, man. You've had enough tonight. You're going to be feeling that last hit for a few days at least. Did he knock any teeth loose?"

"Nah. I'm good. He barely tapped me."

I wanted to punch Ryan a few times myself, but I kept my hands unclenched to avoid the urge. If Nova were there, she would have already been dragging his ass home. Fuck, who was I kidding? If Nova were there, Ryan wouldn't have been within a mile of the underground fights. He sure as hell wouldn't let her close to them. He'd have her home, tucked in bed.

Safe and sound, where she belonged.

Swallowing the knot of emotion that thought always brought with it, I breathed through my anger at him.

"You're already bruised," Vito said, shaking his head. "If *Tetka* sees that, she's going to bury my ass."

"I'm ready for some dinner," Bennie cut in. "I could go for something dripping in grease."

It was even weirder that the twins were trying to be the voices of reason. The two of them were always looking for mischief.

"I'm not hungry," Ryan muttered, back to the emotionless husk once more. "I think I'll just go home."

"Not until you eat," Vito told him forcefully.

"You have to eat." Bennie zipped up the bag and tossed it over his shoulder. "Both of you," he muttered, shoving me toward the door before I could argue with him. Food held little appeal to me these days. It was impossible to find joy in anything without Lis there to share it with me. "I'm thinking burgers and fries. What do you say, Vito?"

"Yeah, *fratello*," his twin agreed. "These two could use some big, juicy meat."

"Fuck you," I grumbled, but I let Bennie guide me out to the SUV.

I just wanted to go home and climb into bed. It wasn't as if I would get any sleep, but at least alone, I could remember Lis without anyone bothering me. But it was hours later before Ryan and I stepped into our apartment.

"Shower," he said with a grunt. Not even looking at me, he started for his room.

"Night," I muttered back. The urge to punch him had eased for the moment, but I knew from experience it would come back burning hot the next time we went to one of the fights.

Walking into my room, I started stripping on my way to the bathroom. After a quick shower, I dropped down onto my bed and grabbed my phone. Opening my saved photos, I started flipping through the hundreds of Lis. Some of them were with me, but the majority were just her.

This was both the best part of my day and the worst.

I got to relieve all the good memories I'd created with Lis. See her beautiful smile, the way her blue eyes lit up whenever she looked at me and I snapped a picture. The silly faces she would make at me. The love that she couldn't hide.

And then I remembered how I'd treated her when we were teenagers, the way I'd just left her the night she'd confessed who she really was, and the way I'd walked away without a word. I'd made the biggest mistake of my life that night.

Maybe if I hadn't left, she wouldn't have gone out with Ciana and Nova. Maybe we would have been home, making love instead.

Perhaps the incident that had happened that night would have still taken place, but I wouldn't have lost them all. Ciana would still be with her psycho baby daddy, and Nova would still be taken from us, but maybe—just maybe—I would have still had Lis.

Tears spilled from my eyes, and I forced myself to close the photo app. But as I reached for my lamp to turn it off, my phone rang. Frowning, I glanced down to see my dad's name on the screen.

Trepidation churned in my stomach, and my

fingers shook as I swiped my thumb to answer. "Dad?"

"Garret," he choked out, but he sounded out of breath, as if he'd been running. My dad wasn't in the worst shape, but he didn't run either. Not without a good reason.

I sat up in bed, knowing I needed to be upright for whatever he was about to tell me.

"I can't find your mom."

Cali

IT WAS BORING as hell doing nothing but lying in bed. I knew it was necessary, and nothing short of a gun pointed at my stomach would have willingly gotten me on my feet, but damn, I would have loved a little bit of change.

Nothing too huge that would overly excite the baby and make her dance around, causing me to cramp even worse than usual. But enough that the idea of watching paint dry on a wall that wasn't inside my childhood bedroom would have been appreciated.

Nova had left the day before, not long after the doctor had excused himself following the ultrasound that had told us the baby was a girl. She was working herself to death, taking care of me and the businesses, along with keeping the men busy and in line. Most nights, she fell asleep beside me in bed while rubbing my baby bump.

I'd missed that the night before. Having her close was comforting. Her presence eased my fear that anything might happen. With her beside me, I knew I was safe until the baby was born. And afterward, my little girl would have Nova as a guardian and protector.

The lawyer had come that morning so I could finalize all the paperwork. Following my death, Nova would be my daughter's sole caregiver. I'd even told him not to allow anyone to list the name of the father, so that even if Garret ever did pull his head out of his ass, he couldn't lay claim to our child.

If he had so effortlessly broken my heart, how cruel would he be to a defenseless little baby? One that he obviously hadn't even wanted to begin with.

Another cramp hit, and I felt the slight dampness between my thighs that told me I was still bleeding. I alternated between simply spotting and a heavier flow, almost like a period, but no matter what, the blood never fully stopped. As Dr. Ortega had said, there was too much damage, nothing was healing, and the baby was only causing tissue that was already torn and bruised to become more distressed.

"Don't give up in there, young lady," I softly chided my little one. "You have a lot more growing to do before you meet the world. The longer you cook in Mommy's tummy, the easier it will be for everyone."

A tiny foot kicked against my palm, making me smile. "Once you're born, I hope I get to see you. Maybe hold you for a few minutes. Then I'll watch over you from the other side. Mommy will be your angel, while your auntie raises you into a warrior just like she is."

A few more kicks followed, making me smile, but my heart felt heavy. I was prepared for my death, but that didn't mean I wasn't sad that I would have to say goodbye to my baby. Just thinking about it was more painful than any beating Manuel had ever inflicted on me.

A light knock had me lifting my head. I was exhausted after a restless night without Nova being home, and my voice projected my tiredness as I called, "Come in."

The door opened, and Nova stepped inside. Seeing her, I instantly began to relax. "You're back!" I exclaimed, and in my happiness at seeing her, the baby kicked excitedly. "I thought you wouldn't be back until tomorrow night."

"I brought you a surprise," she said, staying by the door.

"You know I hate surprises," I complained. But

I'd been so bored that the thought of having some-thing else to do while lying in bed wouldn't go unap-preciated.

"You don't want it?" Nova said with a pout, teasing me. "Okay, well, I guess I'll—"

"Who said I didn't want it?" I grumbled, earning me a grin from my best friend. "I don't like surprises, but I will never turn down a present."

"I didn't have time to wrap it," she said with regret. "And even if I did, I probably wouldn't have been able to find a box big enough."

As she spoke, she stepped away from the door, coming farther into the bedroom.

"Surprise!" Felicity Hannigan shouted softly, star-tling me.

"M-Mrs. Hannigan?" I whispered in disbelief. When I realized she was actually there, I shot a glare at Nova. "You kidnapped your mom?"

She snickered. "Does she look like she's here under duress?"

"Well, no, but how is she here?" Then it hit me. If Nova's mother was here, was the rest of her family as well? My heart started pounding against my ribs, and the baby didn't like that at all. A cramp hit me, and I grimaced, knowing I needed to calm down so the baby would go back to kicking softly instead of beating the hell out of me from the inside. "Wait, is anyone else here? Is—"

"I only brought Mom," Nova hurriedly assured me.

I released my breath in relief, my heart rate instantly slowing down and causing the baby to behave herself once again. With a sigh, I eased back against my many pillows.

"Since you were being stubborn about every-thing, I felt like I needed reinforcements," Nova confessed, making me stiffen for a moment, but I forced myself to relax. "I couldn't think of anyone better to help than my own mother."

Snuggling back into the pillows, I smiled up at my baby's grandmother. "It's great to see you, Mrs. Hannigan, but your daughter wasted your time if she thinks I can be dissuaded from having the baby at home."

The still-beautiful brunette walked over to my bed and sat down on the edge. Taking both of my hands, she gave them a squeeze that made my eyes sting with tears. "We can discuss that later. Right now, tell me how you are feeling. Nova told me everything, and I've been so worried about you, sweet girl."

When I'd been in Creswell Springs the previous summer, I'd gotten to know many of the Hannigan clan. Felicity—or Flick, as most of the residents of the town called her—was one of the sweetest people I'd ever met. She was made to be a mother, with her loving, nurturing touch.

Shyly, I smiled up at her. "Oh, well, I'm fine. I mean, I'm a prisoner of this bed at the moment, but I'm okay with that." I pulled one hand free and rubbed it over the baby. "This little girl is worth being bored out of my mind all day long. If she's okay, then nothing else matters."

"May I?" she asked, her gaze traveling with longing over my distended belly.

I pulled up my shirt before guiding the hand that the older woman held to my belly, pressing her palm to where the baby was still kicking a little. "She's not too active yet, but when she does kick, it's pretty powerful. Right, Nova?"

The blonde walked around the bed and sat in the chair beside my bed. "She tends to be squirmier at night. Sometimes, I'll snuggle up with Cali and rub her belly. Usually, I end up falling asleep talking to the little brat."

"I don't care if she's a brat or not. She's perfect." I pressed Felicity's hand closer. "Right there, do you feel it?"

Her eyes filled with wonder. "That's so amazing. I remember how it felt when Garret and Nova would kick me. I don't think there could be a more magical experience." Her chin trembled, but she quickly sucked in a steadying breath. "But this is something else entirely."

The mention of her son's name set off an explosion of emotions inside me, but I pushed them down, refusing to think of him. Instead, I announced, "I decided on a name while you were gone."

"Thank goodness," Nova teased. "I thought you were going to drive us all crazy trying to find the perfect fit. Well, let's hear it. What will we be calling our baby girl?"

"Justice," I murmured, then lifted my chin in challenge. Not at Nova or her mother, but at the universe in general. "Justice Nova."

"You're giving her my name too?" Nova whispered with tears in her eyes.

"How could I not? If it weren't for you, neither one of us would have made it this far." I held out my hand, and she put hers in mine, our fingers entwining.

"I think it's a beautiful name," Felicity said softly, her hand still rubbing over my belly lovingly.

For the first time in what seemed like forever, I found myself laughing. "Well, it's definitely ironic. I mean, it's pure justice that my daughter will be the one to rule everything Manuel was so desperate to have full control over."

And I hoped he was in hell, watching it all unfold.

"I like it," Nova assured me. "It's both beautiful and badass. Just like our little Justice will be."

"With you as her auntie, I don't doubt it." A yawn escaped me. With Nova home, I was able to relax, and sleep pressed down on me. "Sorry. Apparently it's exhausting lying around doing nothing except growing another person inside you."

"Been there, done that," Felicity said with a dry laugh. "With Nova, I was on bed rest from the beginning of the third trimester. I still went into preterm labor. It was one of the most terrifying experiences of my life. I thought we were going to lose her." She shuddered, and I felt her fear, because it was something I thought about every single day. "And then we actually lost her... Or at least, we thought we did. When they told me she was dead, a part of me died inside."

I blinked at her in surprise. They thought Nova was dead? How was that even possible? Didn't they even think to look for her in Colombia?

"Mom," Nova whispered.

Felicity waved her off, swallowing hard. "It's over now. I have you back. And Cali too. That's something to celebrate. Plus, now we have baby Justice to plan for. We need to get the nursery ready and start stocking up on everything."

My curiosity over Nova's family thinking she was dead evaporated, replaced by a new excitement that I'd been hoping for. "Yes, yes, and yes. Let's get started now," I pleaded. "Let's use my iPad and start ordering baby furniture."

Nova stood and stretched. "You two have fun with that. I have some work to get caught up on."

"I'll text you pictures of things we like," I promised, wanting her input on everything. She was the one who would be using it, after all.

Before she left, Nova rubbed her hand over my belly. The two Hannigan women shared a look before Felicity winked at her daughter. I narrowed my eyes at Nova, following her steps as she walked to the door and closed it behind her. Once she was out of sight, I shot my gaze back to Felicity.

"I'm not stupid. I know you're here to make me conform to whatever it is Nova wants me to do." The older woman grimaced, but I shook my head at her. "My body, my choice. I'm having this baby here."

"But, sweetheart—"

I lifted my hand to cut her off. "Mrs. Hannigan, please. I know the dangers, but my heart is telling me to stay right here."

She was quiet for a long moment before nodding. "I can understand that. For now, let's table this conversation. It's obvious it distresses you, and that's the last thing I want to do."

"Thank you," I whispered. "And while we're discussing things that upset me, I'm going to ask you not to mention Garret in my presence again."

"Cali—"

"I adore you, Mrs. Hannigan. You were there for me last year when I desperately needed someone. But I will ask Guzman to take you back to California if you mention your son's name again."

It wasn't an idle threat. I couldn't handle hearing the name of the man who had torn my heart from my chest. If I was going to keep Justice safe long enough for her to make it in the world without me, then I had to keep everything that had the potential for disrupting that progress far, far away.

"Okay, then." Felicity gave in. "I won't bring up my son again. But only until Justice is here. I can't promise not to speak my mind on that particular subject past her birth."

"Fair enough," I agreed. It wasn't as if I would be around to deal with it anyway.

"It's a deal, then," she said with a kind smile. "Now let's start ordering baby clothes and furniture."

Three weeks later

The cramp woke me from a restless sleep. It was so painful, I couldn't keep from crying out. But it wasn't just the discomfort that had tears stinging my eyes.

I was scared.

The wetness between my legs told me something must have happened. Groaning, I shifted and pulled up my nightgown. The sight of the blood on the insides of my things made me cry out again.

Multiple pairs of feet came running, and moments later, the bedroom door was practically kicked in as Guzman, Felicity, and Maria all stood there, breathing hard.

"Oh dear lord." Felicity pushed through the other two and marched over to the bed. "That's it, Calista. You have to go to the hospital."

"No!" I wanted to shout it, but it came out as a whisper, followed by another cramp. Shit, that hurt. Tears spilled down my face. "It's nothing," I lied. "The baby is fine."

"The baby is *not* fine," she snapped, putting her hands on her hips and glaring down at me. "You might not care about what happens to yourself, young lady, but the rest of us do. And not only are you putting your own life at risk by stubbornly refusing to be admitted to the hospital, but you're putting my granddaughter's life in jeopardy as well. Now, stop acting like a petulant little girl, and grow the fuck up! You're going to the hospital, right this minute."

I felt the color drain from my face as the truth of what she'd just shouted hit me dead center. She was right. I had been putting Justice at risk by refusing to allow Dr. Ortega to admit me to the hospital. My fear of what could be waiting on the outside of the walls surrounding the mansion was nothing compared to what could happen to my baby if I went into labor so early. The hospital was too far away for Justice to survive without the immediate medical attention she would need.

"O-okay," I sobbed. "I-I'll go."

"You're damned right, you'll go," Felicity growled. "Maria, get her things ready. Guzman, have the men prepare one of the cars, and alert Nova that we will be leaving for the hospital in ten minutes."

"No need to tell me," Nova said as she came into the bedroom. Her face was tight and pale. When she saw the amount of blood on the insides of my legs, she closed her eyes. "I'll… Um, I'll call the doctor."

"I'm sorry," I choked out. "I didn't mean… I wasn't thinking… I-I'm so sorry!"

Felicity wrapped her arms around me, and I buried my face in her chest as the sobs tore out of me. I'd been so selfish. Justice deserved better than what I'd put her through. I was already a terrible mother.

"Don't be sorry, sweetheart." Felicity's voice soothed quietly at my ear. "You had your reasons. But now it's time to put all those stubborn thoughts away. You're going to be fine. So will Justice. The two of you are going to be a family, my family." She pulled back and used her thumb to wipe away a few of my tears. "Nova and I won't allow anything else to harm you, sweet girl. Be strong for your daughter, accept that you're going to live a long, happy life with her."

That she knew what I'd been planning all along made my face burn with shame, but she tipped my chin up, refusing to let me hide from her kind eyes. "You can't run away now, Cali. I won't let you. The reasons you have for wanting to let go are no longer important. What you need to focus on is being strong for your little girl."

Garret

I FLOPPED down on my bed with my phone to my ear. "I know, Dad. I'm worried too. But we have to stop thinking the worst." I swallowed hard when I heard his ragged inhale.

Mom running away was my father's worst nightmare. She'd done it before, years before they had gotten married. Back then, it was because she was having trouble getting over the loss of a child—a miscarriage from a beating that had nearly killed her. Losing Nova had sent her running again, and no matter how many favors anyone called in, we couldn't find a single trace of her. Not even Emmie Armstrong had seen or heard from her, and she was the one Mom had run to the last time she'd decided to hide from her pain with a new life.

Every woman I loved was either dead or missing,

and it was destroying my gut. I was pretty sure I had an ulcer at this point. Food was unappealing, and what food I did eat fucked up my gut so badly, it was a wonder I didn't puke blood.

"If I don't get her back soon, I don't know what I'll do," Dad muttered, sounding even more tired than I felt. "At least with her here, I was able to hold on for her sake. But with you in New York, what do I have left?"

"Dad, I need you to stop talking like that. Mom… She just needed a little time to herself to heal. That's what she does. She hides her pain from everyone, especially us. Once she's come to terms with Nova being gone…" I closed my eyes, fighting the fresh burn of tears. "She'll be back, Dad."

"Fuck, I hope so," he muttered. After a pause, he cleared his throat. "I gotta get back to work, son. You stay safe, and if you hear anything, call me."

"Yeah, Dad," I promised, keeping my eyes clenched tight. "You too."

The phone went silent in my ear, and I let it fall to the bed as a few tears slipped through my lashes. It had been months since Nova's death—since I'd lost Lis. But the pain I felt at both of their losses never got any easier. Every mistake I'd ever made with either of them came back to haunt me. Sometimes the memories would hit me out of nowhere, and it was enough to have me clutching at my stomach as I bent in half, my entire body locked with the force of the pain.

It was too late to say I was sorry, too late to make it up to either of them. The "what-if" scenarios played out in my mind every night, keeping me from falling asleep until the early hours of the morning from sheer exhaustion.

Between all the hours I'd been working and even more time I spent trying to find Mom, what little sleep I'd been able to get was starting to catch up to me. I felt sick to my stomach, and I was hoping it was just from the lack of rest, so I'd swallowed two sleeping pills before my shower. With my eyes growing heavy, I barely had the sense to turn off my lamp before I crashed.

Something touching my face tried to break through my drugged brain, but I was too tired to care.

"Garret," a voice I recognized hissed. But there was no way it was real. Nova was dead. I had to be dreaming. Then I felt the sting of a slap. "Wake up, you dumbass."

Pissed that my mind and body were trying to play a sick joke on me, I grunted and tried to turn over, only to get a harder slap. "If I didn't love you so damn much, I would smother you with your own pillow."

My lashes were hard to lift with the effects of the sleeping meds, but when I realized there really was someone standing over me, I reacted instantly. I reached for the gun I kept under my pillow, my thumb already releasing the safety as a light weight landed on top of me. Sharp knees squeezed into my ribs, knocking the air from my lungs from the pain as the person on top of me grabbed my wrists, stopping me from squeezing the trigger.

"Garret," that beloved voice snapped, louder this time. "Stop before you hurt one of us."

Realizing that I wasn't dreaming, I jerked at the sound of my sister's voice. "N-Nova?" I rasped, emotion clogging my throat.

She eased her hold on my ribs enough to let me roll onto my back as she took possession of my gun.

"Nova?" I shook my head in denial. "No, you're dead. I saw you."

"Did you, though?" The snarkiness in her voice made me question everything I knew as truth as she flipped on the light. Blinking at the new brightness of the room, I gazed at my sister for the first time in what felt like a lifetime. "Do I look dead to you, big brother?"

Nova moved to sit beside me on the bed while I

sat up, trying to separate reality from dream. My hands shook as I touched her face and hair before I grasped her wrist and rubbed my thumb over Ryan's name on her skin.

"But I saw you," I muttered to myself. "Even the necklace."

She pulled her hand free of my grip and reached under her hoodie, pulling out a platinum chain with the Russian rings on them that read "Ryan's Heart." "This necklace?"

I wrapped my finger around the chain, skimming my thumb over the two rings. "Yeah, this necklace. It was…" My tormented gaze, full of the nightmarish things I'd seen that night, met hers. "She played us?"

"You would have known that already if you had just talked to me when I tried to contact you," she complained, a pout in her sweet voice.

She was trying to be cute and tease me, but that didn't stop my anger at her. "Why the fuck haven't you come home before now?" I raged. "Do you know what we've gone through? Mom and Dad…" My voice broke. Now I had to tell her. Fuck! "Mom ran away, Nova. She couldn't handle what happened, and she just up and disappeared. We've been looking everywhere for her."

"Not everywhere," she said, as if it was no big deal. "And she didn't run away. I needed her help, so she came with me to Colombia to talk sense into Cali and—"

I saw spots for a moment at the mention of *that* name. Maybe I was wrong. Perhaps this was a dream after all. One where my sister tormented me with the possibility of Lis actually being alive.

"Cali?" I nearly choked on the name, cutting Nova off before she could get my hopes up any further. "Did…you…say…Cali?"

She pressed her lips together in displeasure at being interrupted, but she nodded.

"Lis is alive?" My heart began pounding so hard, it was difficult to breathe, and I had to press my hands to my chest, willing myself to breathe and not pass out.

Small hands cupped my face. "Garret, look at me," she commanded. My eyes snapped open—I didn't even remember closing them. "Take a deep breath, okay? You can't pass out on me. Not now, not ever. We have to get back, and I can't carry your ass out of here on my own."

"B-back?" I whispered, blinking away tears.

"To Cali," my sister murmured with a smile. "She's waiting on you."

"You aren't playing with me, are you, Nova?" I begged her to be honest with me. "I don't know if I can survive this if you're not being real right now."

217

"I wouldn't play that kind of game with you or anyone else," she assured me softly. "When you came down with Dad and the MC, they told you she was dead, right?" Pain lanced through me at the memory, but I nodded, letting a tear spill down my face. "Well, they lied, Garret. They thought it would be safer for everyone to think she was dead, but she's not. Now, get your ass out of this bed and grab a few things. We have to hurry."

———

"From what Mom told me, I'm guessing that Sheena got someone who looked as much like me as possible," Nova explained as we sat on the cargo plane. We'd already been in the air for a while, but the pilot and guards had needed Nova's attention, so we'd only gotten to sit down and talk a few moments before. "That's why she destroyed the girl's face and took her hands and feet." She rubbed her fingers over her tattoo. "She got the necklace right, but she didn't realize I'd gotten a tattoo that could have identified me."

"That sick bitch," I muttered. "But what happened to you and Lis?"

"Ramirez took us to his place in Colombia," she said with a shrug. "I got knocked out during the wreck and woke up in what Cali called Manuel's torture dungeon. He'd been beating her for days by that point."

I balled my hands into fists, rage simmering through me. If I didn't know Ramirez was already dead, I would have been plotting the bastard's death.

"The beating caused some serious damage, and she struggled not to miscarry," Nova went on, knocking the air out of my lungs. "Cali was so stubborn, though, refusing to let the doctor admit her to the hospital so she would have round-the-clock care. She was terrified of going outside, and I think..." She grimaced. "I think she was expecting to die when the baby was born. That was why I went to get Mom. It was all I could come up with to make her see reason, and even then, it took her weeks to convince Cali."

I opened my mouth, but no words came out. I didn't even know how to respond to what my sister was telling me.

"But we eventually got her to go, and yesterday— yeah, it was yesterday," she muttered, checking her watch. "Yesterday, Justice was born. She's so tiny, Garret. But she's a fighter, just like every other Hannigan woman."

"Wait," I choked out, needing her to clarify it for me. "I have a daughter?"

"Come on, Garret," she chided, glaring at me. "You knew she was pregnant."

"No, I didn't." I shook my head adamantly. No, no, no. I'd had no idea the woman I loved was carrying my child. If I had, there was no way I would have left her that night. Fuck, I was an even bigger screwup than I thought. "I swear to you, I had no idea."

"She told you," Nova practically growled, her anger at me flooding the entire plane. "The night she explained who she was, she said she told you everything. And after she confessed she was pregnant, you just left."

"Oh God," I groaned, burying my face in my hands. "I turned everything off that night. All I remember was her saying who she really was, and I kept replaying in my head over and over again all the fucked-up things I'd said to her over the years. Then I left, got wasted, and the next thing I knew, you were slapping me across the face, trying to knock some sense into my dumb ass."

"Well, you know now." Her encouraging smile did nothing to alleviate my guilt. How the fuck was I going to make this up to Lis *and* my daughter? I'd left them both unprotected, and now my baby girl was in a hospital, fighting for her life.

"Justice is just as dramatic as you, by the way,"

my sister continued, trying to comfort me. "She came into the world in a rush, demanding everyone sit up and pay attention to her. That includes you, so don't disappoint her."

"I won't," I vowed reverently. "From this moment forward, my only goal is to protect her and Lis."

And I wouldn't fuck it up this time. No matter what, I was never going to leave either of them again.

"Yeah?" Nova considered me for a moment while she chewed on her lip. "Have you ever been to Colombia before? I mean, other than when you came with Dad?"

"Yeah," I admitted. "A few times. We control the biggest coke pipeline into the US, Nova. Once Matias died, we took over the fields he owned. I had to go down once or twice just to make sure everything was moving smoothly."

She leaned forward. "I own half of the Ramirez business now. The legit business."

After everything else she'd already told me, I hadn't thought there was anything else she could have said that would surprise me, but at that confession, I felt my eyes bulge.

"But if I go back to New York, I won't be able to run the business as I have been. Would you maybe... want to take half of my half—"

"I'll do it for free," I promised, cutting her off. "For you and Cali. I owe you both."

"I wouldn't feel right unless you took a portion of mine," she argued.

"Whatever. I'll do anything you want as long as it gives me a reason to stay close to my girls."

My girls.

Those two words held such a magnitude of power, I slumped down into my chair. I had a family now, one that needed my full attention, but I knew it wasn't going to be easy. Lis was stubborn as hell. "I have a feeling she's going to try her hardest to keep me away. Running the business gives me an excuse to stay close."

Cali

"WHERE IS NOVA?" I asked, still groggy from all the drugs they kept pumping into me.

"She had to take care of something," Felicity murmured quietly, stroking her hand over my hair. "Don't worry, sweet girl. She will be back soon. I promise."

"But where did she go?" I rasped. My throat was raw from where they intubated me during my C-section, so every word—every breath—that rubbed over the tissue was enough to make me grimace. Neither that nor the drugs was enough to make me miss the fact that Nova wasn't there when I'd first woken up hours before, and she still wasn't there.

Nova was my safe place. Without her there, everything felt wrong. Unsafe. Even with Guzman and several other guards changing shifts outside my hospital room doors, Nova was the one who had always been my protector. I needed her there.

Through my drug-hazed mind, I didn't miss the indecision on the brunette's face before she finally repeated, "She will be back soon."

"You sent her after Garret," I whispered accusingly as what energy I'd started to gain vanished like a puff of smoke. "She wouldn't have left me—she wouldn't have left Justice unless you made her."

My daughter's grandmother sighed heavily. "Justice deserves to be held by her father just as much as she does you, Cali. If something were to happen to her before he can do that, you won't be able to forgive yourself."

A dry, pained laugh left me. "Trust me, I wouldn't have lost a moment of sleep over your asshole son never holding *my* daughter," I gritted out. "You might be her grandmother, but where my child is concerned, you have no say in who enters her delicate little life."

"You didn't create Justice alone, Cali," she reminded me, her voice growing firm, turning into that tough-love tone.

But it didn't work on me any longer. My baby had already been delivered, and to my surprise, I'd survived the birth. I wasn't completely sure how I felt about that just yet. Should I be thankful that I would be around to watch my daughter struggle to survive because I hadn't been strong enough to get her to thirty-four weeks gestation? Angry that I wouldn't be waiting on her when she finally lost the battle to survive and passed on? Heartbroken that I would have to watch Justice suffer because there was such a small chance she would make it over all the hurdles in her way?

I closed my eyes, fighting the dizziness from the drugs along with the tears of all the emotions bombarding me. "No, Mrs. Hannigan. I didn't create her on my own. But your son wanted nothing to do with his baby from the moment I told him I might be pregnant. By default, he gave up his right to see or hold her, in my eyes." My lashes lifted, and I gazed up at her with all the anger that was choking me. At her, Garret, even a little at Nova for giving in and going to fetch her brother. "He's your son, so I realize he can do no wrong in your eyes. But he's a worthless coward, and I don't want that kind of person to have a hand in raising my child."

"You're extra sensitive after everything that happened yesterday," she said soothingly. "I know that you're upset, but once you are more clear-headed, you'll realize I'm right."

"No," I snapped. "You're not going to stand there and tell me how I'm feeling and that I'll get over it once the medication wears off. You came here to make me agree to be admitted to the hospital. The job is over. Take your false empathy and manipulations and get the hell away from me."

Her face paled, and her blue eyes began to glitter with tears. "Cali—"

"Guzman!" I shouted, gritting my teeth through the pain I'd just inflicted on my throat. "Guzman!"

The door opened before I could finish calling his name a second time. He entered the room, his hand already under his suit jacket, reaching for his gun as if he'd expected me to be in imminent danger. "What's wrong?" he demanded when he didn't see a threat.

"Get her out of here," I commanded, waving my hand weakly at Felicity. "As soon as Nova returns, I want her and Garret Hannigan on the plane back to the States."

Guzman dropped his hand from his gun. "I'm sorry, Cali, but I won't do that."

Betrayal sliced through me. "Excuse me?"

"Justice deserves to see her father. I won't stand in the way of that. And Felicity has done nothing to cause you harm, so I won't force her to leave. You are incapacitated at the moment, and someone needs to be with Justice until Miss Nova returns."

His tone was gentle yet firm, and in that

moment, I hated him. I hated them all. It was so clear to me that no one had ever been on my side. That the only thing they had cared about was keeping me pregnant for as long as possible. Now that Justice was born, they were all turning their backs on me.

No one had ever been loyal to me when I was a teenager being tortured by my psychotic stepbrother, and it was still the same even though I was the Ramirez heir.

None of them cared except for Nova, and even she had given in to her mother's demands to bring Garret there.

"Get out," I whispered. "Both of you, just go."

"Cali—" Felicity tried once more, but I cut her off again.

"Go!" I screamed so loud it felt like my throat was going to shred open from the pain. "Leave me alone. None of you care about me, so just get the fuck out of my sight."

A small sob came from the woman beside me, but I turned my head away from her and the door where Guzman still stood. Several moments passed before Felicity sighed heavily, and I heard her footsteps as she crossed the room. "We all love you, sweet girl," she said with a sniffle from the doorway. "You simply don't want to see it right now."

"Liar," I whispered as the door closed behind them. "Everyone is a liar."

Letting the tears fall silently down my face, I allowed the meds to take me away from all the pain my heart and body were in. The next time I opened my eyes, they felt swollen and gritty. A nurse was standing by the bed, her gaze on the machines I was hooked to, reading my vital signs before checking my IV and then changing the bag of fluids for a fresh one.

"Oh, you are awake," the woman said with a small smile. "How are you feeling, dear?"

I sighed but took stock of my aching body. My throat hurt even worse than it had earlier, and the rest of my body… There was no way to describe the pain I was in. It surpassed the zero-to-ten levels medical professionals used to rate how badly someone felt.

The nurse watched my face as I considered the answer and grimaced. "That bad, huh?" I nodded, and she pulled a syringe from the cart she had beside her after scanning the code on my wristband. "Let's get you more comfortable. Maybe tomorrow your little one will be ready for some company. Wouldn't you like to hold that gorgeous baby girl?"

"Yes," I murmured. "I want to hold her so badly."

The syringe was placed into the IV line, and

within seconds, I barely felt any pain. I blinked a few times, fighting the heaviness of my eyelids, but they fluttered closed once again while I dreamed of holding my sweet Justice...

"Justice!" When I sat upright in bed, my entire body protested the quick movement, but I ignored it. A voice in my head was screaming at me to get up, to get to my baby. She needed me. Throwing my legs over the side of the bed, I got unsteadily to my feet.

The first step was agonizing, as were the second and third. By the fourth, the IV line in the back of my hand tugged, reminding me I was attached to it and several machines. I ripped the IV out, not caring that blood dripped down my fingers as I undid the blood pressure cuff and then pulled off the stickers that had wires attached to them to monitor my heart.

Lifting my feet, I walked as quickly as I could, the pain from my midsection robbing me of breath, but by the time I got to the door, I was used to it. I put up a mental block so I could handle the pain and pulled the door open.

The guards standing outside the room jerked to attention when they saw me. "Miss Cali." The one on my left tried to touch me, but I flinched away from him.

"Which way to the NICU?" I asked, pushing my hair back from my face, not realizing it was the hand that was bleeding from the IV, and I smeared blood across my cheek.

"Let me get a wheelchair," the guard on the right offered. "I'll take you up there myself."

"No," I gritted out, walking down the hall to where I knew the elevators were. A directory over the call button listed what was on each floor, and I pressed the up button. Behind me was the nurses station, and I heard them call my name, but I blocked them out, just as I blocked out the pain in my body. When someone tried to touch me again, I jerked away, cowering from them. I couldn't stand the thought of anyone's hands on me.

The doors opened, and I stepped inside, pressing the button for the NICU floor. Others entered the elevator with me, but I didn't pay attention to who they were. Vaguely, I heard them speaking to me, but I was focused on one thing—and only one thing.

Getting to Justice.

The ride up to the NICU floor was over quickly, and I stepped off, still unsteady and bent in half, but walking, nonetheless. Moving toward the door that advised me I was in the right place, I tried to turn the handle, but it was locked.

"Justice!" I screamed her name, wanting her to know I was there. "Justice, Mommy is coming, sweet angel."

The doors opened moments later, and someone stepped in front of me, blocking my entrance when I would have gone inside. "Ma'am, you're not in any condition to be in the NICU," she informed me. "This is a sterile environment."

"I need to see my daughter," I snapped at her. "I need to touch her. She needs me!"

Understanding filled her eyes, and she grasped my hand. Lifting it, she showed me the blood that was still dripping off my fingertips. "Let's get you cleaned up, put on a fresh gown, and then you can see your little one. Okay?"

"She needs me," I repeated, my voice quieter.

"Yes, she definitely does," the nurse agreed in a gentle, yet firmly reassuring voice. "And as soon as you're cleaned up and can safely see her, I will take you to her."

A chamber separated the outside from the NICU ward itself. The nurse patched up my bleeding hand and washed away the blood I hadn't realized I'd smeared on my face. She gave me a fresh gown to change into and then helped me with the protective covering. My hair was pulled into a low knot at the back of my head before a hair net was placed over it.

I'd been in some scary places, but there was nothing more terrifying than the NICU. It was mostly silent, the beeping of heart monitors wasn't present, but there was a nurse at a station who did nothing but watch the vitals of the itty-bitty patients who were in her care. I heard no crying babies, and I realized as I passed one incubator after another, that most of the babies were too small and sick to have the energy to make a sound.

My heart lifted into my already aching throat, but I kept my tears at bay as the nurse finally stopped in front of the incubator that had the name "Baby Hannigan" on a card, identifying who the baby was.

I gasped when I got my first look at my little girl. She was by far the tiniest baby in the ward, perhaps the sickest as well. She could have easily fit in the palm of my hands with room to spare. The name tag had her birth weight—one pound, four ounces—but there was a note that said she'd already lost two ounces since she'd been brought to the NICU.

There was oxygen in her nose that was taped to her face to stay in place, as well as an NG tube. Her eyes were covered, and all she wore was a teeny-tiny diaper that would have been too small even to fit on my dolls when I was a little girl. Cords, tubes, wires, and what seemed like a hundred other things were connected to her, helping her to breathe, to nourish her—to keep her alive.

The IV in the top of her head was what finally broke me. The discomfort I'd felt at having one in the back of my hand… *How much did it hurt Justice to have one in her scalp?* My tears fell silently because I didn't want my daughter to hear her mother weeping. I had to be brave, for her sake, if nothing else.

"You can touch her," the nurse murmured softly beside me. "Put your hand through this hole here, and you can hold her hand or stroke her leg."

"I'm scared," I confessed, my voice barely a whisper, but she still somehow heard me.

"I know you are, dear. Every mommy and daddy who comes in here is scared out of their minds. But your little one is tougher than you think." She guided me closer, and taking my hand that wasn't bandaged, she placed it at one of the holes into the incubator. "Your touch will soothe her, give her the courage to keep fighting. Because, Mommy, she needs that more than anything I can do for her."

My tears fell faster, but I nodded and slid my hand inside. I stroked my index finger over her leg before reaching for her hand. She grabbed me, her strength surprising me so much that a half laugh, half sob escaped my throat.

"See," said the nurse with a smile when I looked at her in amazement. "You're already giving your baby the will to fight the biggest war of her new life. The power of a loving touch is an incredible thing."

I turned my gaze back to Justice. "I'm here, little

angel," I told her, hoping she could hear me. "No matter what happens, or who comes and goes from our lives, I swear to you, Justice, I won't ever leave you. So please…" My voice cracked, and I pressed my forehead to the incubator. "Please, sweetheart, don't leave me. You…you are all I have left."

Garret

BY THE TIME the plane landed at the private airstrip close to the Ramirez estate, Nova's foot was the size of a watermelon. Even her toes were swollen. Her ankle was so purple it looked black. It had to have been painful, but she didn't complain once. She'd mentioned hurting it jumping from the building adjacent to my apartment but hadn't gone into detail. It had only taken the flight from NYC for me to realize there was a lot I didn't know about my baby sister.

Once the pilot gave the all clear that we could get off the plane, she stood and grimaced. After thinking I'd lost my sister forever—having seen what I'd thought was her bashed-in face and dismembered body—I couldn't handle the thought of her in even the slightest pain.

TERRI ANNE BROWNING

Lifting her into my arms, I carried her off the plane and to the car that was waiting for us. As we neared, the driver stepped out, and I stopped in my tracks, recognizing the man. He'd been the one who was in charge when we'd come for Ramirez's head, and he'd told me Lis was dead.

My anger began to boil through my veins, and I started to shake with the effort it took to control myself.

"Hey Guzman," my sister greeted the man in Spanish. "Looks like I didn't manage to come home without incident this time."

He saw her foot and shook his head. "That's a first, Miss Nova."

Carefully, I sat my sister on the hood of the car. "Guzman?" I repeated the man's name, staring at Nova for confirmation.

"Yes, he's our head of security," she explained.

"Guzman," I muttered to myself as I turned and punched the man in the face.

"Garret!" Nova shouted, watching as Guzman stumbled back from the force of my hit. "What the fuck are you doing?"

I didn't answer her. Stepping into the other man's personal space, I grabbed him by the shirt and jerked him closer. He didn't flinch. Other than the rapidly swelling bottom lip from my first punch, he appeared completely unaffected by me—and that only pissed me off even more.

"You lied to me," I seethed. "For months, I've been living in hell, thinking Lis was dead. My woman and child needed me, and you kept them both from me."

His eyes scanned my face dispassionately. "She never once mentioned you to me. When your name is mentioned, she goes quiet and withdraws into herself. You hurt her. If you're waiting for me to apologize for keeping you away from her when she's been trying to heal from whatever you did to her, then you will be waiting for the rest of your life. Her well-being is all that I care about."

"That's enough, Garret." Nova hopped down and limped over to us. Grasping one of my wrists, she tried to get me to release my hold. But I was too pissed to let him go. I wanted to pound my fist into his face until he felt half the pain I'd been put through, thinking Lis was dead.

Heaving a sigh, my little sister shifted, and somehow I ended up on my knees—right along with Guzman. Even at this level, the two of us were nearly as tall as Nova, but there was something about my sister that exuded power, making us both watch her like mice watching a cat about to pounce.

"I said that was enough," she said in a tone that

reminded me of... Ah fuck, why did it remind me of Anya? And more importantly, how the hell had she gotten me on my knees to begin with? Not just me, but Guzman as well. Both of us outweighed her by more than a hundred pounds. She shouldn't have had those kinds of skills.

Unless someone had taught her.

Someone who'd been trained as an assassin from childhood.

"Nova," I spoke cautiously, almost afraid of her answer. "Did Anya—"

"We need to hurry and get to the hospital," she cut me off. "I don't like being away from Cali and Justice for this long."

Guzman got calmly to his feet, dusting off his pant legs. "She has been emotional while you were away," he reported. "She guessed where you'd gone and kicked your mother out of her hospital room. Felicity has been in the waiting room since last night, too afraid to upset Cali more if she went back in without you."

Shaking off my daze at Nova's ability to incapacitate me so effortlessly, I jumped to my feet and jogged over to where my sister was getting into the back of the car. "She's going to give me hell, isn't she?"

"Like you don't deserve it?" She huffed and climbed inside. "Ride in the front with Guzman. I'm going to prop my foot up."

"You need to see a doctor," I muttered, closing the door.

"I'll do what I need to after I've checked on Cali and Justice," she said as I took the front passenger seat. "And I'm warning you now, Garret. Keep yourself in check, or I'll kick your ass out of the hospital faster than you can blink."

"You gonna throw me out a window, Nova?" I found myself teasing, glancing back at her over my shoulder.

Without even blinking, she shrugged. "If I have to."

It took a while to get to the hospital, but as soon as Guzman pulled up in front of the entrance, another member of the Ramirez security team was there to park the car for him. Nova stepped out, but after two steps, I couldn't handle the sight of her limping and lifted her into my arms once again.

Guzman led the way to the elevators. When we reached the floor he'd picked, he took a right but stopped after only a few steps. Turning his head, he glared at the woman dressed in scrubs sitting behind the nurses station. "Where are my men?"

She nibbled her lip for a moment before answering. "Miss Ramirez went up to the NICU."

"My mother?" Nova asked.

"She went with the guards," the nurse informed us, before going back to biting at her bottom lip nervously.

"Something isn't right," Nova muttered as I followed Guzman back to the elevators. The doors opened as soon as he hit the up button. "She was way too twitchy."

The head of security nodded, pressing the floor button over and over again as if that would get the elevator to move any faster. As it began to rise, I felt my heart rate increase.

Lis was so close. I would see her again soon.

Her and our daughter.

Nova lightly tapped me on the cheek, forcing my attention on her. "Relax, bro. It's going to be an uphill battle, but as long as you don't fuck it up again, you'll be fine."

My eyes closed just as the elevator stopped. "I don't know how not to fuck it up, Nova."

"Try," she gritted out. "Don't make me have to kill you, Garret. Because I will if you hurt her again."

I almost laughed at the idea that my little sister would or even could make me bleed, let alone kill me. But then I remembered how fast she'd been, putting Guzman and me on our knees like it was nothing—all with a foot four times bigger than it should have been. A voice in the back of my head told me that the little blond angel who barely weighed as much as my left leg wouldn't hesitate to cut my throat if I hurt Lis or our daughter.

"I swear to you, I won't hurt either of them," I vowed. "I love Lis and our daughter, Nova. Even though I haven't met her yet, Justice is already in my heart, and I'll give my own life for hers if I have to."

The elevator doors were slow to open, but as they did and Guzman stepped out, Nova gave a sharp nod. "Good."

Walking out into the corridor, I saw the NICU ward was just a few feet away. Two guards stood on either side of the double doors, but it was my mother, standing by a window trying to peek inside, that caught and held my attention.

"Mom?" I choked out, so happy to see her that I nearly dropped Nova.

Her head was slow to turn, but when she spotted me, her face lit up for a moment with a bright smile. "Hi, honey," she greeted. But then she realized I was carrying Nova for a reason and not for fun, and she jumped into mom-mode. "What happened?"

"Just rolled my ankle," my sister said with a careless shrug. "How are Cali and Justice?"

Mom pushed her hair back from her face with a heavy sigh. "She kicked me out of her room last night. But about an hour ago, she suddenly got out of bed and walked up here."

"What?" Nova half shouted. "She shouldn't be walking. She had a C-section and then the hysterectomy. The doctor said she needed to take things slow."

"She pulled out her IV and unhooked all her monitors," Mom explained. "There was a trail of blood droplets from her room, down the hall to the elevator, and all the way up here. They cleaned it up a while ago, but I can still see it in my head."

"Where is she now?" I demanded, shifting Nova in my arms.

"One of the NICU nurses took her in to see Justice. She's been in there ever since." Mom touched my arm tenderly. "Garret, sweetheart, I need you to be prepared when you go in there. Justice is…"

"Has something happened since I left?" Nova asked with concern.

"The baby has already lost a little weight. She's got more tubes and wires attached to her than when you saw her right after the birth." Mom took a slow breath, steadying herself, and everything inside me clenched as I prepared myself for whatever she was about to tell us.

"There was some slight brain bleeding, but that has already stopped on its own," she explained. "Right now, Justice is having breathing issues, which is putting pressure on her heart. They found an opening between her aorta and pulmonary arteries, which would normally close on its own given time if it was small, but hers is bigger. The doctor said these types can be closed by a catheter or surgery, but hers is so bad that he wants to do surgery to repair it. They want to wait until she's gained more weight to give her a better chance of...of..."

"Of survival," Nova finished for her when Mom began to cry.

She nodded. "Y-yeah."

My strength left me as my brain tried to comprehend everything my mom had just dumped on me. Feeling weak, I carefully set Nova on her feet before I pressed my back to the nearest wall and tried to catch my breath. Putting my hands on my knees, I bent in half, sucking in big gulps of oxygen—but it didn't help. My lungs had stopped working.

"Garret!" Nova snapped my name. Grasping my chin, she lifted my head until our gazes locked. "You're not allowed to have a panic attack," she growled at me. "It's time to grow up and be the man your daughter deserves. I'm not going to allow you to let her down. Do you hear me?"

"I-I hear you." Looking into her eyes, for a moment, I didn't see Nova standing there commanding me, but Aunt Raven. Shaking off the weakness that had overcome me, I straightened my spine and pushed away from the wall. "I'm ready to meet my baby girl."

Cali

I DIDN'T KNOW how long I stood beside that incubator, letting Justice clutch my finger, before a doctor appeared at my side. He and the nurse explained everything that was going on with my baby. The brain bleeding that had thankfully stopped on its own, the lung issues, and scariest of all—the heart problem.

It was a miracle I stood there and was able to listen to the words out of the man's mouth without falling apart, but tears and screaming at the injustice of what my child had to go through could come later. I refused to let her hear her mother be a hysterical mess while every moment of her life was a miracle. A struggle that was no doubt painful and exhausting, but a miracle, nonetheless.

After I'd agreed to a plan of action, the doctor left me there with the nurse, who continued to check Justice every few minutes. Her tubes, her wires, her IV. Making sure the incubator temperature was keeping her warm enough because her body didn't know how to regulate itself yet. I knew the nurse was keeping a close eye on me as well, making sure I didn't collapse.

Honestly, I was surprised I hadn't already fallen to my knees. The block I'd thrown up in my mind so I could withstand the pain I was going through phys-ically was starting to crack, and my entire body shook. I didn't know if I was cold or going into shock from the combination of stress and pain, but some-thing was definitely happening.

Yet I just stood there, letting Justice cling to my finger while I stroked what little I could of her with my other hand. I ached to pick her up and hold her against my chest, but the nurse had explained that, while skin-to-skin contact would work wonders for Justice, she wasn't ready for that yet. She needed to stay in her incubator for a few more days before that could happen. I would just have to make do with what contact I did get with her.

With my energy fading by the minute, I leaned on the incubator a little, trying to remain upright. Fighting the agony my body was no longer able to control, I folded my arm and rested my head on it, looking down at Justice. Tears leaked out of my eyes and down my nose, but with the mask over her eyes, she couldn't see me cry.

Behind me, I heard voices murmuring, but I ignored them. My vision was blurry, but I could still make out the image of the tiny body that I would fight to protect until my last breath.

A hand touched my arm, and I jerked. I lifted my head, and I came face-to-face with Nova. Tears glittered in her eyes, and she started to hug me, but I took a step back. "How could you?" I whispered, her betrayal cutting through me all over again. "I trusted you."

"Let's not talk about that here," she urged in her sweet, quiet voice. "We don't want to argue and upset Justice. She needs as much peace and rest as she can get."

"What would you know about what she needs?" I hissed. "You left us. Like everyone else, you abandoned us. I thought I could trust you, but you only broke my heart too."

"That's bullshit, Cali," she said firmly, her jaw tightening. "I will never abandon you. You and Justice are my family."

A humorless laugh left me, making my throat throb all over again. "Your family can go to hell. I'm done with all of you."

Her green eyes dropped to Justice, and a single tear spilled down her cheek. "I'm sorry I wasn't here. Believe me when I say that I wanted to be. But Mom was right. Garret does deserve to see his daughter. In your heart, you know that as well. You're just too hurt to see the truth. With everything that has happened, your brain and body are overwhelmed. Should you even be out of bed?" she demanded with concern.

"I should be with my baby," I snapped.

At my raised voice, I felt Justice jerk, her hold tightening on my finger before relaxing. Guilt that I'd caused her even a moment of distress slammed me. Bending, I looked at her closer, trying to see if I'd caused her any physical harm.

But the sudden movement drained what was left of my energy reserve, and I felt myself sliding down, down, down…

Strong arms caught me before I hit the floor, lifting me into the air. I knew who it was and refused to even look at his face as he adjusted me in his hold. Keeping my gaze locked on the incubator, I gritted out, "Tell him to put me down, Nova."

"If he does that, you'll fall," she argued. "Let him take you back to your room. The two of you can talk and—"

"Tell him to put me down. Now!" I whisper-shouted, so as not to disturb my baby.

"Lis, please." Garret's voice rolled over me, making my pain level go from one hundred to ten million in a heartbeat. Even my eyelashes hurt, but that was nothing compared to the agony in my abdominal muscles from being scrunched up in his arms.

It was so bad, my vision started to go dark around the edges. But my hand was still inside the incubator, Justice's little fingers wrapped so trustingly around my digit. I tried to breathe through the pain, to keep conscious, for her…

The next thing I knew, I was lying in my bed in the private hospital room.

Blinking, I took stock of myself. There was a fresh IV line in my hand, the heart monitors were back, and so was the blood pressure cuff. My pain level had been cut in half, so a nurse must have given me a dose of medication. But there was something else I quickly became aware of.

My boobs felt full and sore—and wet. Looking down at my chest, I saw two huge spots on my gown from where breast milk had leaked from my nipples.

"Shit," I muttered, tugging the material away from my skin, but that only caused more milk to leak down my chest and onto my stomach. "Shit, shit, shit."

"Baby," a deep voice from my right tried to soothe. "What's wrong?"

"Get out," I told Garret without looking at him. Keeping my focus on my chest, I tried to sit up.

Firm hands pressed my shoulders back into the mattress. Blowing out a huff, I slapped at his arms until he released me and stepped back before hitting the call button for the nurse. She must have been close, because the door opened moments later.

"Miss Ramirez?" she greeted as she pushed her cart into the room. "What's wrong, dear?"

"I'm leaking," I explained, waving the hand without the IV in it at my chest.

"That's a good thing. And once you're off the pain medication, you can start pumping to feed your baby." She left the cart and walked over to the bed. "Let me get you a fresh gown. Do you have a nursing bra packed? We have pads to insert, and if your nipples start to crack, we can put some cream on them."

"I don't know," I muttered. Nova and Felicity had been the ones to pack all the things they said I would need following giving birth, so I wasn't aware of what was in my case. Even after Felicity had convinced me to allow Dr. Ortega to admit me to the hospital, I hadn't been completely convinced I would survive the delivery.

Now that I was very much alive, I was thankful to be there so I could help Justice. She needed me in her corner, to give her a reason to continue to fight. I didn't know what the future held for her, if she would always have health issues, delays in her development, if she would ever be fully healthy. But I would always love and protect her.

We just had to get over this hurdle first. It was going to be long, and already scared the hell out of me, but I wasn't going to give up on her.

The nurse went to the closet where my case was stored and started going through my things. After several minutes of my lying there, keeping the damp gown away from my boobs, she finally returned with a white nursing bra.

The woman's gaze went to where Garret stood. He'd remained quiet the entire time, but I'd felt his presence. I'd tried to block my mind from thinking about his being there, but that was impossible. All I could do was pretend, and that must have worked, because he barely seemed to be breathing.

"Sir, do you mind stepping out while I get Miss Ramirez comfortable?"

"I mind," he muttered. "I can help you."

The tension in my entire body must have alerted

the nurse to how I felt about that offer. She put her hands on her hips and gave him a hard look. "Thank you, but we will manage just fine on our own." When he didn't move to exit, she glanced down at me, and I shook my head, silently telling her I didn't want him there. "Out. Or I'll have the men standing guard at the door remove you."

"Then have them remove me," he told her matter-of-factly. "I'm not letting this woman out of my sight ever again. I already thought I lost her once. I'll be damned if I allow that to happen again. And to ensure that doesn't happen, I'm going to be her shadow for the rest of my goddamn life."

Rolling my eyes, I picked up my phone that was within reach on the side table. Swiping my thumb over the screen, I lifted it to my ear and waited.

"Hello?"

"Nova, come remove your brother from my room, or I'm going to have security throw him out the window."

"The windows don't open, dear," the nurse informed me, amusement filling her voice.

"Did you hear that, Nova?" I bit out. "The windows don't open, and I'm going to have him thrown out one of them. Come save the worthless asshole before his death is even messier."

"Lis—"

"Nova!" I shouted into the phone when he used *that* name, in that pained, pleading tone that had always affected me in the past. "Now."

"All right," she said with a huff. "Give him the phone."

"Just come get him, Nova. For fuck's sake." I hung up before she could argue and tossed the phone back onto the nightstand.

"Lis, please."

"Eat a dick, Garret," I snarled, still not looking at him. "Read the room. Your presence is unwanted."

"I can't leave you," he said stubbornly.

"When Nova gets here, you will," I assured him with confidence.

"No. You don't understand. I physically can't leave you. Just the thought of you being out of my sight makes me sick. I'm not leaving, not even if they try to take me out of here in handcuffs. The last time I walked away from you, I didn't see you again for months. I thought you were fucking dead!"

I saw him move out of the corner of my eye; moments later, his hands were on either side of my head as he leaned over me. I tried not to look up at him, to avoid his gaze, but his breath brushed over my cheek, and I was powerless to control the direction my eyes traveled.

His tormented green eyes locked with mine, and I

sucked in a pained breath at the anguish I saw there. "Ignore me all you want. Pretend like I don't exist. But do not expect me to go anywhere you aren't. Because I fucking won't, Lis."

Garret

HER HAIR WAS a tangled mess around her face and across her pillow. The hospital gown she wore was drenched in breast milk. Her complexion was blotchy from all the shit she'd been through in the past few days. Her blue eyes, slightly glazed from a combination of discomfort and painkillers, shot flames up at me.

And for the life of me, I couldn't remember seeing a more beautiful woman in my life.

Just the sight of her was enough to take my breath away, causing my heart to pound against my ribs. That she was there, in front of me, breathing and very much alive, was enough to bring fresh tears to my eyes. I'd never missed anyone as much as I'd missed her during the time I'd thought she was gone from this world forever.

Now that she was right in front of me, it was a struggle not to touch her constantly. I needed that physical contact to remind myself that I had her back, because this could all so easily turn into a dream and the love of my life might turn into a wisp of smoke before my eyes. But touching her, feeling her soft skin, the heat of her body, the heart beating in her chest—that told me without a shadow of a doubt that she was truly there.

From the time she'd lost consciousness in the NICU, I'd been by her side, staying out of the way of the nurses and doctors as they'd come and gone. But I'd be damned if I allowed anyone to take her out of my line of vision ever again. Walking out on her the night she'd confessed everything to me had turned out to be the worst decision of my life—and I'd made some fucked-up mistakes over the years.

While she'd been out, Nova and Mom had been on my case to go up to the NICU to visit with Justice, but as much as I wanted to see my daughter, it felt wrong to do so without her mother with me. That, and the thought of being anywhere Lis wasn't made my stomach churn in an ugly kind of way that wouldn't be good for anyone, my little girl included.

Angrily, Nova had called me a coward for not being with Justice, and I'd shut her up by agreeing. I *was* a coward, a scared boy trapped in a man's body. I was terrified out of my mind, but not for the reasons my sister thought. I trusted Nova and Mom to keep my baby girl safe, but the last time I hadn't been there for Lis, when she'd needed me the most, I'd thought she'd died.

I wouldn't survive that again. It would be worse than Ryan without Nova. After getting Lis back, only to lose her again, it would be the end of me too. Not even for Justice could I walk through life without the other half of my soul beside me.

"Sir," the nurse tried to urge me. "It won't take me long to help Miss Ramirez get showered and changed. The longer you delay that, the more uncomfortable she will be."

"We can't have that," I murmured and lifted Lis carefully into my arms. But I'd forgotten about the monitors she was attached to and the IV.

With an exasperated huff, the nurse unhooked her from everything, leaving the IV port in the back of Lis's hand. "She needs to walk, sir. The more movement she has, the better. We want to avoid blood clots."

"She can walk on her own afterward," I told the woman as I carried Lis into the adjoining bathroom. I stood there with her in my arms while the nurse got the shower ready.

The entire time, Lis remained quiet, keeping her

gaze averted, looking at anything but me. She still continued to hold the gown away from her chest, but it only made wet spots appear elsewhere, like on her stomach as her milk supply leaked from her nipples.

I gritted my teeth, trying my damnedest not to think about her nipples. It was fucked up to think about her body like that when she'd only recently given birth. Her body had been through so much trauma since the last time I'd been with her, I didn't know if she would want me ever again. But even if we couldn't have a sexual relationship, I didn't care. All I wanted was her—and Justice. My tiny family was all I needed.

The bathroom was small and the nurse kept giving me dirty looks as she prepared everything for the shower, but I hadn't been kidding when I said I wasn't going anywhere Lis wasn't. Even if that meant I watched her use the toilet, I couldn't be away from her.

Maybe what I was feeling would eventually calm down enough to let her do small things on her own without me hovering over her, but for the moment, I was an obsessed clinger, openly stalking the woman I loved.

"You can set her down now," the nurse instructed in a cool tone. "Miss Ramirez is entitled to privacy while she bathes."

"Her name is Lis Brewer," I corrected her, carefully placing Lis on her feet but keeping my hands on her hips when she swayed slightly. "And soon it will be Hannigan."

Lis snorted. "My name is Calista Ramirez. Cali to my friends, and you are as far from a friend as they come." Her hands covered mine and tried to shove them off her, but I held firm, not trusting her legs to keep her upright on their own. I heard her swallow hard. "Get out, Garret. I just want to get clean. It's not like I can go anywhere without you seeing me leave."

"What if you fall?"

"That's what the nurse is here for," she snapped and finally lifted her blue eyes to look at me. "Please."

Muttering a curse, I helped her sit on the closed toilet seat and then backed out of the bathroom. But I left the door cracked and stayed right in front of it, just in case she needed me.

I listened to the sounds of the water running, the nurse's voice speaking quietly to Lis as she helped her wash her hair and body. I heard several moans coming from her, but I couldn't tell if they were in pleasure or pain. While she got washed up, I texted my sister to ask about Justice, but I didn't get a reply back. That only told me that she was in the NICU where phones weren't permitted because of the sensitive machinery connected to most of the precious patients in the ward.

I texted Mom next in hopes that she wasn't with Nova.

Mom: *The doctor just came in. Nova is inside speaking to him now. If Justice gains enough weight, they might do the surgery next week.*

A new fear squeezed my lungs, and I had to force in my next breath.

Mom: *That's what he was saying when he went in with Nova a little while ago. I won't know more until they come out. How is Cali?*

I heard a groan from behind the bathroom door and clenched my fingers around my phone for a moment before forcing them to loosen their hold.

Me: *Hurting. Angry. Broken.*

Me: *Her milk came in. Right now, she's taking a shower with the nurse's help.*

Mom: *Nova is upset that you aren't up here with Justice, but I think you're making the right decision to stay close to Cali. She needs to see that you're here for her, not just the baby.*

At least Mom wasn't giving me grief and making me feel like I was abandoning my child because I wasn't up in the NICU. The guilt still churned in me, though. I wanted to be up there with Justice, but she had a full team of nurses and doctors—plus Nova and my mom—to look after her. Cali wasn't letting anyone close. If I weren't forcing the issue, she would have already had me kicked out of the hospital.

My baby girl might have been fighting for her life, but her mother was just as fragile. Maybe more so. Justice had a strong spirit, just like every other Hannigan woman I knew. Lis was vulnerable. She thought no one cared, but I was going to prove to her that she was the center of my world.

Somehow.

The door pushed outward, and the nurse stepped through, guiding Lis out of the bathroom. I rushed forward to assist when she wobbled slightly on her feet. My arm went around her waist, taking some of her weight, but she stopped mid-step at my touch.

"Fuck, can't you just leave already?" she muttered. "It's what you're good at after all."

Ignoring her comment, I lifted her off her feet a few inches and carried her toward the bed.

"No," she cried. "That hurts!"

Instantly, I had her back on her feet, but I didn't release her. Her hands touched her midsection, her face pale from renewed pain. "I'm sorry, blue eyes. I didn't realize."

"Carrying me like that makes the C-section incision stretch. And when you lifted me upstairs in the NICU, you scrunched me up, and the pain became too much." She tried to shrug off my touch, and I released one hand from her hip but kept the other in place as a precaution—and because touching her was the only thing that didn't cause *me* pain. "Garret, damn it, I'm not helpless. Just back up and give me some room to breathe."

Scrubbing my free hand over my face, I took a half step away from her, but that was as far as my body would allow me to go. Any farther than that and my feet wouldn't listen to my brain.

"I'll just get that wheelchair so you can go up to visit with your sweet baby girl," the nurse commented as she walked toward the door.

"Thank you," Lis muttered, fidgeting with her clothes.

Glancing down, I saw that she'd changed into a pair of pajama bottoms and a matching top. Her stomach was still slightly rounded from carrying Justice, and a few inches of her empty baby bump peeked out, showing me her bruised bikini line from the C-section incision.

"Holy fuck," I breathed, pulling the top of her pants down enough to see the scar that went from one pelvic bone to the other. "Jesus, Lis. No wonder you're in so much pain. Nova told me what they had to do to get Justice out of you, but I had no idea this was the result."

"She told you?" Lis tossed at me, sounding even angrier than she had only moments before. "What exactly did she explain to you?"

A warning went off in my head, screaming at me to handle this with caution, but I honestly didn't know how or even why I needed to. "She said you had a C-section—"

"Yeah? And did she tell you that they had to rip out everything once Justice was pulled from my body?" she demanded. "Did she tell you there was so much trauma from where Manuel beat me—for days —that nothing was healing? And the bigger our daughter grew, the more damage my body sustained, until I couldn't keep her safely inside where she needed to be? Did your sister explain to you that I will never be able to have another baby? I'm twenty-two years old and already going into menopause!"

"No," I said quietly, everything she'd just shouted at me hitting me like a ton of bricks. Her pain was a physical entity, one that weighed me down, made me ache for her. "Nova didn't mention any of that, Lis. She only told me about Justice." I cupped her face, wiping away her angry tears with my thumbs. "Listen to me, baby. Please listen. I didn't even know you were pregnant until I got on the plane with my sister the other night. The news that you were alive was all I needed for her to say before I was running for the nearest exit. Once we got in the air, she told me what happened—Ramirez took the two of you and that you were in the hospital recovering from preterm labor. She said our baby girl needed me, but I knew she was wrong. Justice needs all of us, but you are the one who needs me."

"I don't need anyone except Justice. It's just her and me from now on. No more liars who say they want the best for me, but then put me through hell all over again." She slapped my hands away. "And what do you mean, you didn't know I was pregnant? I *told* you, Garret. I said I thought I was pregnant, and you walked away as if we meant nothing to you."

Swallowing the lump in my throat, I made my own confession. "You told me who you were, and I realized how stupid I'd been. I didn't know how I hadn't recognized you. Nova said it was my brain shutting down so I wouldn't have to face how badly I'd treated you when we were kids. Maybe she's right. Fuck, I don't know. But you said 'Calista Ramirez,' and every vile thing I'd ever said to you on social media flooded into my head. I didn't hear anything else that you said after that. Eventually, I got so sick of my own past behavior, and I left. Nothing you said past your name penetrated my mind that night, Lis."

"Bullshit," she hissed. "You can't use that as an

excuse for abandoning me and your child. You walked away, and then Manuel found me again. You weren't fucking there when I needed you!"

"I know," I choked out. "I know I messed up, but if you'll give me a chance, I'll make it up to you."

"Make it up to me?" she repeated with a dry laugh. "How do you make up for the fact that he beat me until I couldn't even stand? I was unconscious for days while he did only God knows what to my body. I struggled every damn day to keep Justice safely inside my body, but it was too much… Too much," she whispered brokenly, shaking her head. Tears spilled down her face, and my knees threatened to give out. I'd let her go through all of that. Alone. How the fuck did I make up for all that pain and suffering? How did I prove to her that I wasn't the same man I'd been before I'd thought I lost her forever?

"I wasn't strong enough." Her voice cracked as more tears spilled from her pretty eyes. "I couldn't protect her. And you… You were supposed to protect us both, but you weren't here."

Cali

GARRET'S THROAT WORKED, making it obvious he was having difficulty swallowing, but before my heart could soften or he could come up with some lame excuse, the nurse walked into my room with the promised wheelchair. Scrubbing away my tears with the backs of my hands, I took the offered seat and didn't give the father of my child another glance as the woman wheeled me away.

I didn't need to look over my shoulder to know that he followed behind. The two guards fell in behind him from the sound of the number of heavy footfalls. I pushed my damp hair back from my face. My body felt cleaner, but my mind wasn't the least bit refreshed. If anything, it was more clouded and confused than ever.

On the elevator ride up to the NICU, I replayed

the night I'd made my confessions to Garret. He'd sat on my couch with this blank look on his face, which made his story that he'd blocked everything I'd said out of his mind plausible, but that wasn't a good enough excuse for not coming for me when I'd needed him the most. Whatever he'd been feeling at the time, he'd still abandoned me at my lowest.

And not just me, but our baby as well.

We'd been through hell, and he'd been doing what, exactly?

Living it up in New York, forgetting all about my existence? Like I'd once told Nova—out of sight, out of mind. He was the same as every other man on the planet. Predictably unreliable.

Not just the male population, it seemed, I reminded myself as the elevator doors opened and I saw Felicity standing near the ward's doors with Guzman. From the time she'd arrived after Nova had gone to California to bring her to Colombia, she'd felt like a mother figure to me. The first one I'd had since before my own mother had passed away.

But she'd only been playing the long game, waiting until her granddaughter was born before she showed her hand. While I was incapacitated, she'd forced Nova to fetch Garret, knowing that her son was the last person I wanted near me. She couldn't even give me time to recover from having my entire life turned upside down—yet again—before she was demanding someone bring the one person I didn't want in my life crashing back into it.

She and Guzman could talk about how they only wanted Justice to have her father in her life, because they were so worried that my baby wouldn't be around long enough to see him later on. But even if, God forbid, she didn't make it through the obstacles that were being thrown into her path, she didn't need someone like Garret Hannigan in her life.

My daughter was strong and brave. She didn't need any man to hold her hand to make it in this world. All she needed was me—and Nova, although I was still upset with her for giving in to the pressure her mother had put on her to bring her brother down from New York.

Everyone else could take their good intentions and ulterior motives and get the hell away from my child. It was obvious neither Justice nor I could depend on any of them. Even Guzman, whom I'd put in charge of security, had betrayed me by allowing Garret to be brought back into my life. But I only had myself to blame for that. I'd been shown over and over again that no man could be trusted.

Not just men, but everyone. Even Nova had betrayed me, although I knew it was because of her mother pressuring her, but she'd still given in.

Proving to me that, like always, I was at the bottom of the totem pole when it came to anyone's loyalty.

But I wasn't ever going to let Justice feel like she wasn't good enough, like there wasn't anyone who would make her their most important priority.

The nurse started to pause when Felicity and Guzman approached, but I made a noise that must have alerted her to the fact that I wanted nothing to do with either of them. Even if she had stopped, I would have gotten to my feet and walked into the NICU under my own steam. Thankfully, I didn't have to put myself through the extra pain of getting out of the wheelchair.

Before he could follow us, I turned my head and glared up at Garret. "No," I told him in my coldest voice. "Stay here with the other traitors."

"Lis, don't do this to me," he begged. "I need my eyes on you."

"And I need mine on my baby."

"She's mine too," he argued, making me laugh.

"You walked away from her once already. I think she'll be just fine without you standing around doing nothing. You're good at it, after all."

"Lis—"

"Let's go," I directed the nurse, and the double doors opened.

In the chamber that separated the outside from

269

the ward itself, I washed my hands and pulled on the protective covering before letting the nurse pull my hair into the surgical-style cap that was more net than cloth. Once I was covered up so that I wouldn't carry any outside germs in to the babies within the ward, she pushed me inside, where another nurse took over and wheeled me over to where Nova was standing with the doctor I remembered from my last visit.

Their conversation paused when I reached them. Nova grasped my hand and gave it a squeeze. Glancing down, I noticed she had a splint on her foot, but there wasn't time to ask about it as the two of them turned to face me and the doctor gave me a full report on Justice.

"As long as she's gained enough weight, we feel like next week will be a good time to do the surgery to repair the opening in her heart," he finished. "What we're hoping is that you can take a few days to let the pain medication leave your system before we start feeding her your breast milk. Once she starts getting those nutrients, and we see that she is gaining weight, we will begin prepping her."

My hand turned over in Nova's, clutching her fingers hard. "What are her chances?" I croaked out in a tight voice.

He glanced over at the baby in the incubator for a

long moment before gazing down at me. "Her chances without it are a hell of a lot smaller. Her lung issues are already putting more pressure on her heart, and her blood pressure isn't where it needs to be. The sooner we can get her to a more stable weight, the better."

"And my breast milk is the key?"

"We're giving her formula now, but her stomach isn't handling it as we would like. There are several options for someone in her condition, but so far, Justice hasn't tolerated any of them, which means she's losing more weight. Her digestive system simply can't endure the proteins in the formulas. Hopefully, your breast milk will be easier for her to digest."

"How soon can I start giving her my milk?" I asked, already calculating the last time I'd had a dose of pain medication.

"We're going to have you start pumping now if you are on board with stopping the opioid painkillers," the doctor told me. "If you are, then once the milk tests negative for the medication, we will start putting it in her NG tube instead of experimenting with the different formulas."

"Whatever you need me to do," I assured him. I was still in a lot of pain, but what was my discomfort compared to my child starving to death?

"What I need is for you to get plenty of rest, eat a well-balanced diet but avoid several different food groups so she's not yet exposed to them, and pump as often as possible." He patted my arm. "Getting you strong again means we can get your baby stronger too."

"I'll eat whatever the nurse puts in front of me," I promised. "I'm sure they will have me producing the nutrition Justice needs in no time."

"About that…" Nova said hesitantly, glancing from the doctor down to me. "After tomorrow, you're going to be released. But the nutritionist has been in contact with Maria, and she knows exactly what you should and shouldn't eat."

"Wait," I protested, surprised. "I can't be released yet. Justice is still here."

"And she will remain in the ward for quite some time," the doctor agreed. "To be completely honest, I don't know when your daughter will be able to go home."

"Then I'm not going home either," I told him between clenched teeth.

"Cali, you have to go home to rest. We can travel back and forth to the hospital every day to visit with Justice, but for the most part, we have to let the medical professionals do their job and—"

"I have no problem with them doing what they

need to help my baby, Nova!" I snapped, then quickly lowered my voice again. "What I have an issue with is not being near her twenty-four seven. If you think I'm leaving this hospital for even a moment without my child in my arms, then you are all crazy."

"Cali…" Nova started, her sweet tone attempting to soothe.

"No," I hissed at her. "Make a donation, whatever amount of money they want. Kill someone if you fucking have to. But make sure I don't have to leave this hospital without her, Nova. If you want to make up for bringing Garret here, then make this happen. Or I'll tell them not to let you into this ward, just like I did with your mother."

Putting her hands on the armrests of my wheel-chair, Nova bent slightly so our gazes locked. "You are being unreasonable. No other parents get that kind of special treatment, and some of their babies are just as sick as Justice—if not more so. This isn't about proving where my loyalty is. Of course it's with you and Justice. If I didn't care about either of you, do you think I would have stayed in Colombia all this time when I should have gone back to the States and kicked not just my dad's ass, but Garret's and Ryan's too?"

She blew out a heavy sigh while that sank in. My

heart clenched, because I knew she was right. After Manuel's death, she could have so easily left me behind and gone home. Unlike me, she had an entire family waiting on her, not to mention the man she'd planned on marrying. Instead, she'd waited for them to come get her and taken care of me.

Nova touched my chin with one hand, her eyes pleading with me to understand. "You have to start accepting there are some things that we can't change, Cali. Things that I can't fix, no matter how badly I want to. You leaving this hospital without a baby in your arms, at least for the moment, is the reality you have to face."

I pressed a fist to my chest. "I-I can't. The thought of leaving her here—alone—I can't breathe, Nova."

"I promise you, she will be safe here," my friend vowed. "I'll put guards outside this ward twenty-four hours a day. No one will get past the entrance who isn't supposed to be in here. Justice will always be safe as long as there is still air in my lungs."

"Please," I whispered brokenly, looking into the incubator where Justice remained motionless. "Please, don't make me go without her."

"She's safer here, babe. Just as you will be safer at home."

"How will it be safer for me at home, when my

heart is here?" I demanded. "How can you even ask that of me?"

"If it were up to me, none of us would leave this place until Justice is ready to go home. But it isn't up to me." She hugged me, and after a slight hesitation, I wrapped my arms around her and pressed my face into her chest. "I'm sorry," Nova murmured in my ear, her voice catching in her throat. "I wish I could make this easier on you, but it's completely out of my control."

Garret

I STOOD outside the NICU double doors waiting for Lis to say goodbye to Justice for the day. She'd been discharged by her doctor earlier, but she'd spent as much of the afternoon visiting with our daughter as was allowed.

Only she and Nova could come and go from the ward. Lis had given the nurses and doctor instructions that no one else could go near Justice. Not even I, her daddy, could step inside. My daughter might have my last name on paper, but Lis hadn't listed me as the father. She'd said Hannigan was Nova's last name, and she'd thought that my sister would end up as Justice's guardian if she'd died during the birth. That was the only reason my daughter didn't have the Ramirez surname.

But it was all bullshit. I could read it in her eyes

whether she knew it or not. She hated Manuel, so there was no way she would allow our baby to have his last name. If she would give me a chance, I'd change hers in a heartbeat, but the stubborn woman wouldn't even hear me out.

"This isn't right," Mom complained as she paced back and forth in front of the double doors. "She shouldn't be keeping you from Justice. You're her father. You have just as much right to be back there as she does."

"Mom, I'm not arguing with you about this again," I muttered, scrubbing my hands over my face. I needed a shave, and I would have given my left nut for a shower, but that could wait. I had more important things to worry about than being twitchy over the stubble on my jaw.

"But she's your daughter too."

"And what have I done to earn the right to call myself her daddy?" I snapped, causing her to flinch. Sighing, I lowered my voice. "Mom, thank you for being loyal to me when it comes to this, but Lis is right. She deserves your support more than I do, and you're not being fair to her at all. All you know is what she and Nova have told you about what happened during the time Ramirez held them captive. Neither one of them has probably told you the full truth, but knowing that sick

277

son of a bitch, it wasn't pretty. And where the fuck was I?"

"You didn't know." She tried to excuse for me.

"That doesn't matter. It was my duty to protect her and our baby. To protect Nova too. But I was back in New York, chasing my own ass because I didn't know where to look for them. When Nova called, I should have listened to her and not automatically assumed it was Sheena O'Brion playing a sick game on us all. If I had flown down here, just one time, and demanded entrance to the mansion, I would have discovered the truth and been here for Lis while she'd struggled through the pregnancy."

"But you did come looking for her," Mom growled, shooting Guzman a dirty glare where he stood with two of the other guards.

He shrugged, used to her giving him hell over what had happened when I'd come with Dad and the MC for Ramirez's head. "I'm not going to apologize for protecting those girls when no one else did. I would do it all over again if given the option. You had your chance to keep them safe, and you blew it. Miss Nova might be able to protect herself, but no one has ever looked out for Calista as she deserved. I made the mistake of agreeing with you to send your daughter to fetch your son. Now, that? I would definitely undo in a heartbeat if given the chance."

"You said if it were you, you would want to know your child had been born. You agreed that you would want to have the chance to hold her, if only once," Mom reminded him. "And now you regret it?"

"Absolutely," Guzman said to her, unblinking.

"Why?" she demanded angrily.

"Because he still hasn't stepped up and even held his child."

"No one has been able to hold her yet!" Mom exclaimed in exasperation.

"But has he spent more than two minutes in there?" the head of security shot back, just as angry. "No. He doesn't want to leave Calista's side. Which I understand. But sometimes, you have to divide your priorities. Justice is just as important as Cali. Where is his need to love and protect his daughter?" He gave me a look of disgust. "To you, your baby girl is just a name, an idea. When in reality, she's a helpless little angel, fighting for every breath she takes. Get over yourself, motherfucker, and fight for your daughter as hard as you are for the woman you claim to love."

"There's nothing I can do for Justice right now," I growled at the other man. "She has people taking care of her around the clock. She won't even know if I'm there or not. Lis needs me more than Justice."

"She might not know, but *you* will," he said with

condemnation thickening his tone. "What are you going to tell her when she's old enough to hear stories about the time she was in the hospital? She's a goddamn superhero, fighting a battle no one else can fight for her, but where are you going to be in the story? What part are you going to play? The man who is supposed to love her most in the world—are you even going to be there? Or are you too much of a coward to write yourself into the tale?"

Guzman rolled his eyes when I remained quiet, the lump filling my throat making it impossible to speak. "Or maybe you will lie and tell her you were there every step of the way. The shameless coward who couldn't bring himself to even look at his brave little girl, telling her how he stood by her incubator and held her hand, giving her the strength to keep fighting. When in truth, all you did was whine that her mother wouldn't give you the time of day."

"Cali won't let him in to see Justice," Mom argued for me while I stood there, bowled over by the reality of what he'd just dumped on me. "She doesn't want him in there."

"She doesn't want him near her either, but that hasn't stopped him yet, has it?"

Mom started to snap back, but there really wasn't anything she could say in my defense. Because he was right. About everything.

I was a coward.

The one and only time I'd gone into the NICU was to get Lis out of there. The entire time, I'd kept my eyes averted from where Justice lay so silently, unable to bring myself to look at that pitiful little body. I'd seen the incubator, the tubes and wires connected to it, but I hadn't been able to look inside at the precious little angel I'd helped create.

"My biggest regret in life was abandoning my own daughter," Guzman confessed, choking up. Clenching his jaw, he swallowed roughly several times before shrugging off the emotions. "Now, she doesn't even know who I am. Don't be like me, boy."

I was still coming to terms with what a coward I was when the doors opened, and Nova walked out with her arm around Lis. Her doctor and nurses had been encouraging her to move more and more, despite her having had major surgery only days before. But it wasn't the pain in her body that had her clinging to my sister as they left the NICU.

Lis was sobbing so hard, her entire body trembled from the force of it. "Please," she whispered brokenly. "I know I have to, but please don't make me."

Nova didn't say anything as she kept her arms around Lis. Glancing at Guzman, she nodded toward the elevators, and he instructed one of the men to call for the car to be brought to the front entrance.

"Mom," Nova murmured, keeping her voice soothing for Lis's sake, but her eyes were hard as they trailed to Mom. "We should get going."

"I can stay—" Mom started to offer, but that only had Lis's head snapping up.

"No!"

Mom pressed her lips into a firm line but nodded. As they walked toward the elevator, Lis dug in her heels until Nova was practically dragging her. My sister was a strong little thing, but she couldn't take all of Lis's weight, and she nearly stumbled.

Without hesitation, I lifted Lis into my arms and stepped into the elevator as soon as the doors opened. At first, she struggled against me, but I simply pressed my face into her hair and inhaled the floral scent as we rode down to the ground floor. Guzman stepped out first, then my mother, with me following with Lis still in my arms, while Nova brought up the rear.

Mom and Nova climbed into the back, and I sat Lis beside my sister.

"Garret," she sobbed, grabbing hold of my hands when I tried to buckle her seat belt. "Please. Let me stay. Just a few more hours. Then I'll go home. I'll rest and eat and pump later. Please."

Swallowing with difficulty, I got her fastened in before turning my hands over in hers. "You're going to go home and do all those things now, Lis," I instructed firmly. "Once you've had a full night's sleep, you can come back in the morning. Guzman will drive you here as soon as you've had a complete breakfast."

Her tears gutted me, the plea in her blue eyes stealing the breath from my lungs. "What if something happens while I'm not here?" she cried. "What will she do if there's no one to hold her hand when they have to do something that hurts?"

"She will have someone to hold her hand for that," I promised.

"Nova is going with me," she argued. "And everyone is forcing me to leave. There won't be anyone—"

"I'll be here," I told her, my tone leaving no room for argument. "Her daddy will hold her hand while her mommy goes home and gets the rest she needs."

"But—"

I leaned in and tenderly pressed my lips to hers. It was the first time I'd gotten to kiss her in months, and it eased something inside me that had been tense, even though I'd seen with my own eyes that she was alive. It wasn't a passionate kiss, and she didn't kiss me back, but it quieted her arguments. When I finally forced myself to pull away, she touched her lips as if in a daze.

Stepping back, I slowly released her hands and closed the door. Guzman was sitting in the front passenger seat, and I met his gaze. There was a brief flash of respect in his eyes, before he gave me a chin lift and the driver pulled away.

After they were out of sight, I turned and went back into the hospital. Up on the NICU floor, I made sure the guards outside the doors didn't need a break before going inside. A nurse met me at the hand-washing station.

"Sir, Miss Ramirez has instructed us not to let you in," she said with regret.

"Call Nova Hannigan. I'm sure she will tell you that I have full access now." With a huff, she went to make the call, and I continued to wash my hands.

It was a process, like a doctor prepping for surgery. Washing up to my elbows, getting under my nails, scrubbing every inch in between. Rinse. Repeat. Once I was dry, I pulled on the protective covering that went over my clothes. By that time, the nurse had spoken to my sister and didn't give me any more trouble as I walked through the ward and straight up to my daughter's incubator.

Since my arrival, I'd told myself I was prepared to see Justice. That she wouldn't have anything to worry about because her daddy was there to make it all better. But I'd been too scared to even look at her, let alone attempt to make anything better for her.

Disgusted with myself, I pushed the self-deprecation down and finally looked at my baby girl for the very first time. Seeing that tiny body, smaller than a baby doll, attached to so many machines nearly brought me to my knees. It was a hard pill to swallow that I, a grown-ass man, wasn't even a tenth as strong or as brave as that little baby who would barely fit in one of my hands.

Blinking back tears, I gently placed one of my hands into the incubator and stroked my thumb over her fist. She reacted by wrapping her itty-bitty fingers around my digit and holding on. "Hey there, beautiful girl," I murmured, unsure if she could hear me or not, but needing to talk to her. "Daddy's here now. You don't have to worry. Just concentrate on getting better for Mommy. Daddy will take care of the rest."

Cali

SLOWLY, reality entered my sleep-fogged brain.
The ache in my body lessened with each passing day,
but I was still so sore that it was slow moving first
thing in the mornings.

Beside me, Nova mumbled in her sleep and
turned just enough to get comfortable. Her foot
wasn't nearly as swollen as it had been when she'd
first returned from New York, but it was still bruised.
She had it propped up on a high stack of pillows,
while her head rested on my arm. Night after night,
we fell asleep in my bed, with her promising
tomorrow would be better than the previous day.

It had been three weeks since I'd been released
from the hospital, leaving my little angel in the
NICU. During that time, she'd gained a little weight,
but we kept having other setbacks that delayed her

heart surgery. But today was the day. Justice was finally going to have the opening in her heart closed. It was the most troublesome of her disabilities caused by her extremely premature birth, and with it, we hoped that she would begin to thrive.

The night before, it had been difficult for both Nova and me to fall asleep, but once she had, it had been with a restlessness that had my friend tossing and turning for hours. I'd hugged her to me, wishing it were my little girl in my arms rather than her aunt. Around one, my brain had finally relented and let me get a few hours of sleep.

A glance at the clock showed me that we still had another two hours until we had to be at the hospital before Justice was taken into surgery. I hated being so far away from her. Even if the hospital itself wasn't more than an hour away, it might as well have been a thousand miles that separated me from her when I returned to the mansion each night.

But saying goodbye to my baby was a little easier, knowing that her daddy was there for her. Garret hadn't left the hospital once since my release. It had surprised me at first. He'd been so adamant that he couldn't handle me being out of his sight, but that had changed when I was released and had to leave our little girl behind. I needed to rest and recover from the C-section and hysterectomy. That meant traveling back and forth throughout the day so that I didn't overtire myself and eating the right foods regularly in order to produce enough milk to feed Justice.

Garret, however, slept in the waiting room each night. He was the first parent through the NICU doors each morning. He knew every move the nurses made where our daughter's care was concerned. I got a texted update at six every morning, when he went into the ward and spoke to the night nurse. Then another message after one of the many doctors came in to check on her. By the time I got to the hospital, I knew everything that had happened from the moment I'd left the previous night.

When he'd stayed behind the day I was released, I'd been torn. I didn't want him hanging around when he'd barely even looked at her to begin with. But at the same time, I'd been thankful to have someone there to hold her hand and report to me if something happened in the middle of the night. Mostly, I just didn't want Justice to be alone. I didn't want her to think that she'd been abandoned.

I wanted to hate him, but that became harder and harder to feel toward him when he was taking such good care of our little one.

All while handling the business side of things for the Ramirez company.

SACRIFICED

Nova had confessed to me that she'd given her brother half of her own holdings that I'd signed over to her. At first, I'd been upset, but then I realized it only made sense. Nova did a good job handling the company, but she wasn't a businesswoman at heart. Garret, on the other hand, had a degree in business, as well as apprenticing with the Vitucci family—in both the legal and not-so-legal aspects of their family-run businesses.

Between his long nights sleeping in the waiting room, followed by the even longer days, I'd expected Garret to be dead on his feet after three full weeks. But if he was exhausted, it didn't show. There were no dark circles under his eyes. Every morning when I saw him, he had a smile for me—even if it was grim at times depending on if Justice had a bad night or not.

Over the last week, she'd had more bad nights than good. Her surgery became more important with each passing day.

With a gasp, Nova suddenly sat upright in bed, her foot falling off the stack of pillows. "Did we over-sleep?" she mumbled, rubbing at her eyes.

It was still dark outside the window, but we always left the bathroom light on. I was a grown woman and still needed a night-light. It made me feel pathetic; the monster who had tortured me most of

289

my life was dead and gone, but I couldn't sleep without it on. I picked up my phone to show her the clock on the display. "We still have time," I assured her, easing into a sitting position beside her.

She sighed. "Thank goodness. Sit tight. I'm going to grab us some food, and then we can get ready. It won't hurt anything if we show up at the hospital earlier than expected. I won't be able to sit still if we wait around here, so I know you won't either."

While she rushed around, pulling on a cardigan over her sleep shorts and tank top and left the bedroom, I texted Garret.

Me: *Have you seen her yet this morning?*

Garret: *You should still be sleeping, blue eyes. But yes, I've seen her. She had a difficult night. Her apnea alarm went off more than usual, according to the night nurse. But her vitals are stable, and the doctor said the surgery is still going ahead as scheduled.*

I was scared to death of Justice going through this surgery, yet I was relieved that everything was proceeding as planned. Any number of things could go wrong. She very well might not even make it through the operation. But like her cardiologist had once told me, her chances without it were a hell of a lot smaller than with it.

Garret: *I wish you would get more rest, but I know you're too anxious to listen. Try to eat some-*

thing before you leave. I'll call Guzman and make sure everything is ready for you by the time you leave. Bring your pump and supplies with you so you don't get uncomfortable while we wait. The surgeon said it could take a while, depending on how every-thing goes.

I was torn on how to respond to his second text. Part of me wanted to yell at him that I could tell Guzman myself, and I sure as hell didn't need him to remind me to bring my breast pump. I didn't go anywhere without it and enough snacks to keep me constantly producing the milk that was helping Justice gain weight.

At first, she hadn't been able to tolerate my breast milk, but as I'd eliminated certain foods from my diet, she'd started digesting it better and gained the weight needed.

Another part of me—which was secretly bigger—melted over how he was always watching out for me, even from the hospital. He was constantly texting Maria to tell her to make my favorites, and the ones that had the ingredients Justice couldn't tolerate, he'd found substitute recipes so I could still eat things I enjoyed without it harming our baby. He knew more about Guzman's every move than I did, and the head of security was rarely away from me unless I was taking a nap.

The bedroom door opened, and Felicity walked in, carrying a tray. It held fruit and gluten-free cereal with non-dairy milk and a glass of orange juice. I set the phone aside and gave her a small smile as she placed the tray over my lap. Our relationship was still strained, but I was slowly getting over her forcing Garret back into my life.

I'd relented and began allowing her in to see Justice a few times each day. With her son having full access to her granddaughter, she wasn't nearly as prickly with me, but that didn't mean I was going to trust her fully. She'd let me down when I'd needed her to have my back the most. I'd learned at a young age that forgiveness was one thing, but putting my full faith in someone again was a recipe for heartache.

"Maria is already packing your food for the day," Felicity said with a smile. Her bloodshot eyes suggested she'd had just as much of a restless night as Nova and I had. "The car is already out front, so as soon as you are dressed, we can leave. But not until you eat everything on this tray."

My stomach was in knots, the food on the tray holding zero appeal, but I knew if I didn't eat, my milk supply would be low for the day, and even a few ounces less than usual was unacceptable. I would not be the reason my daughter didn't get the nutrition she needed.

After forcing down the majority of the meal, I drained the glass of juice and eased out of bed. A shower and change of clothes later, I left my hair to air-dry and climbed into the back of the SUV with Guzman's help. Once I was settled, I realized he still held on to my hand.

When I glanced up, he gave me an odd look while his fingers squeezed mine gently. "She's going to be okay, little one."

Emotion clogged my throat, and all I could do was nod, giving him a smile that felt tremulous. Releasing my hand, he lifted his to stroke over my damp hair. It was a tender, parental action that made something flip in my brain. I blinked at him a few times at a faded memory of being a small child and having my father do the same thing.

I shook it from my head, feeling oddly queasy all of a sudden.

My real father had died when I was a toddler. I didn't remember much about him, and the few times I'd asked my mother what he'd died of, she'd just said, "This life, this life took him from us, Cali." As I'd gotten older and seen what Matias's lifestyle was like, I realized it could have been a thousand different things that could have ended my biological father's life.

He'd been the reason we'd moved to Colombia in the first place. She'd met him when she was seventeen, while he'd been in the States studying at some university—which one, I didn't know because my mother had never gone into detail. When her family found out she was pregnant with me, they'd kicked her out, and my father had quit school to return home.

Not long after his death, my mother had met Matias, and they'd dated for a year or so before getting married.

"Cali?"

I jerked at the sound of Nova's voice beside me. Blinking away the memories of my childhood, I glanced over at her. "Yeah?"

"We're here," she murmured, nudging my leg with her knee. "Guzman has been standing there waiting for you to take his hand for like two minutes."

Startled, I looked up at the head of security, and instantly, the old memory replayed in my head. A shadowy man, his work-roughened hand stroking over my hair. The gruff way he'd called me "little one" in Spanish. Indigestion made me belch, and I had to fight to keep bile from lifting into my throat, but I placed my hand in Guzman's rough palm and let him help me out.

Nova exited behind me, carrying the case that held all my breast pump supplies, while Felicity carried the cooler that had my food for the day. As we all entered the hospital, the driver pulled away, leaving only Guzman as our private security until we reached the NICU, where two fresh guards had taken over for the night shift.

As was our routine, Nova and Felicity went to the waiting room, where another guard was stationed, while I went into the NICU. I washed up and got ready to enter the ward, my heart thumping at triple its normal rate as I walked to where Garret was already waiting with the day nurse and a doctor I didn't recognize.

Seeing me, Garret held out his hand, and I grasped it without thinking, desperately needing his touch. "Baby, this is the anesthesiologist."

I nodded in greeting before my gaze went to Justice. "So, this is it? She's really going to have the operation today? There isn't another delay?"

"It's really happening," the man informed me, his tone thankfully soothing. "Miss Justice is the first on the schedule this morning, and I assure you, I'll be with her the entire time. The procedure can take anywhere from one to three hours, depending on any issues the cardiologist might run into while he's in there. You will be alerted via text during the entire process. When she's put under, when the cardiologist has opened her up…"

I clutched at Garret, wrapping my other hand around his arm as I reminded myself that this was all necessary for our little girl's survival. I swallowed with difficulty, but I didn't hide my face against him as I really wanted to.

The doctor continued when I straightened my shoulders, showing him I could take whatever else he had to explain to us. "And so on. Once she's closed up, she will go to recovery until the anesthesia wears off. That can take an hour or several, it just depends on how well she tolerates everything. When she wakes up, we will assess her pain levels. But again, you will get text alerts about every change in her and her condition."

"O-okay," I said, proud of myself when my voice didn't crack too loudly. I didn't want Justice to hear how nervous I was. She needed good vibes and to know her parents were confident in the medical staff to patch her up. To get her back to us safe and sound.

"I just need to get your signatures on the consent for treatment, and I'll get out of your way," the doctor said with a kind smile. "Miss Justice will be prepped while the rest of us are scrubbing in. Take a moment to be with her, and then she will be taken down to the OR."

My eyes widened at the speed everything was moving. If I hadn't gotten up earlier than planned, would I have missed this chance to kiss her before she went into surgery?

Garret's name had been added to her birth certificate, so he signed first, and then the clipboard was offered to me. Almost blindly, I scribbled my name across the appropriate line, before shoving it back at Garret to give to the doctor. I was too busy moving closer to the incubator so I could take Justice out for one more skin-to-skin moment.

Unbuttoning my shirt, I lifted her to my chest and held her as I'd been taught with all the cords and tubes still connected to her tiny body. Blinking back my tears, I touched my trembling lips to her forehead. "You're going to do great," I whispered to her. "The doctors are going to take good care of you, sweet girl. Mommy and Daddy won't be far, so don't be scared."

Garret came up beside me, his huge hand on her back practically swallowing her up. He rubbed his thumb over her arm, and he bent to brush his lips over her small cheek. "Daddy loves you, princess," he told her, his voice thick with emotion. "Don't be afraid."

Our gazes locked over her little head, the both of us fighting the tears that wanted to spill over, but we refused to let them in front of her. I nearly whimpered when I saw the love that was in his green eyes.

At that moment, I wanted to believe it, but I was almost more afraid of loving him back than I was of letting Justice go into surgery.

Garret

THE MOMENT the nurse took Justice from Lis, I knew I only had a matter of seconds to get her out of there before she lost it. The baby was placed back in the incubator, and Lis began to shake as she tried in vain to hold on to her emotions. Pulling her into me, I hid her face in my chest as I guided her out of the ward and down the corridor to the waiting room.

Immediately after the door shut behind us, a sob left her that was hauntingly similar to the heart-broken sound my own mother had made months before. When I'd taken her home following what we'd thought was Nova's funeral and she'd curled up on my sister's bed—that sound had echoed in my head for weeks. But the one that came from Lis would remain with me until my dying day. The cry stabbed through my heart, and I gripped her tighter, rocking her against me as I allowed my own tears to flow freely.

"What's happened?" Mom demanded, touching a hand to both of our backs.

"They just took her for surgery," I informed her quietly.

"Already?" Nova whispered, wrapping her arms around us from the other side.

"Yeah," I choked out, trying to remain strong for my woman. But thinking of Justice, all alone as she went through something grown adults were frightened of, was killing me. She shouldn't have had to go through this at such a vulnerable age—or at all, damn it. Closing my eyes, I breathed in the light floral scent of Lis's shampoo in an attempt to ground myself. "We... Um, we should get texts telling us what's going on with her as it happens."

"Okay," Nova said, trying to sound brave for us. "Let's get you two into a chair. Cali needs to eat again. And she's going to need to pump soon."

My legs felt unsteady as I found the first chair and dropped down on it, pulling Lis into my lap. She curled into a ball in my arms, trying to make herself as small as possible to either hide from her pain or hold it in—I wasn't sure which. I cupped the back of her head, holding it against my shoulder as I kissed her brow. "Baby, you need to eat."

"My stomach feels sick," she sniffled, rubbing her running nose against my shirt.

"Mine too, babe," I admitted. "But you need to eat for Justice."

More tears filled her already swollen eyes, but she gave a tiny nod. Nova pushed a mug of something into my hands, and I lifted it to Lis's lips, urging her to drink the soup.

"It doesn't have egg, dairy, or wheat in it, does it, sis?" I asked as Lis continued to drink.

"No," she assured me, dashing her fingers over her own tears. "Maria makes all of Cali's food separately from everyone else's. There's actually a smaller kitchen that was meant for staff use in the past. She's using it just for Cali's meals so there isn't any cross contamination."

My throat was too tight to respond, so I just nodded and continued to hold the mug to Lis's lips. A wrap of some kind was placed in my hand, and I lifted my brows, again to confirm it was free of all the foods that would hurt Justice. Her digestive system found them difficult to process. If Lis ate any of them, even if it was just a trace amount, it would affect our daughter.

"Gluten-free tortilla wrap. Grilled chicken, lettuce, and tomato with a little Italian dressing that is completely allergen-friendly," Nova explained patiently.

I exchanged the soup for the wrap, holding it to Lis's mouth so she could take small bites. Luckily, she got half of it down, and then she grew uncomfortable. While Nova had been making sure Lis was fed, Mom was busy setting up the breast pump, getting everything ready to go.

Shooting a glare at the guard, I jerked my head at the door, and he quickly excused himself. On his way out, I realized that Guzman was absent, but I didn't have time to wonder where the head of security was or what the fuck he was doing.

Mom brought over the pump and Lis tried to get off my lap, but I locked my arms around her, holding her in place. She huffed but didn't argue as she widened her already unbuttoned shirt and then pulled at the cups of her nursing bra, freeing both breasts at the same time so she could pump.

While she worked on gathering milk for Justice, I ate a little of the food in the cooler. My stomach was tied up in knots, but I forced the food down so that I would be alert for Justice's sake.

We'd already gotten the notification that Justice was sedated, and a short time later, we received a message that the pediatric cardiologist had opened her chest. I could picture it all in my head, and it made the chicken wrap sit heavy in my stomach. But I fought the urge to puke, needing to be strong for Lis's sake.

Time seemed to stand still, yet pass in the blink of an eye. Every time my phone buzzed with a new text, my gut would clench and the urge to puke would intensify until I read the message.

"The opening has been closed," I read aloud, and all three women seemed to release their held breaths as one.

Another half an hour passed before the next text came in. "They just took her into recovery," I choked out. I was still holding on to Lis, and she curled her arm around my neck, letting out a small, relieved laugh.

"It's over?" she said with a tiny whimper.

"Her surgery is," I confirmed. "Now we wait until we can see her."

"But she's okay, right?" Lis asked, lifting her head. Her blue eyes drilled into mine, begging—demanding—that I give her an affirmative answer.

"There was no news of any complications," I said instead, not wanting to give her false information in case something happened between Justice going into the recovery ward and us seeing our baby again.

"Time to eat," Mom said with a smile.

Without hesitation, Lis took the wrap from Mom and ate it a little quicker than she had the first one, before swallowing it down with a fresh mug of soup. Guzman still hadn't joined us, and I was getting curious as to where the hell he was, but I wasn't about to leave Lis to go find him.

Another hour passed, and a new text message with it. "She's starting to come out from the seda- tion," I announced. "But they seem to be having issues with her pain level. The cardiologist has been with her the entire time, but he will be out to speak to us soon."

"What does that mean?" Nova asked from beside me where she was eating the orange she'd just peeled.

"I don't know, except she's in a lot of pain."

"I don't like this," Lis whispered, turning on my lap. "Does it say when we can see her?"

"No, babe. It just gave an update. Don't worry. The doc will give us a detailed report soon." She bit her lip and laid her head on my shoulder. I kissed her brow, to comfort myself just as much as her. "It's going to be okay."

"Yeah," she murmured unsteadily.

It wasn't much longer before the door opened, and the cardiologist came in. He wasn't smiling, but he didn't look upset either, so I had to take that as a good sign. I started to stand with Lis, but he waved me back into the chair and walked over to join us.

"Everything went as well as I could have hoped for during surgery," he informed us. "She remained stable throughout the entire procedure. The opening was slightly bigger than anticipated, but it was easy to close."

"That's all good news," Lis murmured, almost to herself, and I rubbed my hand up and down her back.

"Once the sedation started wearing off, Justice quickly let us know that she was in pain. Her vitals became unstable, and we've been working to keep her comfortable to avoid any more issues." He scrubbed his hands over his face and into his hair before squeezing the back of his neck. "She's stable now, but the next few days are going to be critical. We will have to ensure her pain is consistently under control, while also watching to make sure she doesn't encounter complications such as hypoglycemia or hypocalcemia. We will also monitor her closely for any signs of infection."

"Wh-what can I do to help her?" Lis rasped.

"Everything that you've been doing prior to surgery. Getting her the nutrition she needs. Physical contact, although you can't do the skin-to-skin for a brief time as her chest heals. Stay as calm as you can while visiting with her. Keeping her as stress-free as possible is key at the moment."

"Okay." She nodded in acceptance. "We will do whatever Justice needs us to do. When can I see her?"

"She's going to be in the recovery unit overnight. I'll be there with her, personally monitoring her round-the-clock. If she becomes distressed, I can handle it immediately. Tomorrow, if she's showing signs that her pain levels aren't as intense, we can move her back to the NICU, and you can see her then."

"No," Lis growled. "That's unacceptable. She needs to know we're here, that we didn't leave her."

The doctor patted her on the arm. "I assure you, dear, she isn't aware of anything other than when she's in pain. I realize your instinct as her mother is to be with her, but you need to put your faith in me to treat her during this critical time. I promise that I will treat your baby as my own child."

"I've been that child who was supposed to have people treat her as if she were their own. That shit didn't end well." Lis shifted, getting into the doctor's personal space, turning into the dangerous momma bear that only wanted to protect her cub. "I'm her mother. I'll know if she's in pain or not. Just let me see her. Let me touch her hand, her foot. Anything!"

Her plea was agony to hear, but I wrapped her in my arms and rocked her as the doctor told us he would keep us informed as the day went on, but that we should think about going home to rest. I barely noticed his exit from the waiting room.

"No!" Lis cried, her nails biting through the material of my shirt and slicing the skin on my chest. But I didn't feel the discomfort of the scrapes. My heart was too heavy, too full of fear for my child, to feel anything. All I wanted to do was take away the pain that Justice was experiencing. "I can't leave her. Even if I can't be with her, I can't leave. Not now. Not this time. She's in *pain*, Garret."

"We won't," I vowed, kissing the top of her head. "I promise, baby. We'll stay here all night. We won't leave Justice."

She curled into a ball on my lap again, needing me to make it all better. To protect her and our baby girl. But as much as I wanted to, I knew I couldn't protect Justice from what she was going through at that moment. "We can't leave her," she whispered brokenly.

"We won't." I kissed her brow, her cheek, the top of her head again. "We will stay right here until the end of time, if that's what it takes. No one will move us until we have seen Justice again."

"P-promise?" she sobbed into my chest.

"I swear it, baby." Clenching my eyes closed, I prayed that I hadn't just lied to her.

For both our sakes.

Cali

I THOUGHT...HOPED—FUCKING *prayed,* even though I'd given up on God hearing my pleas long ago—that after Justice had her heart repaired, that would be the end of it. Everything else would begin to resolve itself because there wasn't so much pressure on her poor little heart.

Instead, it led to a weeklong battle of her blood pressure skyrocketing to stroke level one minute, only to crash the next. It was a hundred times more stressful than when I was pregnant with her or the weeks before her surgery took place. Her entire itty-bitty body swelled to more than twice its size because of fluid retention. According to the cardiologist and the nurses, it was normal following heart surgery.

With medication, the edema began to ease, but we were told that Justice would likely be on the drug for a while. I hated when they gave me timelines like that. What the fuck did "for a while" even mean? I needed it broken down for me in days, weeks, months—I would even accept years, damn it. But her recovery was a wait-and-see process, not one that could be measured by a calendar.

As the days passed, Justice thankfully started showing signs of improvement. She was taking more milk, acting like she was starving more often than not, and no longer seemed to be in the excruciating pain she had been in. Every time I saw her wiggle around without her vitals setting off alarms that would make my heart stop, I was able to relax a little more.

Maybe it would be a slow process, but I could accept that. Slow was better than not at all, or her getting worse.

Having Garret at my side, day and night, as we urged our daughter to fight—cheering her on through even the smallest of victories—made it easier. Without realizing it, I began to appreciate that he was there for the long haul this time around. If he could help me through the most terrifying moments a parent had to live through, then I figured he wasn't ever going to go anywhere.

Did I still want to slap the stupid out of him for shutting down on me the night I confessed everything to him all those months before? Hell yeah. But I didn't. Having to go through the same fear of losing Justice was more than enough punishment for him to experience without me adding physical violence to the torture.

"I need to make a phone call," Garret murmured quietly in my ear after the cardiologist had given us the latest update on Justice.

I leaned into him for a moment before nodding and turning my attention back to the day nurse. She had her own report to give us, and with Nova beside me, we listened intently for the next twenty minutes.

"She's healing really well, Mommy," the nurse said with a smile as she finished. "And by this time next week, it is likely that we can start the skin-to-skin again. That also means that we can start training her to bottle-feed as well."

"Really!" I whisper-shouted, bouncing from one foot to the other. "I can possibly start feeding her myself soon?"

She laughed quietly. "It's on our goal chart."

I turned to Nova, and we grabbed each other's hands at the same time, the two of us doing a little happy dance that had the nurse laughing even harder.

"Now comes the part I know you're not going to

want to hear, but it needs to be said," the nurse said, growing serious once again.

I stopped dancing and frowned at her. "What?" I mumbled, sounding petulant even to my own ears.

"With Miss Justice doing so well, we all think that you and Daddy need to go home and get a full night's sleep." I opened my mouth to argue, but she lifted a hand to stop me. None of us had gone back to the mansion since Justice's surgery. Not even Felicity or Nova. As for Guzman, he spent more time in the chapel than anywhere else.

The first time I'd seen him coming out of the small room, I'd been on my way back from the bathroom. He hadn't spotted me, and I'd watched him scrub away a stray tear before he'd released a pent-up sigh and then walked back to the waiting room. The moment had left me speechless.

And with questions I wasn't sure I wanted the answers to.

That faded memory kept haunting me, whether I was awake or asleep. I relived it at least once a day, and I disliked where it took my mind, along with the possibilities I kept coming up with.

Shaking those thoughts away, I blinked at the nurse. "Thanks for the suggestion, but—"

"No buts," she tutted. "If you don't get enough sleep, you're going to end up in a hospital room of your own. Then you won't get to visit with Justice at all. Go home, shower, eat, sleep for more than a few hours at a time, and then come back first thing in the morning."

"She's right, Cali," Nova said. "Consider it an early birthday present to me. It's the day after tomorrow, and I think all of us getting a full eight hours of sleep would be the best gift I've gotten all year."

I bit my lip, torn between wanting to stay near my baby and knowing that what the nurse said was true. Then there was Nova, who had been my saving grace —my own personal guardian angel—and I'd completely forgotten that she was turning eighteen in just a couple of days.

"Okay." I gave in after a moment. "But if anything changes, someone better call me."

"We will, Miss Ramirez," the nurse assured me with a kind smile. "And you can be right back here first thing in the morning. I'll even call you with an update on Justice before the end of my shift this evening."

"O-okay," I choked out. Unable to stop myself, I reached into the incubator, and Justice grasped my finger as always. Her grip got stronger by the day. Smiling, I whispered, "Love you, sweet angel. Mommy and Daddy will be back tomorrow. I promise."

As I pulled back, Nova threaded her arm through mine, and we left the NICU together. "She's getting so big," my friend exclaimed as soon as we were outside the ward. "And not in the bad, scary way with all that fluid buildup. I mean, she's doubled in size since her birth. And there's all that peach fuzz on her head! I wonder what color her eyes will be?"

"Probably green like every other Hannigan in the world. Except for Max, but that doesn't count. Bash's DNA is just too dominant," Felicity commented, overhearing our conversation. She was standing with Guzman, waiting on us. There was a three-person limit per patient in the NICU, but she'd gone in with Nova and Guzman earlier to visit with her grand-daughter.

They hadn't stayed long, and I'd seen Guzman heading straight for the chapel before I'd gone in to speak to the doctor. Now he was back from doing whatever he did in there; I suspected it was lighting a candle and praying for Justice, but I wasn't sure.

"Mom, we're going back to the mansion for the day," Nova informed her mother. "I'm going to eat half the batch of enchiladas that Maria was working on when I spoke to her earlier, and then I'm going to sleep for the next twelve hours."

Guzman opened the waiting room door for us,

while Felicity laughed at her daughter's enthusiasm. "I like that plan. I hope Maria made enough."

"I'm hungry too," I said with a laugh. "I've been forcing food down for days, but my stomach is finally working again, and I would kill for a giant cheeseburger from that diner back in New York."

"Me too!" Nova and Felicity said in unison, making the three of us laugh.

"See you soon," Garret said, drawing my gaze just as he hung up his phone and quickly pocketed it. I eyed him suspiciously, but it wasn't me he avoided looking at when he crossed to us. It was his mom and sister. "What's all the commotion, ladies?"

"We're going home," I told him with a sigh. "The nurse talked me into it, and I think we should all get some rest tonight."

His green eyes widened. "You sure, baby? I can stay, and you can go back for a nap."

"No." I shook my head and reached for his hand. "Let's go home. Please?"

His fingers entwined with mine, and he pulled me into his space. "Okay. Guzman can drive Mom and Nova, and I'll drive us."

From the glint in his eyes, I could see he had something he wanted to tell me, so I nodded and followed the others out of the waiting room. Both SUVs were waiting by the time we got to the lobby. I hugged Felicity and Nova as Guzman waited for them to get into the back of the first car.

Once they were settled, Guzman turned to me. "I would like a word later, if you have time, little one."

My muscles, which had only just started to relax now that Justice seemed to be out of the woods, tightened with tension all over again, but I found myself agreeing before taking the front passenger seat of the second SUV. Garret shut my door and exchanged a few words with the head of security before taking his place behind the wheel.

"Okay," I said, forgetting about Guzman for the moment and eyeballing my baby's father. "What did you do, and how likely is it that your sister is going to slit your throat for doing it?"

He snorted in amusement, and it was in that moment that I realized he actually had no clue how deadly his sister could be when provoked. Felicity didn't seem to suspect it either, from what I could tell. Which was bizarre to me, because the Hannigan family appeared so close. How the hell did no one know that the sweet little blonde they loved so much had the skills of an assassin?

I kept those thoughts to myself, while Garret took his time pulling onto the road that would take us back to the mansion. Only then did he answer. "You know that Nova turns eighteen the day after tomorrow?"

"I'd forgotten about it until she mentioned it earlier," I admitted, a little crestfallen at letting it slip my mind.

"Well, I just arranged her present," he said, throwing me a smug grin before turning his gaze back on the road ahead. "Ryan is flying out to California to pick up my dad. They should be here by morning."

"Oh dear lord," I muttered, covering my face with both hands. "Garret, your mom and sister are going to murder you."

"Nah," he said with a laugh. "Trust me on this, babe. If it weren't for how sick Justice has been, I know Mom would have already gone back to Creswell Springs to get Dad. The two of them would have been down here straightaway, because my dad would want to be close to his first grandbaby just as much as Mom. As for Nova…"

My neck hurt from how tense I was as I waited for him to continue.

"Nova doesn't belong here, blue eyes. Her place is in New York, with Ryan." I quickly turned my head away to hide the sudden tears that filled my eyes. Garret grasped my wrist and tugged, urging me to look at him again. "Baby, I know she's like a security blanket for you. From what I've been told, she saved you from Manuel. But just because she's in New York doesn't mean she's going to love you any less."

"I should be used to this by now," I whispered. "Everyone leaves me eventually."

"Hey, I'm not ever going to leave you again," he promised, his voice so full of conviction, I couldn't help but believe him. Trusting him became a little easier each day. "And Nova isn't leaving forever. She will visit us as often as she can. You and Justice mean the world to her."

"But are you sure this is what Nova wants?" I asked, legitimately concerned for his well-being if it turned out that she didn't want to see Ryan.

He laughed deeply. "There is no Ryan without Nova. They are meant to be, Lis. Just like you and me."

"Are we?" I murmured quietly.

"Abso-fucking-lutely," he growled. "The first thing we're doing as soon as Justice is released from the hospital is getting married. We'll have to wait a little while for the honeymoon because neither one of us will want to leave her right away after she's home. Maybe for our five-year anniversary, we'll take a long trip together while Nova watches our baby girl."

My heart rate started increasing with every word out of his mouth. "That…That's a lot of plans you've made for our future, gangster. During any of these ideas for a wedding and honeymoon, did the thought of actually asking me to marry you happen to pop up anywhere?"

"Plenty of times. I'm just waiting for the perfect time to propose, blue eyes." He lifted my hand and kissed my ring finger without taking his eyes off the road. "And then there's the whole fear that you might say no…"

There was a hint of real fear in his voice that tugged at my heartstrings. Turning my head toward the side window, I hid my smile. "Guess you will just have to ask and find out, huh?"

He was quiet for a few miles before blowing out a long exhale. "Yeah, I guess I will."

Cali

AFTER DINNER, Felicity and Nova went up to bed. I was glad that they didn't wait around, because I wasn't sure if I could have kept Garret's surprise a secret from either of them if they had.

I was tired but restless. With all the time I'd been cooped up in the hospital both personally and then watching over Justice, I wanted fresh air. While Garret went into the office to handle something that had come up with work, I stepped out into the garden. Before she'd gotten sick, this had been my mother's favorite place, especially in the evening with the sun setting in the distance, casting a beautiful kaleidoscope of oranges, yellows, and reds across the horizon.

Stopping at her favorite bench, I sat and watched as the day turned to twilight. The temperature was in the high sixties, but it was quickly starting to lower, turning the air crisp. I loved this time of year the most. The chill in the air had always meant Christmas was just around the corner. My wish was that the following year, Justice would be home—happy and healthy—and we would start decorating for the holiday. She might not be walking by then, but she could sit and watch the lights while Garret put the star on top of the tree. Her sweet giggles would fill the entire house, and I wouldn't have a worry in the world...

"Little one?"

Pulled from my fantasy, I looked up to find Guzman standing a few feet away. His stance was tense and unsure. Seeing the vulnerability in him had me sitting up a little straighter. "Guzman, did something happen? The hospital—"

"Hasn't called," he rushed to assure me. "I was hoping... Do you have time for our chat?"

The faded memory that had been haunting me flashed before my eyes, and I lowered my gaze to the flowers on the ground in front of me. "Yes," I responded. "If you need to speak to me, now is as good a time as any."

I heard him shuffle his weight from one foot to the other several times before he walked over to the bench and sat beside me. I'd only known Guzman a short time before I'd gone to the States with Manuel that last time and then ran away. Back then, and in the months since I'd returned, I hadn't witnessed him being anything but confident. I'd quickly put my trust in him and appointed him the head of security, but the truth was, I barely knew him.

"Your mother always loved those flowers."

"Heliconia, the false bird of paradise," I murmured, smiling at the beautiful flower that Matias had planted throughout the garden for my mother. "She would sit here and just look at them for hours."

But then a realization hit me, causing me to snap my head up and around to look at him. "How did you know that?" I demanded. "You didn't work here when my mother was alive. It was only a few years ago that you were hired."

He grimaced and clasped his hands together. It took him several moments before he finally answered, and it only left me with more questions. "Before I came to work here, I was in prison... In America."

"What for?" I asked, curious about his past.

"Matias Ramirez set me up," he said with a casual shrug, while the air around us seemed to snap and crackle with the emotions that vibrated off him. "He'd seen your mother and me at a party, and he fell for her on sight. But she was my wife. Loyal and in love with me. At least, I thought she was. When she got pregnant with you, she'd given up her entire life in the States to come back to Colombia with me."

The oxygen in my lungs whooshed out, and for a moment, I felt light-headed. "You…and…my…m-mother?" I whispered, unable to formulate a full sentence all at once.

"She was the love of my life. My wife. The mother of my child." There was pain in his voice, but his eyes bored into mine, demanding I believe him. Oddly enough, I did. "And Matias stole her from me. He stole you both. I was in New York on business. My family didn't have the money that Ramirez did, but we weren't poor. I had to travel regularly. The last time, he had one of his people plant drugs in my luggage. As I got off the plane, the police were already waiting to search my things. There was enough cocaine in my checked bag to put me away for a decade."

I jumped to my feet, needing to pace, to think. He'd just dumped a lot on me, but he wasn't done.

"My family spent a lot of money to get me released, but they ended up bankrupting their company for nothing. By the time I accepted that I would be in prison for years, your mother had filed for divorce. I didn't want to lose her, but not signing would have denied her the freedom she deserved. My family hadn't liked her to begin with, and they were making her miserable. I agreed to the divorce, thinking she would return to America and her family."

Leaning forward, he rested his forearms on his thighs. His face tightened in anger. "But I was wrong. Two years later, a lawyer brought me adoption papers. Matias Ramirez wanted to adopt my little girl." His voice changed, turning colder. "I was told if I didn't sign them, Ramirez would arrange for one of the inmates to kill me in my sleep and my signature wouldn't be needed. I signed, but I didn't sleep for more than a week, thinking he would still arrange to have me murdered."

"Matias was ruthless when it came to getting what he wanted," I admitted. "But...he was good to me."

"No, little one, he wasn't," Guzman denied hoarsely. "He didn't protect you. He didn't pay attention when you needed him the most. He might have given you material things, said he loved you, left his billions to you. But where was he when you were being harmed by his sadistic son?"

I flinched and turned my head away, shame staining my cheeks.

"It wasn't your fault, Calista. The adults in your life failed you."

"I-I know," I agreed weakly, but a part of me still felt like if I had only been stronger, braver, then I could have stopped Manuel myself.

"When I got out of prison, I was angry. I returned to Colombia, determined to confront your mother. If nothing else, I at least wanted to have custodial rights to you. But I learned right away that she had died, and when Ramirez found out I was trying to see you, he gave orders to kill me on sight."

I stopped pacing to look down at him. "Then how did you get a job here?"

"It took a while, but Matias started losing his memory, and Manuel took over. He didn't know who I was. That idiot didn't know anything but how to snort coke. He was the one who hired me. But you were in the States more often than not at the time. I had to prove myself, so I was given work that kept me away from the mansion. Matias was ill, and Manuel took you with him every time he took the old man for treatments in New York. I was making plans to steal you away when you returned."

"And then I ran away." Nova had helped me escape my tormentor.

"Yes," he agreed. "My first thought was to find

you, but Manuel was so angry. He kept talking about what he was going to do to you if he got his hands on you. He was manic and high most of the time, talking nonsense. I didn't know who Sheena O'Brion was, but he kept mentioning her. I decided to stick around, just in case. When he took you and brought you back here, I was gone. He'd ordered several men to watch the coke fields, said he was going to take them back and to await his signal. I guess he was waiting for Vitucci's guard to be down from the loss of Nova, and then he would take the fields back by force."

"Probably," I muttered.

"I was there for a week before Maria called me, so it was before you were even taken from New York. She hadn't seen Manuel bring you in, but when she heard female screams coming from the dungeon, she let me know right away. She remembered me from before, when your mother was my wife. She knew you were my daughter."

I sucked in a surprised gasp. "She tried to help me once, but it didn't end well for her. She was lucky Manuel didn't kill her."

"She's never mentioned it to me…" He drifted off, his eyes going vacant for a moment as he considered what I'd told him. Shaking his head, he continued. "I was just coming in the door when Nova shot the bastard on the stairs." His lips tilted up in a ghost of a smile. "She nearly shot me but stopped at the last second. Her reflexes are...unnaturally well trained."

"And then some," I said with a tight laugh. "I think Anya Vitucci got her hands on Nova at a young age. But she hasn't confided in me whether that is true or not."

"I've heard of the Vitucci queen," Guzman said, his voice full of awe. "If what you say is true, then Nova is a very valuable asset."

"She's probably going to leave us in a few days," I confided. It surprised me that I so easily believed him, but the pain and anger in his voice as he'd explained left no doubt in my mind that he spoke the truth.

Yet I didn't know how I felt about all of it. My mother told me my father died; obviously, that was a lie. All that time, I'd had someone out there in the world who cared about me, wanted to be a part of my life—would have protected me from Manuel, damn it.

And she'd denied me that.

Maybe she didn't know what would happen to me after her death, but she should have at least told me that my biological father was still alive. It should have been my decision to make if I wanted him to be a part of my life or not. After she was gone, I'd needed someone, and though Matias had loved me in his own way, he'd been blind to the danger I was in beneath the roof we shared.

My mother had been selfish, something I never would have suspected from her. But as I looked back, it all became glaringly obvious to me. She was definitely not the person I had thought her to be.

We were both quiet for a long moment before I glanced at Guzman again. "Is Guzman your real name?"

"My full legal name is Juan Guzman Gómez. It's the name that should have been on your original birth certificate."

"I never saw it," I admitted. "I've only seen the one that has Matias as my father after he adopted me."

"I figured as much," he said sadly.

"Do you have any family left?"

He shook his head. "My parents both passed while I was in prison, and I didn't have any siblings."

"I'm sorry."

"As am I," he said gently. "I'm sorry I failed you."

"You didn't." I tried to reassure him. "You couldn't have known what was going on here. Matias fucked you over."

"That he did, little one. That he did."

Another long silence descended on us, but it didn't feel uncomfortable. I was still unsure how I felt about having a father again, but I felt no resentment for him in my heart.

"Why are you telling me all of this now?"

He took both of my hands in a tender hold. "I've wanted to confess everything from the moment you arrived in Colombia again. But you were already under so much stress with the difficult pregnancy. Then once Justice was born, you were in so much pain—both physically and emotionally. I didn't want to add more to your shoulders. Since the baby's heart surgery, I've struggled with the decision to tell you or not. I have spent many hours in the chapel, praying for my granddaughter to get well, but also for a sign to show me what I should do."

"You're right," I said, looking down at his much bigger hands holding my smaller ones. "I wouldn't have been ready to hear any of this during that time. But I...I'm not sure what to do with this new information." His face tightened with grief, and I quickly continued. "I don't blame you for anything, Guzman. Over the past several months, you have been with me when I've needed a parental figure the most. I'm very thankful for that. I just... I don't know how to wrap my mind around this, that's all."

"I understand," he said, sadness causing him to sound choked up.

"Give me a few days. Let my brain catch up. And then we can talk again."

"Talk about what?" Garret's voice demanded, causing my head to snap up to find him standing nearby. But his gaze wasn't on me. Those pissed green orbs were on how Guzman was holding my hands. "What the fuck is going on here?"

I rolled my eyes at him. "Oh, shut up, Garret."

"Shut up?" he repeated, practically seething. "I come out here to see if you're all right, and I find you with the head of security—"

"Who is also my father," I snapped back.

"Your…" His voice trailed off, and his whole stance relaxed. "Oh. Yeah, okay, that explains a lot." The dumbass stepped closer. "Are you ready for bed, baby?"

Guzman got to his feet, releasing my hands as he did, only to put them on my shoulders. Lowering his head, he kissed my brow. "Take all the time you need to process, little one. I'm not going anywhere."

"Thank you," I rasped, watching him walk through the garden and toward the garage in the distance.

Garret wrapped his arm around me from behind, and I leaned into him, needing his strength but still pissed at him. "You're such a dickhead."

"Not going to argue with you, blue eyes. I'm a

jealous man who loves you. I see someone else touching you, my brain goes crazy."

"Idiot," I muttered.

"Again, I'm not going to argue with you."

"Good," I said, and I actually found myself snickering. "Let's go to bed."

"You don't have to tell me twice. I'm ready for a full night's sleep in an actual bed."

Garret

I WAS the first one up the next morning. It was still dark outside, and I rushed to get everything ready for the day. I'd gotten a call from the night nurse that Justice had an easy night, which was a relief, but not the sole reason I was in a rush to get to the hospital.

With my daughter out of the danger zone, all we had to do now was play the waiting game. It was going to take time before she was able to come home, but she only got stronger as each day passed. Which meant it was time for Mom and Nova to get their shit together.

I directed Maria to pack enough food for everyone, then found Guzman. He was outside, talking to the men who already had the vehicles pulled in front of the mansion. I took him aside, telling him what I needed him to do.

"Hannigan I can handle, but Vitucci?" He raised skeptical brows at me. "It doesn't matter that Ramirez is dead. He's not going to trust anyone but you."

"I told Ryan to expect you," I informed him. "Once he's back here, you can join us at the hospital, or stay if you don't feel comfortable leaving him to roam free in the mansion."

"I still don't understand why Vitucci is coming, but I'll deal with it for you," he muttered unhappily. "As long as you can promise me that neither Hannigan's nor Vitucci's presence will upset Calista."

"It won't. This has nothing to do with Lis and everything to do with my mom and Nova." I patted him on the back. "And when all of that is sorted out, you and I need to sit down and have a long talk. Maybe you'd like to have some input into the ring I buy for your daughter."

"The ring should have come first," he grumbled at me, but there was a new glimmer in his eyes. "I would like to be a part of anything that has to do with Calista and Justice. Thank you."

I gave him another hard slap on the back before jogging back into the mansion. Upstairs, I made sure Mom and Nova were up and ready to go before checking in on Lis. I heard the shower running and knocked on the door before sticking my head into the steamy bathroom. "Baby?"

"Ten minutes," she called. "I swear, I only need ten minutes."

"Take your time, blue eyes," I told her. "Justice had a good night."

"Yay!" she squealed happily. "Okay, but I still only need ten minutes."

"I'll be downstairs."

"All right."

I turned but paused, my hand still on the door. "Lis?"

"Yeah?" she yelled over the loud spray of the water.

"I love you, babe."

"I..." I heard her clear her throat. "I love you, Garret."

If she weren't still recovering from giving birth, and a full hysterectomy, I would have dived into the shower with her then and there. Instead, I practically sprinted out of there before my dick decided to do something dumb. My heart felt full to the point of bursting, and I walked downstairs with a stupid grin on my face.

"Looks as if the full night's sleep did someone good," Mom murmured with a yawn. She lifted a travel mug to her lips and took a long swallow. "Glad at least one person got one."

"Me too," Nova grumbled, pulling her hair up into a knot on top of her head, her movements a little aggressive. "I tossed and turned all night, even though I was exhausted."

I slung an arm around both their shoulders and turned them toward the front door. "Let's get you two settled in the back of the SUV. You can nap on the way to the hospital."

"Mr. Garret," Maria called, appearing with the cooler of food and the bag with all of Lis's pumping supplies. "Everything is all ready to go."

"Thanks, Maria," I said, taking my arm from around my sister to accept both cases from her. "Remember what I said earlier."

She smiled up at me. "Everything will be taken care of. Please give baby Justice my love."

I winked and then escorted the other two women out to the SUV. Opening the back door, I didn't wait for them to get in before securing the cooler and other case in the trunk area. Once everything was in place, I pressed the button to lower the back gate and went inside to check on Lis.

She was coming down the stairs as I walked in. Maria met her at the last step with a food storage container of fresh fruit, a refillable water bottle, and a hug. "Any request for dinner tonight?"

"Ajiaco?" she suggested, licking her lips. "With whole ears of corn, please."

"I know what my girl likes in her chicken soup," Maria said with a laugh. "Now, you get going. That baby is going to want to see her momma."

"Thanks, Maria," she called, skipping over to where I stood. I took the container of fruit from her so I could clasp her hand in mine, and we exited the mansion.

I helped her into the front passenger seat and then went around to the driver's seat before returning her breakfast to her.

"Where's Guzman?" Mom questioned with a frown from the back seat.

"Some business came up," I told her as I concentrated on driving rather than looking at her in the rearview mirror.

"This fruit is so juicy and sweet," Lis commented. "Felicity, did you and Nova eat breakfast?"

"We did, sweetheart," Mom told her, easily distracted. "Did you sleep well last night? You seem energized."

"Surprisingly, yes. Considering everything," she mumbled, looking out the window.

I reached over and put my hand on her thigh,

giving her leg a gentle squeeze. After her talk with Guzman the night before, I'd thought it would take a while before she fell asleep. Yet it was only a matter of minutes after we'd lain down in her bed before she'd been sound asleep, her head pillowed on my chest and the rest of her body wrapped around mine.

I'd fought my own need for sleep for a while, simply enjoying having her in my arms again, before finally giving in.

Nova fell asleep on the drive to the hospital, but Lis and Mom kept up a quiet conversation along the way. The guards had already switched shifts, and we passed them in the lobby. I paused long enough to ask if there had been any activity I needed to know about, but as usual, everything had been quiet. It wasn't that I was expecting anything to happen. With Manuel dead, and many people still thinking Lis had died with him, there were no enemies to come in search of trouble.

But it put my mind at ease, knowing that the NICU was protected, especially when I wasn't around. Playing with Justice's safety was the last thing I would ever do.

Upstairs, Lis and I went straight into the ward. The doctor was doing his rounds, and we got our morning report. Her vitals had remained stable all night, as the night nurse had told me on the phone, and the doctor was even lowering her pain medication dosage a little more but upping her magnesium. He had nothing critical to tell us, other than he expected Justice to be a guest in the NICU for quite some time. Nothing new about that information. We were prepared for her to be there for longer than many of the other tiny patients.

We stayed with Justice long enough to hold her hand and love on her as best we could before Lis needed to pump. Promising our baby girl we would be back soon, I guided her mother out of the ward and toward the waiting room.

As I pushed the door open, the elevator dinged down the corridor, and I paused. Lis looked up at me questioningly, but I turned my head to see who stepped off. When the guards I'd had Guzman send to the airstrip appeared first, I held my breath, waiting for my dad to exit next.

The moment my eyes landed on him, I knew he'd been having an even rougher time of it than I'd originally suspected. His clothes were wrinkled, as if he'd been wearing the same outfit for days, and his hair was longer than I could ever remember seeing it, looking just as unkempt as the rest of him. His green eyes were bloodshot, and he looked like he could use a little time in a hospital room himself from how gray his skin was.

I smelled the whiskey on him the closer he got, his blurry eyes demanding answers. "Where is she?" he rasped. "Where is your mother, Garret?"

Urging Lis aside, I opened the door wider and waved him inside.

"What's going on?" I heard Mom's voice from the waiting room. "Did I hear…?"

Her voice trailed off as Dad stepped into the doorway. Over his shoulder, I saw her entire face rapidly transform. First with concern, then anger, but lastly, the kind of longing that I'd felt myself when I'd been without Lis.

"You're here," Mom said, giving him a disdainful look. "For fuck's sake, Jet. When was the last time you showered?"

"Hell if I know," he croaked, just standing there eating up the sight of her. "Are you real, Felicity?"

"Get over here and kiss me, you big dummy, and find out."

With a growl, he pushed away from the doorway and was across the room in a matter of a few long strides. Swinging Mom up into his arms, he kissed her in a way that had me quickly averting my gaze. No kid ever wanted to see their parents making out, and there was no other way to describe how Dad attacked Mom's mouth right then.

It was several minutes before Lis nudged me, and

I finally glanced back at the couple. Dad had Mom on her feet once again, his hands tangled in her hair as he glared down at her. "Don't you ever fucking do that to me again. I know losing Nova was hard, but we're supposed to face everything together, love. You can't disappear on me and expect me to continue living as if my heart isn't missing from my chest."

She slapped her hands against his chest. "You're the one who fucked up, mister. Coming down here, leaving our daughter behind! Telling me that she was dead, even though I heard her voice when she called us."

"Ah, baby, please don't do this now. Tomorrow is her birthday. I'm barely holding on. Don't you think I miss her too? But we have to be strong. Nova was—"

"Nova is," Mom corrected.

"Baby, she's gone."

"Where did I go?" Nova asked, coming up behind me. "Did I miss something while I was in the bathroom?"

Dad jerked around at the sound of my sister's voice. When I moved so he could see her, the huge biker lost control of his legs and fell to his knees. "N-Nova?"

She stepped forward hesitantly. "Hi, Daddy."

"You're..." His voice became too choked for him

to get another word out as huge tears fell from his green eyes.

"I'm here," Nova murmured softly, taking another step closer. "I've been here in Colombia the entire time."

"H-how?" he breathed raggedly.

"It's a long story," Mom told him. "But that will have to wait. I think our son expected you to arrive a little more put together than you currently are. Let's arrange with the hospital to get you a shower and some clean clothes, and then you can meet our granddaughter."

"Grand...granddaughter?" he repeated, his eyes widening so much they nearly popped out of his head. "We have a granddaughter?"

"Yes, honey," Mom told him with a loving smile. "And she's so beautiful."

"Okay, just give me a minute here. This is a lot to take in." Unsteadily, he got to his feet. "Nova, princess. If you're real, Daddy needs a hug. Right now."

With a half sob, half laugh, she ran and threw herself into his arms. "I'm real, Dad," she assured him, hugging him tight. "I'm so sorry I didn't come home sooner, but Cali needed me. And..." She pulled back to glare up at him. "You just left me here!"

"No, baby girl, no," he cried, the tears pouring

unabashedly from his eyes. "If I had known you were here, I never would have left without you. We all thought Sheena had taken you from us. That she was playing her sick games, even from the grave. Please, sweetheart, you have to believe me. I would have never—"

"It's okay, Daddy. I believe you." She hugged him tight again. "But Mom is right. You need a shower in the worst way."

Laughing, he nodded. "Yeah, princess. I seriously do. And you need to go see Ryan."

"Ryan?" she gasped, turning to glare at me. "You called Ryan?"

"He doesn't know yet," I said, holding my hands up in surrender in case she attacked me. "But Dad is right. You should go back to the mansion. Your man is waiting there. Guzman is waiting downstairs to drive you."

"You're such an asshole," Nova muttered. Giving Dad one last hug, she turned and made a run for it, slapping me on the arm as she passed. "I love you, dumbass!" she called over her shoulder as she stabbed at the call button for the elevator.

Beside me, Lis released a pent-up breath. "That was a close call," she said with a teasing grin. "I feared for your life there for a few minutes. I'm actually surprised she didn't shank you as she ran by."

Laughing, I pulled her into my arms. "Nova's harmless."

"Sure she is, babe," she said, rolling her eyes. "You're so blind."

"Blindly in love with you."

"And cheesy," she said with a huff. "But it's kind of cute, so I guess I'll keep you."

CALI

TWENTY-ONE MONTHS.

That was how long Justice spent in the NICU. It was the longest premature stay in history, but the day we buckled our baby into the car seat and carried her out of that hospital was one of the happiest days of my life.

There had been ups and downs during the nearly two years my baby girl had been a patient. She'd had two other minor surgeries during that time, but thankfully, we'd had more ups than downs.

Now, at the age of six, she had a few health issues that she had to see her specialists for every few months. We had graduated to seeing her cardiologist every month in the beginning, to every three, and then six months. Now, it was once a year, with the possibility of stopping altogether when she was ten.

Her eyesight was the biggest issue, but she looked so adorable in her glasses—and we had to be extra careful with her food allergies—but other than that, she was a happy and mostly healthy girl who ran through the mansion at the speed of sound, lighting up our entire lives so effortlessly, the times I didn't have a smile on my face were rare.

Honestly, we had been scared she would have developmental delays. Yet she was so smart, it was hard to keep up. She was already reading at a sixth-grade level. We'd started with smaller picture books, but that hadn't lasted long before she grew bored. Garret had started giving her graphic novels, which she loved, but then she'd found Harry Potter and it had been huge chapter books ever since.

But while her brain was as big as an elephant's, her body size was still in the tenth percentile when compared to other children her age. Many people confused my six-year-old for a three- or four-year-old because of her small stature.

"Daddy, I want to put the star on the tree!" Justice said as she picked up the tinsel-and-glitter star we'd made together the year before. Everything on the Christmas tree was handmade by us. Justice wouldn't have it any other way, and we were all too happy to decorate the tree with love instead of fancy ornaments, the way my mother used to insist on every year.

"Okay, princess," Garret said, handing her the star that had been carefully wrapped, as if it were made of the finest porcelain instead of papier-mâché. She held it tightly, crinkling it a little, as her father lifted her high into the air, making her squeal with delight before placing it on top of the tree.

Watching them, my heart nearly burst out of my chest with love for my two favorite people. These two, they were my entire world. If given the choice of erasing every bad thing that ever happened to me in the past but having to give either of them up to gain it, I wouldn't do it. The past no longer haunted me as it once did, and it was all because of my little family.

"Beautiful!" Felicity said as she walked into the family room, holding a tray loaded with cups of dairy-free hot chocolate and the allergen-friendly cookies she and Justice had made together with Maria earlier that day. "That's the prettiest tree I've ever seen."

Sitting on her father's shoulders, Justice inspected our handiwork before nodding in agreement. "It is pretty, GiGi. What do you think, Mommy?"

"Gorgeous," I agreed. "But I think next year we should add a few more ornaments. Especially since your cousins will be joining us next Christmas."

Nova and Ryan alternated the holidays with us and the Vitucci family. Sometimes, they stayed in New York if it was their turn to be with Ryan's family, but most of the time, they went to Ciana's island for Christmas—or any other holiday—unless it was our turn to host.

The Hannigan clan came as often as they could, as well. Garret's aunts and uncles loved coming down for a visit and stayed for weeks at a time. As for Felicity and Jet, they lived with us, only leaving on rare occasions to visit Nova and her two kids in New York.

Ryan and Garret had started working together. I didn't ask, and my husband never offered to discuss the details of their partnership, but only an idiot would have thought it involved anything but the cocaine fields and the pipeline into the States.

Jet worked with his son, coordinating. Again I didn't ask, and no one willingly offered details. Felicity and I were of the same mind-set where our husbands and work were concerned—if we needed to know, they would tell us. And so far, we didn't need to know.

"But there's no room," Justice said with a huff.

"Then we'll just have to get a bigger tree," I told her. "Or maybe we could put up two." Because of her allergies, we couldn't have a live tree, but the artificial one we did have was beautiful. There was plenty of room for a second tree beside it.

"Okay. But Wrenley and Gabriel will have to help us make the ornaments," Justice said.

"Your cousins will be all too happy to help," Garret assured her as he set her on her feet. "Now run and tell your grandfathers that it's time for a snack." He popped her lightly on the bottom, urging her to hurry.

Giggling, she took off, her tiny legs reminding me of a cartoon character with how fast she was. For someone so small, she moved like the wind.

"How does she have so much energy?" Felicity asked with a shake of her head. "We've been going nonstop all day, and I'm exhausted."

"That's because you're old, GiGi," Justice informed her as she ran back into the family room, both Jet and Guzman following slowly behind her.

"Justice Nova!" Garret and I scolded at the same time.

"Rude, young lady," her father muttered, but I caught him trying to hide his grin.

"I'm only being honest, Daddy," our child said with a roll of her green eyes. "You said it isn't right to lie."

"But sometimes the truth can hurt people we love. Look at Gigi. Her heart is all sad now."

Justice gasped and threw her arms around her grandmother's waist. "I'm sorry, GiGi. I didn't mean to make your heart hurt because you're so old."

Felicity snorted with laughter and bent to kiss her granddaughter's head. "It's fine, Justice. You're right. It's only the truth."

"You might be old, but you're still the most beautiful woman I've ever set eyes on," Jet said, kissing his wife.

"Gross. Old people kissing is wrong."

I covered my face with my hands, trying to hide my expression from my child. It was hard not to laugh at the words that left her mouth on a daily basis. She was so full of sass.

I blamed Garret; he was too blunt around her. And then when Nova and her two kids came to visit, they were just as bad. Especially Wrenley. Good lord, when those two girls were in the same room together, it was hard not to crack up, even when they both needed to be reprimanded for the things they said.

Picking up a mug of the dairy-free hot chocolate, Guzman walked over to where I stood beside the tree. I might not call him "Dad," but he was very much a part of our family. Justice called him "Papa," just as she called Jet "Poppy."

He was there for every milestone in my daughter's life. I couldn't make up for what Matias had done to him, or cost him, but with Justice, he got to experience it as he should have been allowed to with me.

"You girls did a beautiful job on the tree," he commented, inspecting the tree with a loving eye.

"Look, Papa," Justice said, coming over to show him the new ornament she'd made with his name on it. He already had two, almost completely identical to the new one, but he gushed over it just as he had the others. "I made it last night just for you. This one is for Poppy and GiGi. And this one..." She lifted the egg-shaped ornament from the tree. "This one Daddy and I made this morning for Mommy."

I glanced down at it, frowning when I realized I hadn't spotted it earlier. "Very pretty," I murmured, taking it from her when she offered it to me.

It was one of those plastic easter eggs that came apart, but it had been painted with gold glitter to match many of the other ornaments. Something rattled around inside as I transferred it from one hand to the other, and I lifted my brows as my gaze searched for my husband's.

He winked but didn't say anything. Curious, I popped the egg apart and gasped when I saw the diamond band inside.

"What's this?"

"Surprise!" Justice squealed, bouncing up and down. "Daddy and I picked it out yesterday."

"Actually, we picked it *up* yesterday," her father corrected, coming over to take the ring from the bottom half of the egg. "It's been fitted to your size."

Grasping my hand, he lifted it and placed the ring on my finger that already had a solitaire engagement ring and a platinum wedding band. "I know it's a few days early, but I wanted to give you something special."

I melted against him. "Every day with you and Justice is special." From the moment we brought our baby home from the hospital, I'd been living the perfect happily ever after. There were still the occasional moments of worry for Justice and her health, but my life was so perfect now that, at times, I had to pinch my arm to remind myself this was all real.

"Gross, they're going to kiss," Justice muttered unhappily. "Papa, can we make more cookies with Maria in the kitchen? Everyone keeps kissing."

"Papa kisses Maria," I reminded her.

"Oh yeah," she sighed. "Fine. I'm going to go read in my room. There's too many old people kissing down here."

"Brat," Garret called after her, but I grabbed hold of his shirt and pulled his head down, taking the kiss I needed.

My fear after having a full hysterectomy was that my sex drive would diminish with it. But I couldn't keep my hands off my husband. We made love so often that, if it were possible for me to have more babies, the mansion would have been overrun with half a dozen kids.

But all we would ever be blessed with was Justice, which was completely fine for both of us. Only having one child, and with a house full of grandparents who loved spending their time with her, made it easy to sneak away and make love anytime we wanted.

"I have an early present for you too," I murmured, looking up at the man I loved through my lashes. "But I left it upstairs."

His green eyes glittered with passion. "It's only fair if I get mine today."

"Mm-hmm."

With a feral-sounding growl, Garret swooped down and grabbed me around the legs, tossing me over his shoulder. "See you old people later," he called as we left the family room.

Made in the USA
Coppell, TX
16 September 2022